AND THEN THE WORLD EXPLODED

The main door lay blown off its trunnions, and beyond was the ruin of the cannon. She heard screams, running, bang and hiss of firearms. Men boiled around or sprawled unmoving.

Enormous shone the bulk of a suit of combat armor. The wearer called her name, and even amplified by the helmet, she knew the voice was Flandry's.

Suddenly fingers closed on her arm. Around her shoulder she saw the alien, Glydh. He swung her before his body as a hostage. Flandry spun his blaster nozzle to needle beam, aimed, and fired. Glydh's brow spurted steam, brains, blood, shattered bone across Kossara, and his heavy corpse bore her down. Her head struck the floor. Lightning filled the universe.

Flandry reached her, stood over her, shielded her. A spacecraft's flank appeared in the entry. It had sprouted a turret, whose gun sprayed every doorway where an enemy might lurk. Kossara let darkness flow free . . .

A Knight of
Ghosts and Shadows

POUL ANDERSON

SPHERE BOOKS LIMITED
30/32 Gray's Inn Road, London WC1X 8JL

First published in Great Britain by Sphere Books Ltd 1978
Copyright © Poul Anderson 1975

TRADE
MARK

Set in Linotype Juliana

Printed in Great Britain by
Hazell Watson & Viney Ltd
Aylesbury, Bucks

To
my lady Dorothea of Paravel
and Hal Ravn her lord
(Dorothy and Wilson Heydt)

How shall we tell it, brothers, the tale of Bodin's raid? Whence can we draw the words of wrath and sorrow, the words of valor and vengeance? Who today is a poet such as Andrei Simich, singer of heroes?

For Andrei, words ran to command, baying and belling like a pack of hounds in pursuit through mountains where echoes fly. The words of Andrei thundered like tundra beneath a herd of gromatz, shrieked like wind around the wings of the orlik as it stoops upon its prey, roared like a dyavo hunting — then sounded low and sweet, whether deadly as the call of a vilya or innocent as the song of a guslar in springtime.

Human and zmay together thrilled at the lays of Andrei when he celebrated the olden heroes, Yovan Matavuly who led the Founders the long lightless way to this our Morning Star, Toman Obilich who slew wild Vladimir on the crown of the Glacier, Gwyth who dared the storms of the Black Ocean, Stefan Miyatovich — great ancestor of Gospodar Bodin — who in the depths of the Night Years cast back the reavers from our very homes. Ah, well could Andrei Simich have sung the deeds of Bodin!

But his voice is departed. That the glory of Bodin Miyatovich go not from memory, let us find what poor plain words we may.

CHAPTER ONE

Every planet in the story is cold—even Terra, though Flandry came home on a warm evening of northern summer. There the chill was in the spirit.

He felt a breath of it as he neared. Somehow, talk between him and his son had drifted to matters Imperial. They had avoided all such during their holiday.

Terra itself had not likely reminded them. The globe hung beautiful in starry darkness, revealed by a viewscreen in the cabin where they sat. It was almost full, because they were accelerating with the sun behind them and were not yet close enough to start on an approach curve. At this remove it shone white-swirled blue, unutterably pure, near dewdrop Luna. Nothing was visible of the scars that man had made upon it.

And the saloon was good to be in, bulkheads nacreous gray, benches padded in maroon velvyl, table of authentic teak whereon stood Scotch whisky and everything needed for the use thereof, warm and flawlessly recycled air through which gamboled a dance tune and drifted an odor of lilacs. The *Hooligan*, private speedster of Captain Sir Dominic Flandry, was faster, better armed, and generally more versatile than any vessel of her class had a moral right to be; but her living quarters reflected her owner's philosophy that, if one is born into an era of decadence, one may as well enjoy it while it lasts.

He leaned back, inhaled deeply of his cigarette, took more smokiness in a sip from his glass, and regarded Dominic Hazeltine with some concern. If the frontier was truly that close to exploding – and the boy must go there again . . . 'Are you sure?' he asked. 'What proved facts have you got – proved by yourself, not somebody else? Why wouldn't I have heard more?'

His companion returned a steady look. 'I don't want to

make you feel old,' he said; and the knowledge passed through Flandry that a lieutenant commander of Naval Intelligence, twenty-seven standard years of age, wasn't really a boy, nor was his father any longer the boy who had begotten him. Then Hazeltine smiled and took the curse off: 'Well, I might want to, just so I can hope that at your age I'll have acquired, let alone kept, your capacity for the three basic things in life.'

'Three?' Flandry raised his brows.

'Feasting, fighting and – Wait; of course I haven't been along when you were in a fight. But I've no doubt you perform as well as ever in that department too. Still, you told me for the last three years you've stayed in the Solar System, taking life easy. If the whole word about Dennitza hasn't reached the Emperor – and apparently it's barely starting to – why should it have come to a pampered pet of his?'

'Hm. I'm not really. He pampers with a heavy hand. So I avoid the court as much as politeness allows. This indefinite furlough I'm on – nobody but him would dare call me back to duty, unless I grow bored and request assignment – that's the only important privilege I've taken. Aside from the outrageous amount of talent, capability, and charm with which I was born; and I do my best to share those chromosomes.'

Flandry had spoken lightly in half a hope of getting a similar response. They had bantered throughout their month-long jaunt, whether on a breakneck hike in the Great Rift of Mars or gambling in a miners' dive in Low Venusberg, running the rings of Saturn or dining in elegance beneath its loveliness on Iapetus with two ladies expert and expensive. Must they already return to realities?

They'd been more friends than father and son. The difference in age hardly showed. They bore well-muscled height in common, supple movement, gray eyes, baritone voice. Flandry's face stood out in a perhaps overly handsome combination of straight nose, high cheekbones, cleft chin – the result of a biosculp job many years past, which he had never bothered to change again – and trim mustache. His sleek seal-brown hair was frosted at the temples; when Hazeltine accused him of bringing this about by artifice, he had grinned and not denied it. Though both wore civilian garb, Flandry's iridescent puff-sleeved blouse, scarlet cummerbund, flared blue trousers, and curly-toed beefleather slippers opposed the other's plain coverall.

Broader features, curved nose, full mouth, crow's-wing locks recalled Persis d'Io as she had been when she and Flandry said farewell on a planet now destroyed, he not knowing she bore his child. The tan of strange suns, the lines creased by squinting into strange weathers, had not altogether gone from Hazeltine in the six weeks since he reached Terra. But his unsophisticated ways meant only that he had spent his life on the fringes of the Empire. He had caroused with a gusto to match his father's. He had shown the same taste in speech—

('– an itchy position for me, my own admiral looking for a nice lethal job he could order me to do,' Flandry reminisced. 'Fenross hated my guts. He didn't like the rest of me very much, either. I saw I'd better produce a stratagem, and fast.'

('Did you?' Hazeltine inquired.

('Of course. You see me here, don't you? It's practically a *sine qua non* of a field agent staying alive, that he be able to outthink not just the opposition, but his superiors.'

('No doubt you were inspired by the fact that "stratagem" spelled backwards is "megatarts". The prospect of counting your loose women by millions should give plenty of incentive.'

(Flandry stared. 'Now I'm certain you're my bairn! Though to be frank, that awesomely pleasant notion escaped me. Instead, having developed my scheme, I confronted a rather ghastly idea which has haunted me ever afterward: that maybe there's no one alive more intelligent than I.')

– and yet, and yet, an underlying earnestness always remained with him.

Perhaps he had that from his mother: that, and pride. She'd let the infant beneath her heart live, abandoned her titled official lover, resumed her birthname, gone from Terra to Sassania and started anew as a dancer, at last married reasonably well, but kept young Dominic by her till he enlisted. Never had she sent word back from her frontier home, not when Flandry well-nigh singlehanded put down the barbarians of Scotha and was knighted for it, not when Flandry well-nigh singlehanded rescued the new Emperor's favorite granddaughter and headed off a provincial rebellion and was summoned Home to be rewarded. Nor had her son, who always knew his father's name, called on him until lately, when far enough along in his own career that nepotism could not be thought necessary.

Thus Dominic Hazeltine refused the offer of merry chit-chat and said in his burred un-Terran version of Anglic, 'Well, if you've been taking what amounts to a long vacation, the more reason why you wouldn't have kept trace of developments. Maybe his Majesty simply hasn't been bothering you about them, and has been quite concerned himself for quite some while. Regardless, I've been yonder and I know.'

Flandry dropped the remnant of his cigarette in an ashtaker. 'You wound my vanity, which is no mean accomplishment,' he replied. 'Remember, for three or four years earlier – between the time I came to his notice and the time we could figure he was planted on the throne too firmly to have a great chance of being uprooted – I was one of his several right hands. Field and staff work both, specializing in the problem of making the marches decide they'd really rather keep Hans for their Emperor than revolt all over again. Do you think, if he sees fresh trouble where I can help, he won't consult me? Or do you think, because I've been utilizing a little of the hedonism I fought so hard to preserve, I've lost interest in my old circuits? No, I've followed the news and an occasional secret report.'

He stirred, tossed off his drink, and added, 'Besides, you claim the Gospodar of Dennitza is our latest problem child. But you've also said you were working Sector Arcturus: almost diametrically opposite, and well inside those vaguenesses we are pleased to call the borders of the Empire. Tell me, then – you've been almighty unspecific about your operations, and I supposed that was because you were under security, and didn't pry – tell me, as far as you're allowed, what does the space around Arcturus have to do with Dennitza? With anything in the Taurian Sector?'

'I stayed mum because I didn't want to spoil this occasion,' Hazeltine said. 'From what Mother told me, I expected fun, when I could get a leave long enough to justify the trip to join you; but you've opened whole universes to me that I never guessed existed.' He flushed. 'If I ever gave any thought to such things, I self-righteously labeled them "vice".'

'Which they are,' Flandry put in. 'What you bucolic types don't realize is that worthwhile vice doesn't mean lolling around on cushions eating drugged custard. How dismal! I'd rather be virtuous. Decadence requires application. But go on.'

'We'll land now, and I'll report back,' Hazeltine said. 'I don't know where they'll send me next, and doubtless won't be free to tell you. While the chance remains, I'll be honest. I came here wanting to know you as a man, but also wanting to, oh, alert you if nothing else, because I think your brains will be sorely needed, and it's damn hard to communicate through channels.'

Indeed, Flandry admitted.

His gaze went to the stars in the viewscreen. Without amplification, few that he could see lay in the more or less 200-light-year radius of that rough and blurry-edged spheroid named the Terran Empire. Those were giants, visible by virtue of shining across distances we can traverse, under hyperdrive, but will never truly comprehend; and they filled the merest, tiniest fragment of the galaxy, far out in a spiral arm where their numbers were beginning to thin toward cosmic hollowness. Yet this insignificant Imperial bit of space held an estimated four million suns. Maybe half of those had been visited at least once. About a hundred thousand worlds of theirs might be considered to belong to the Empire, though for most the connection was ghostly tenuous ... It was too much. There were too many environments, races, cultures, lives, messages. No mind, no government could know the whole, let alone cope.

Nevertheless that sprawl of planets, peoples, provinces, and protectorates must somehow cope, or see the Long Night fall. Barbarians, who had gotten spaceships and nuclear weapons too early in their history, prowled the borders; the civilized Roidhunate of Merseia probed, withdrew a little – seldom the whole way – waited, probed again . . . Rigel caught Flandry's eye, a beacon amidst the great enemy's dominions. The Taurian Sector lay in that direction, fronting the Wilderness beyond which dwelt the Merseians.

'You must know something I don't, if you claim the Dennitzans are brewing trouble,' he said. 'However, are you sure what you know is true?'

'What can you tell me about them?' Hazeltine gave back.

'Hm? Why – um, yes, that's sensible, first making clear to you what information and ideas I have.'

'Especially since they must reflect what the higher-ups believe, which I'm not certain about.'

'Neither am I, really. My attention's been directed elsewhere, Tauria seeming as reliably under control as any division of the Empire.'

'After your experience there?'

'Precisely on account of it. Very well. We'll save time if I run barefoot through the obvious. Then you needn't interrogate me, groping around for what you may not have suspected hitherto.'

Hazeltine nodded. 'Besides,' he said, 'I've never been in those parts myself.'

'Oh? You mentioned assignments which concerned the Merseia-ward frontier and our large green playmates.'

'Tauria isn't the only sector at that end of the Empire,' Hazeltine pointed out.

Too big, this handful of stars we suppose we know . . . 'Ahem.' Flandry took the crystal decanter. A refill gurgled into his glass. 'You've heard how I happened to be in the neighborhood when the governor, Duke Alfred of Varrak, kidnapped Princess Megan while she was touring, as part of a scheme to detach the Taurian systems from the Empire and bring them under Merseian protection – which means possession. Chives and I thwarted him, or is "foiled" a more dramatic word?

'Well, then the question arose, what to do next? Let me remind you, Hans had assumed, which means grabbed, the crown less than two years earlier. Everything was still in upheaval. Three avowed rivals were out to replace him by force of arms, and nobody could guess how many more would take an opportunity that came along, whether to try for supreme power or for piratical autonomy. Alfred wouldn't have made his attempt without considerable support among his own people. Therefore, not only must the governorship change, but the sector capital.

'Now Dennitza may not be the most populous, wealthy, or up-to-date human-colonized planet in Tauria. However, it has a noticeable sphere of influence. And it has strength out of proportion, thanks to traditionally maintaining its own military, under the original treaty of annexation. And the Dennitzans always despised Josip. His tribute assessors and other agents he sent them, through Duke Alfred, developed a tendency to get killed in brawls, and somehow nobody afterward could identify the brawlers. When Josip died, and the Policy Board split on accepting his successor, and suddenly all hell let out for noon, the Gospodar declared for Hans Molitor. He didn't actually dispatch troops to help, but he kept order in his part of space, gave the Merseians no opening – doubtless the best service he could have rendered.

'Wasn't he the logical choice to take charge of Tauria? Isn't he still?'

'In spite of Merseians on his home planet?' Hazeltine challenged.

'Citizens of Merseian descent,' Flandry corrected. 'Rather remote descent, I've heard. There are humans who serve the Roidhunate, too, and not every one has been bought or brain-scrubbed; some families have lived on Merseian worlds for generations.'

'Nevertheless,' Hazeltine said, 'the Dennitzan culture isn't Terran – isn't entirely human. Remember how hard the colonists of Avalon fought to stay in the Domain of Ythri, way back when the Empire waged a war to adjust that frontier? Why should Dennitzans feel brotherly toward Terrans?'

'I don't suppose they do.' Flandry shrugged. 'I've never visited them either. But I've met other odd human societies, not to speak of nonhuman. They stay in the Empire because it gives them the Pax and often a fair amount of commercial benefit, without usually charging too high a price for the service. From what little I saw and heard in the way of reports on the Gospodar and his associates, they aren't such fools as to imagine they can stay at peace independently. Their history includes the Troubles, and their ancestors freely joined the Empire when it appeared.'

'Nowadays Merseia might offer them a better deal.'

'Uh-uh. They've been marchmen up against Merseia far too long. Too many inherited grudges.'

'Such things can change. I've known marchmen myself. They take on the traits of their enemies, and eventually—' Hazeltine leaned across the table. His voice harshened. 'Why are the Dennitzans resisting the Emperor's decree?'

'About disbanding their militia?' Flandry sipped. 'Yes, I know, the Gospodar's representatives here have been appealing, arguing, logrolling, probably bribing, and certainly making nuisances of themselves on governmental levels as high as the Policy Board. Meanwhile he drags his feet: If the Emperor didn't have more urgent matters on deck, we might have seen fireworks by now.'

'Nuclear?'

'Oh, no, no. Haven't we had our fill of civil war? I spoke metaphorically. And . . . between us, lad, I can't blame the Gospodar very much. True, Hans' idea is that consolidating all combat services may prevent a repetition of what we just went through. I can't say it won't help; nor can I say it will. If nothing else, the Dennitzans do nest way out on a windy limb. They have more faith in their ability to protect themselves, given Navy support, than in the Navy's ability to do it alone. They may well be right. This is too serious a matter – a whole frontier is involved – too serious for impulsive action : another reason, I'm sure, why Hans has been patient, has not dismissed the Gospodar as governor or anything.'

'I believe he's making a terrible mistake,' Hazeltine said.

'What do you think the Dennitzans have in mind, then?'

'If not a breakaway, and inviting the Merseians in – I'm far from convinced that that's unthinkable to them, but I haven't proof – if not that, then insurrection ... to make the Gospodar Emperor.'

Flandry sat still for a while. The ship murmured, the music sang around him. Terra waxed in his sight.

Finally, taking forth a fresh cigarette, he asked, 'What gives you that notion? Your latest work didn't bring you within a hundred parsecs of Dennitza, did it?'

'No.' Hazeltine's mouth, which recalled the mouth of Persis, drew into thinner lines than ever hers had done. 'That's what scares me. You see, we've collected evidence that Dennitzans are engineering a rebellion on Diomedes. Have you heard of Diomedes?'

'Ye-e-es. Any man who appreciates your three primaries of life ought to study the biography of Nicholas van Rijn, and he was shipwrecked there once. Yes, I know a little. But it isn't a terribly important planet to this day, is it? Why should it revolt, and how could it hope to succeed?'

'I wasn't on that team myself. But my unit was carrying out related investigations in the same sector, and we exchanged data. Apparently the Diomedeans – factions among them – hope the Domain of Ythri will help. They've acquired a mystique about the kinship of winged beings ... Whether the Ythrians really would intervene or not is hard to tell. I suspect not, to the extent that'd bring on overt conflict with us. But they might well use the potentiality, the threat, to steer us into new orbits ... We've barely started tracing the connections.'

Flandry scowled. 'And those turn out to be Dennitzan?'

'Correct. Any such conspiracy would have to involve members of a society with spaceships – preferably humans – to plant and cultivate the seed on Diomedes, and maintain at least enough liaison with Ythri that the would-be rebels stay

17

hopeful. When our people first got on the track of this, they naturally assumed the human were Avalonian. But a lucky capture they made, just before I left for Sol, indicated otherwise. Dennitzan agents, Dennitzan.'

'Why, on the opposite side of Terra from their home?'

'Oh, come on! You know why. If the Gospodar's planning an uprising of his own, what better preliminary than one in that direction?' Hazeltine drew breath. 'I don't have the details. Those are, or will be, in the reports to GHQ from our units. But isn't something in the Empire always going wrong? The word is, his Majesty plans to leave soon for Sector Spica, at the head of an armada, and curb the barbarians there. That's a long way from anyplace else. Meanwhile, how slowly do reports from an obscure clod like Diomedes grind their way through the bureaucracy?'

'When a fleet can incinerate a world,' Flandry said bleakly, 'I prefer governments not to have fast reflexes. You and your teammates could well be quantum-hopping to an unwarranted conclusion. For instance, those Dennitzans who were caught, if they really are Dennitzans, could be freebooters. Or if they have bosses at home, those bosses may be a single clique – may be, themselves, maneuvering to overthrow the Gospodar – and may or may not have ambitions beyond that. How much more than you've told me do you know for certain?'

Hazeltine sighed. 'Not much. But I hoped—' He looked suddenly, pathetically young. 'I hoped you might check further into the question.'

Chives entered, on bare feet which touched the carpet soundlessly though the gee-field was set at Terran standard. 'I beg your pardon, sir,' he addressed his master. 'If you wish dinner before we reach the landing approach zone, I must commence preparations. The tournedos will obviously require a red wine. Shall I open the Château Falkayn '35?'

'Hm?' Flandry blinked, recalled from darker matters. 'Why ... um-m ... I'd thought of Beaujolais.'

'No, sir,' said Chives, respectfully immovable. 'I cannot recommend Beaujolais to accompany a tournedos such as is contemplated. And may I suggest drinking and smoking cease until your meal is ready?'

Summer evening around Catalina deepened into night. Flandry sat on a terrace of the lodge which the island's owner, his friend the Mayor Palatine of Britain, had built on its heights and had lent to him. He wasn't sleepy; during the space trip, his circadian rhythm had slipped out of phase with this area. Nor was he energetic. He felt – a bit sad? – no, pensive, lonesome, less in an immediate fashion than as an accumulation from the years – a mood he had often felt before and recognized would soon become restlessness. Yet while it stayed as it was, he could wonder if he should have married now and then. Or even for life? It would have been good to help young Dominic grow.

He sighed, twisted about in his lounger till he found a comfortable knees-aloft position, drew on his cigar and watched the view. Beneath him, shadowy land plunged to a bay and, beyond, the vast metallic sheet of a calm Pacific. A breeze blew cool, scented with roses and Buddha's cup. Overhead, stars twinkled forth in a sky that ranged from amethyst to silver-blue. A pair of contrails in the west caught the last glow of a sunken sun. But the evening was quiet. Traffic was never routed near the retreats of noblemen.

How many kids do I have? And how many of them know they're mine? (I've only met or heard of a few.) And where are they and what's the universe doing to them?

Hm. He pulled rich smoke across his tongue. *When a person starts sentimentalizing, it's time either to get busy or to take antisenescence treatments. Pending this decision, how about a woman? That stopover on Ceres was several days ago, after all.* He considered ladies he knew and decided against them, for each would expect personal consideration – which was her right, but his mind was still too full of his son. Therefore: *Would I rather flit to the mainland and its bright lights, or have Chives phone the nearest cepheid agency?*

As if at a signal, his personal servant appeared, a Shalmuan, slim kilt-clad form remarkably humanlike except for 140 centimeters of height, green skin, hairlessness, long prehensile tail, and, to be sure, countless more subtle variations. On a tray he carried a visicom extension, a cup of coffee, and a snifter of cogac. 'You have a call, sir,' he announced.

How many have you filtered out? Flandry didn't ask. Nor did he object. The nonhuman in a human milieu – or vice-versa – commonly appears as a caricature of a personality, because those around him cannot see most of his soul. But Chives had attended his boss for years. 'Personal servant' had come to mean more than 'valet and cook'; it included being butler of a household which never stayed long in a single place, and pilot, and bodyguard, and whatever an emergency might require.

Chives brought the lounger table into position, set down the tray, and disappeared again. Flandry's pulse bounced a little. In the screen before him was the face of Dominic Hazeltine. 'Why, hello,' he said. 'I didn't expect to hear from you this soon.'

'Well' – excitement thrummed – 'you know, our conversation— When I came back to base, I got a chance at a general data scanner, and keyed for recent material on Dennitza. A part of what I learned will interest you, I think. Though you'd better act fast.'

CHAPTER TWO

Immediately after the two Navy yeomen who brought Kossara to the slave depot had signed her over to its manager and departed, he told her: 'Hold out your left arm.' Dazed – for she had been whisked from the ship within an hour of landing on Terra, and the speed of the aircar had blurred the enormousness of Archopolis – she obeyed. He glanced expertly at her wrist and, from a drawer, selected a bracelet of white metal, some three centimeters broad and a few millimeters thick. Hinged, it locked together with a click. She stared at the thing. A couple of sensor spots and a niello of letters and numbers were its only distinctions. It circled her arm snugly though not uncomfortably.

'The law requires slaves to wear this,' the manager explained in a bored tone. He was a pudgy, faintly greasy-looking middle-aged person in whose face dwelt shrewdness.

That must be on Terra, trickled through Kossara's mind. *Other places seem to have other ways. And on Dennitza we keep no slaves . . .*

'It's powered by body heat and maintains an audiovisual link to a global monitor net,' the voice went on. 'If the computers notice anything suspicious – including, of course, any tampering with the bracelet – they call a human operator. He can stop you in your tracks by a signal.' The man pointed to a switch on his desk. 'This gives the same signal.'

He pressed. Pain burned like lightning, through flesh, bone, marrow, until nothing was except pain. Kossara fell to her knees. She never knew if she screamed or if her throat had jammed shut.

He lifted his hand and the anguish was gone. Kossara crouched shaking and weeping. Dimly she heard: 'That was five seconds' worth. Direct nerve stim from the bracelet, triggers a center in the brain. Harmless for periods of less than a minute, if you haven't got a weak heart or something.

Do you understand you'd better be a good girl? All right, on your feet.'

As she swayed erect, the shudders slowly leaving her, he smirked and muttered, 'You know, you're a looker. Exotic; none of this standardized biosculp format. I'd be tempted to bid on you myself, except the price is sure to go out of my reach. Well . . . hold still.'

He did no more than feel and nuzzle. She endured, thinking that probably soon she could take a long, long, long hot shower. But when a guard had conducted her to the women's section, she found the water was cold and rationed. The dormitory gaped huge, echoing, little inside it other than bunks and inmates. The mess was equally barren, the food adequate but tasteless. Some twenty prisoners were present. They received her kindly enough, with a curiosity that sharpened when they discovered she was from a distant planet and this was her first time on Terra. Exhausted, she begged off saying much and tumbled into a haunted sleep.

The next morning she got a humiliatingly thorough medical examination. A psychotech studied the dossier on her which Naval Intelligence had supplied, asked a few questions, and signed a form. She got the impression he would have liked to inquire further – why had she rebelled? – but a Secret classification on her record scared him off. Or else (because whoever bought her would doubtless talk to her about it) he knew from his study how chaotic and broken her memories of the episode were, since the hypnoprobing on Diomedes.

That evening she couldn't escape conversation in the dormitory. The women clustered around and chattered. They were from Terra, Luna, and Venus. With a single exception, they had been sentenced to limited terms of enslavement for crimes such as repeated theft or dangerous negligence, and were not very bright or especially comely. 'I don't suppose anybody'll bid on me,' lamented one. 'Hard labor for the government, then.'

'I don't understand,' said Kossara. Her soft Dennitzan accent intrigued them. 'Why? I mean, when you have a worldful of machines, every kind of robot – why slaves? How can it . . . how can it pay?'

The exceptional woman, who was handsome in a haggard fashion, answered. 'What else would you do with the wicked? Kill them, even for tiny things? Give them costly psychocorrection? Lock them away at public expense, useless to themselves and everybody else? No, let them work. Let the Imperium get some money from selling them the first time, if it can.'

Does she talk like that because she's afraid of her bracelet? Kossara wondered. *Surely, oh, surely we can complain a little among ourselves!* 'What can we do that a machine can't do better?' she asked.

'Personal services,' the woman said. 'Many kinds. Or . . . well, economics. Often a slave is less efficient than a machine, but needs less capital investment.'

'You sound educated,' Kossara remarked.

The woman sighed. 'I was, once. Till I killed my husband. That meant a life term like yours, dear. To be quite safe, my buyer did pay to have my mind corrected.' A sort of energy blossomed in look and tone. 'How grateful I am! I was a murderess, do you hear, a murderess. I took it on myself to decide another human being wasn't fit to live. Now I know—' She seized Kossara's hands. 'Ask them to correct you too. You committed treason, didn't you say? Beg them to wash you clean!'

The rest edged away. *Brain-channeled,* Kossara knew. A crawling went under her skin. 'Wh-why are you here?' she stammered. 'If you were bought—'

'He grew tired of me and sold me back. I'll always long for him . . . but he had the perfect right, of course.' The woman drew nearer. 'I like you, Kossara,' she whispered. 'I do hope we'll go to the same place.'

'Place?'

'Oh, somebody rich may take you for a while. Likelier, though, a brothel—'

Kossara yanked free and ran. She didn't quite reach a toilet before she vomited. They made her clean the floor. Afterward, when they insisted on circling close and talking and talking, she screamed at them to leave her alone, then enforced it with a couple of skilled blows. No punishment followed. It was dreadful to know that a half-aware electronic brain watched every pulsebeat of her existence, and no doubt occasionally a bored human supervisor examined her screen at random. But seemingly the guardians didn't mind a fight, if no property was damaged. She sought her bunk and curled up into herself.

Next morning a matron came for her, took a critical look, and nodded. 'You'll do,' she said. 'Swallow this.' She held forth a pill.

'What's that?' Kossara crouched back.

'A euphoriac. You want to be pretty for the camera, don't you? Go on, swallow.' Remembering the alternative, Kossara obeyed.

As she accompanied the matron down the hall, waves of comfort passed through her, higher at each tide. It was like being drunk, no, not drunk, for she had her full senses and command of her body ... like having savored a few glasses with Mihail, after they had danced, and the violins playing yet ... like having Mihail here, alive again.

Almost cheerfully, in the recording room she doffed her gray issue gown, went through the paces and said the phrases designed to show her off, as instructed. She barely heard the running commentary:

'Kossara Vymezal [mispronounced, but a phonetic spellout followed], human female, age twenty-five, virgin, athletic, health and intelligence excellent, education good though provincial. Spirited but ought to learn subordination in short order without radical measures. Life sentence for treason, conspiracy to promote and aid rebellion. Suffers from hostility to the Imperium and some disorientation due to hypnoprobing. Neither handicap affects her wits or basic emotional stability. Her behavior on the voyage here was cold but acceptable.

'She was born on the planet Dennitza, Zoria III in the Taurian Sector. [A string of numbers] Her family is well

24

placed, father being a district administrator. [Why no mention of the fact Mother was a sister of Bodin Miyatovich, Gospodar and sector governor? O Uncle, Uncle ...] As is the rule there, she received military training and served a hitch in the armed forces. She has a degree in xenology. Having done field work on planets near home, several months ago she went to Diomedes [a string of numbers] – quite remote, her research merely a disguise. Most of the report on her has not been made available to us; and as said, she herself is confused and largely amnesiac about this period. Her main purpose was to help instigate a revolt. Before much harm was done, she was detected, arrested, interrogated, and sentenced by court-martial. There being little demand for slaves in that region, and a courier ship returning directly to Terra, she was brought along.

'We rate her unlikely to be dangerous, given the usual precautions, and attractive both physically and personally—'

The camera projected back the holograms it had taken, for its operator's inspection, and Kossara looked upon her image. She saw a big young woman, 177 centimeters tall, a bit small in the bosom but robust in shoulders, hips, and long free-striding legs, skin ivory-clear save for a few freckles and the remnant of a tan. The face was wide, high in the cheekbones, snub in the nose, full in the mouth, strong in chin and jawline. Large blue-green eyes stood well apart beneath dark brows and reddish-brown bangs; that hair was cropped below the ears in the manner of both sexes on Dennitza. When she spoke, her voice was husky.

'– will be sullen unless drugged, but given the right training and conditions, ought to develop a high sexual capacity. A private owner may find that kindness will in due course make her loyal and responsive—'

Kossara slipped dreamily away from the words, the room, Terra ... the whole way home. To Mihail? No, she couldn't quite raise him from the dust between the stars – even now, she dared not. But, oh, just a few years ago, she and Trohdwyr ...

[She had a vacation from her studies at Shkola plus a furlough from her ground defense unit in the Narodna Voyska. Ordinarily she would have spent as much of this time as *he* could spare with her betrothed. But a space force had been detected within a few light-years of the Zorian System which might intend action on behalf of some other claimant to the Imperium than Hans Molitor whom the Gospodar supported, or might use such partisanship as an excuse for brigandage. Therefore Bodin Miyatovich led some of the Dennitzan fleet out to warn off the strangers, and if necessary fight them off. Mihail Svetich, engineer on a Meteor-class torpedo craft, had kissed Kossara farewell.

Rather than fret idle in Zorkagrad, she flitted to her parents' home. Danilo Vymezal, voivode of the Dubina Dolyina, was head of council, chief magistrate, and military commander throughout a majestic country at the northern rim of the Kazan. Soon after she reached the estate, Kossara said she wished for a long hunt. Her father regarded her for a moment before he nodded. 'That will do you good,' he said. 'Who would you like for a partner? Trohdwyr?'

She had unthinkingly supposed she would go alone. But of course he was right; only fools went by themselves so far into the wilderness that no radio relay could pass on a distress call from a pocket transceiver. The old zmay was welcome company, not least because he knew when to be silent.

They took an aircar to a meadow on the unpeopled western slope and set forth afoot. The days and nights, the leagues and heights, wind, rain, sun, struggle and sleep were elixir. More than once she had a clear shot at a soaring orlik or a bull yelen poised on a crag and forbore; those wings or those horns were too splendid across the sky. But at last it was sweet fire in the blood to stand before a charging dyavo, feel the rifle surge back against her shoulder, see fangs and claws fall down within a meter of her.

Trohdwyr reproved : 'You were reckless, Dama.'

'He came at me from his den,' Kossara retorted.

'After you saw the entrance and took care to make much noise in the bushes. Deny it not. I have known you longer than your own memory runs. You learned to walk by cling-ing to my tail for safety. If I lose you now, your father will dismiss me from his service, and where then shall a poor lorn dodderer go? Back to his birth village to become a fisher again, after these many years? Have mercy, Dama.'

She chuckled. They set about making camp. This was high in the bowl of the Kazan, where that huge crater bit an arc from the Vysochina. The view could not have been imagined by anyone who had not seen it, save God before He willed it.

Though treeless, the site bore a dense purple sward of mahovina, springy underfoot and spicy to smell, studded by white and gold wildflowers; and a nearby canebrake rustled in the breeze. Eastward the ringwall sloped down to timberline. Beyond, yellow beams of evening fell on a bluish mistiness of forest, as far as sight could reach, cloven by a river which gleamed like a drawn blade. Westward, not far hence, the rim stood shadowy-sharp athwart rough Vysochina hills. Behind them the snowpeaks of Planina Byelogorski lifted sungold whiteness into an absolute azure. The purity of sky was not marred by a remote northward thread of smoke from Vulkana Zemlya.

The air grew cold soon after the sun went behind the mountains, cold as the brook which bubbled iron-tasting from a cleft in the crater's lip. Kossara hunched into her jacket, squatted down, held palms forth to the fire. Her breath drifted white through the dusk that rose from the lowlands.

Before he put their meal on a spit above coals and dancing flamelets, Trohdwyr drew a sign and spoke a few words of Eriau. Kossara knew them well: 'Aferdhi of the Deeps, Blyn of the Winds, Haawan who lairs on the reefs, by this be held afar and trouble us not in our rest.' Hundreds of kilometers and a long lifetime from the Black Ocean, he remained an old-fashioned pagan ychan. Early in her teens, eager in her faith, Kossara had learned it was no use trying to make an Orthochristian of him.

Surely the Pantocrator didn't mind much, and would re-ceive his dear battered soul into Heaven, at the last.

She had never thought of him as a zmay. Not that the word had any particularly bad overtones. Maybe once it had been a touch contemptuous, four hundred years ago when the first immigrants arrived from Merseia; but later it came to mean simply a Dennitzan of such ancestry. (Did the growth of their original planet into a frightening rival of Terra have anything to do with that?) However, from him and his family she had learned Eriau – rather, the archaic and mutated version they spoke – at the same time as she was learning Serbic from her parents and Anglic from a governess. When finally prevailed upon to stop scrambling these three into a private patois, she kept the habit of referring to Trohdwyr's people by their own name for themselves, 'ychani': 'seekers'.

For he had been close to the center of her child-universe. Father and Mother were at its very heart, naturally, and so for a while were a doll named Lutka, worn into shapelessness, and a cat she called Butterfeet. Uncle Bodin approached them when he and Aunt Draga visited, or the Vymezals went to Zorkagrad and he took her to the zoo and the merrypark. Three younger siblings, two brothers and a sister, orbited like comets, now radiant with love, now off into outer darkness. Trohdwyr never shone quite as brightly as any of these; but the chief gamekeeper to three generations of her house moved in an unchangeable path, always there for her to reach when she needed him.

'Kraich.' Having started dinner cooking, he settled back on the tripod of clawed feet and massive tail. 'You've earned a double drink this evening, Dama. A regular sundowner, and one for killing the dyavo.' He poured into cups from a flask of shlivovitza. 'Though I must skin the beast and carry the hide,' he added.

The hoarse basso seemed to hold a note of genuine complaint. Startled, Kossara peered across the fire at him.

To a dweller in the inner Empire, he might have been any Merseian. No matter how anthropoid a xenosophont was, the basic differences usually drowned individuality unless you knew the species well. Trohdwyr roughly resembled a large man – especially in the face, if you overlooked endless details of its heavy-boned, brow-ridged, wide-nosed, thin-lipped construction. But he had no external earflaps, only elaborately contoured holes in the skull. Totally hairless, his skin was pale green and faintly scaled. A sierra of low triangular spines ran from the top of his forehead, down his back to the tail's end. When he stood, he leaned forward, reducing his effective height to tall-human; when he walked, it was not on heels and soles but on his toes, in an alien rhythm. He was warm-blooded; females of his race gave live birth; but he was no mammal – no kind of animal which Terra had ever brought forth.

By a million signs Kossara knew him for Trohdwyr and nobody else, as she knew her kinfolk or Mihail. He had grown gaunt, deep furrows lay in his cheeks, he habitually spurned boots and trousers for a knee-length tunic with many pockets, he wore the same kind of curve-bladed sheath knife with knuckleduster handle which he had given her and taught her to use, years before . . .

'Why, I'll abandon it if you want,' she said, thinking, *Has time begun to wear him down? How hurtful to us both.*

'Oh, no, no, Dama. No need.' Trohdwyr grew abashed. 'Forgive a gaffer if he's grumpy. I was – well, today I almost saw you ripped apart. There I stood, you in my line of fire, and that beast – Dama, don't do such things.'

'I'm sorry,' Kossara said. 'Though I really don't believe I was taking too big a chance. I know my rifle.'

'I too. Didn't you learn from me?'

'But those were lightweight weapons. Because I was a girl? Today I had a Tashta, the kind they've issued me in the Voyska. I was sure it could stop him.' Kossara gazed aside, downslope toward the bottom of the Kazan, which night had already filled. 'Besides,' she added softly, 'I needed such a moment. You're right, I did provoke the dyavo to attack.'

'To get away from feeling helpless?' Trohdwyr murmured.

'Yes.' She could never have opened thus to any human except Mihail, maybe not even to him; but over the years the ychan had heard confessions which she did not give her priest. 'My man's yonder.' She flung a hand toward the first stars as they twinkled forth, white upon violet above the lowlands. 'I have to stay behind in my guard unit – when Dennitza will never be attacked!'

'Thanks to units like yours, Dama,' Trohdwyr said.

'Nevertheless, he—' Kosara took her drink in a gulp. It burned the whole way down, and the glow spread fast to every part of her. She held the cup out for a refill. 'Why does it matter this much who's Emperor? All right, Josip was foul and his agents did a great deal of harm. But he's dead now; and the Empire did survive him; and I've heard enough from my uncle to know that what really keeps it going is a lot of nameless little officials whose work outlasts whole dynasties. Then why do we fight over who'll sit crowned in Archopolis for the next few years?'

'You are the human, Dama, not I,' said Trohdwyr. After a minute: 'Yet I can think how on Merseia they would be glad to see another Terran Emperor whose spirit is fear or foolishness. And . . . we here are not overly far from Merseia.'

Kossara shivered beneath the stars and took a strong sip.

'Well, it'll get settled soon,' she declared. 'Uncle Bodin told me he's sure it will be. This thing in space is a last gasp. Soon' – she lifted her head – 'Mihail and I can travel,' *exploring together the infinite marvels on worlds that circle new suns.*

'I hope so, Dama, despite that I'll miss you. Have plenty of young, and let them play and grow around me on the manor as you did, will you?'

Exalted by the liquor – how the smell of the roasting meat awakened hunger! – she blurted: 'He wanted me to sleep with him before he left. I said no, we'll wait till we're married. Should I have said yes? Tell me, should I have?'

'You are the human,' Trohdwyr repeated. 'I can simply answer, you are the voivode's daughter and the Gospodar's niece. But I remember from my childhood – when folk still lived in Old Aferoch, though already then the sea brought worse and worse floods – a female ychan of that town. I knew

30

her somewhat, since a grown cousin of mine used to come in from our village, courting her—'

The story, which was of a rivalry as fierce as might have stood between two men of different clans in early days on Dennitza, but which ended after a rescue on the water, was oddly comforting: almost as if she were little again, and Trohdwyr rocked her against his warm dry breast and rumbled a lullaby. That night Kossara slept well. Some days afterward she returned happily to Dubina Dolyina. When her leave was up, she went back to Zorkagrad.

There she got the news that Mihail Svetich had been killed in action.

But standing before the slave shop's audiovisual recorders, Kossara did not think of this, nor of what had happened to Trohdwyr himself on cold Diomedes. She remained in that one evening out of the many they had had together.]

The chemical joy wore off. She lay on her bunk, bit her pillow and fought not to yell.

A further day passed.

Then she was summoned to the manager's office. 'Congratulations,' he said. 'You've been bought, luckier than you deserve.'

It roared in her. Darkness crossed her eyes. She swayed before his desk. Distantly she heard:

'A private gentleman, and he must really have liked what he saw in the catalogue, because he outbid two different cepheid houses. You can probably do well for yourself – and me, I'll admit. Remember, if he sells you later, he may well go through me again instead of making a deal directly. I don't like my reputation hurt, and I've got this switch here— Anyhow, you'll be wise if you show him your appreciation. His name is Dominic Flandry, he's a captain of Naval Intelligence, a knight of the Imperium, and, I'll tell you, a favorite of the Emperor. He doesn't need a slave for his bed. Gossip is, he's tumbled half the female nobility on Terra, and commoner girls past counting. Like I said, he must think you're special. The more grateful you act, the better your life is likely to be ... On your way, now. A matron will groom and gown you.'

She also provided a fresh euphoriac. Thus Kossara didn't even mind that the servant who came to fetch her was hauntingly like and unlike an ychan. He too was bald, green, and tailed; but the green was grass-bright, without scales, the tail thin as a cat's, the posture erect, the height well below her own, the other differences unreckonable. 'Sir Dominic saw fit to dub me Chives,' he introduced himself. 'I trust you will find his service pleasant. Indeed, I declined the manumission he offered me, until the law about spy bracelets went into effect on Terra. May I direct you out?'

Kossara went along through rosiness, into an aircar, on across the city and an ocean, eventually to an ornate house on an island which Chives called Catalina. He showed her to a suite and explained that her owner was busy elsewhere but would presently make his wishes known. Meanwhile these facilities were hers to use, within reason.

Kossara fell asleep imagining that Mihail was beside her.

CHAPTER THREE

It was official: the Emperor Hans would shortly leave Terra, put himself at the head of an armada, and personally see to quelling the barbarians – war lords, buccaneers, crusaders for God knew what strange causes – who still harassed a Sector Spica left weak by the late struggle for the Imperial succession. He threw a *bon voyage* party at the Coral Palace. Captain Sir Dominic Flandry was among those invited. Under such circumstances, one comes.

Besides, Flandry reflected, *I can't help liking the old bastard. He may not be the best imaginable thing that could happen to us, but he's probably the best available.*

The hour was well after sunset in this part of Oceania. A crescent moon stood high to westward; metrocenter starpoints glinted across its dark side. The constellations threw light of their own onto gently rolling waves, argent shimmer on sable. Quietness broke where surf growled white against ramparts. There walls, domes, towers soared aloft in a brilliance which masked off most of heaven.

When Flandry landed his car and stepped forth, no clouds of perfume (or psychogenic vapors, as had been common in Josip's reign) drifted from the palace to soften salt odors. Music wove among mild breezes, but formal, stately, neither hypersubtle nor raucous. Flandry wasn't sure whether it was composed on a colony planet – if so, doubtless Germania – or on Terra once, to be preserved through centuries while the mother world forgot. He did know that a decade ago, the court would have snickered at sounds this fusty-archaic.

Few servants bowed as he passed among fellow guests, into the main building. More guardsmen than formerly saluted. Their dress uniforms were less ornate than of yore and they and their weapons had seen action. The antechamber of fountains hadn't changed, and the people who swirled between them before streaming toward the ballroom wore clothes as gorgeous as always, a rainbow spectacle. However, fantastic collars, capes, sleeves, cuffs, footgear were passé. Garb was continuous from neck or midbreast to soles, and, while many men wore robes rather than trousers, every woman was in a skirt.

A reform I approve of, he thought. I suspect most ladies agree. The suggestive rustle of skillfully draped fabric is much more stimulating, really, and easier to arrange, than cosmetics and diadems on otherwise bare areas of interest. For that matter, though it does take more effort, a seduction is better recreation than an orgy.

There our good Hans goes too far. Every bedroom in the palace locked!

Ah, well. Conceivably he wants his entourage to cultivate ingenuity.

Crown Prince Dietrich received, a plain-faced middle-aged man whose stoutness was turning into corpulence. Though he and Flandry had worked together now and then in the fighting, his welcome was mechanical. Poor devil, he must say a personal hello to each of three or four hundred arrivals important enough to rate it, with no drug except stim to help him. Another case of austere principles overdone, Flandry thought. The younger brother, Gerhart, was luckier tonight, already imperially drunk at a wallside table with several cronies. However, he looked as sullen as usual.

Flandry drifted around the circumference of the ballroom. There was nothing fancy about the lighting, save that it was cast to leave unobscured the stars in the vitryl dome overhead. The floor sheened with diffracted reflections from several score couples who swung through the decorous measures of a quicksilver. He hailed acquaintances when he glimpsed them, but didn't stop till he had reached an indoor arbor where champagne was available. A goblet of tickle in his hand, roses around him, a cheerful melody, a view of pretty women in motion – life could be worse.

It soon was. 'Greetin', Sir Dominic.'

Flandry turned, and bowed in dismay to the newcomer beneath the leaves. 'Aloha, your Grace.'

34

Tetsuo Niccolini, Duke of Mars, accepted a glass from the attendant behind the table. It was obviously not his first. 'Haven't seen you for some while,' he remarked. 'Missed you. You've a way o' puttin' a little spark into a scene, dull as the court is these days.' Shrewdly : 'Reason you don't come often, what?'

'Well,' Flandry admitted. 'his Majesty's associates do tend to be a bit earnest and firm-jawed.' He sipped. 'Still, my impression is, your Grace spends a fair amount of time here regardless.'

Niccolini sighed. He had never been more than a well-meaning fop; but in these last years, when antisenescence and biosculp could no longer hold wrinkles, baldness, feebleness at bay, he had developed a certain wry perspective. Unfortunately, he remained a bore.

Shadows of petals stirred across a peacock robe as he lifted his drink. 'D'you think I should go to my ancestral estates and all that rubbish, set up my own small court along lines I like, eh? No, m'boy, not feasible. I'd get nothin' but sycophants, who'd pluck me while they smiled. My real friends, who put their hearts into enjoyin' life, well, they're dead or fled or sleepin' in an oldster's bed.' He paused. ''Sides, might's well tell you, H.M. gave me t'understand – he makes himself very clear, ha? – gave me t'understand, he'd prefer no Duke o' Mars henceforth visit the planet 'cept for a decent minimum o' speeches an' dedications.'

Flandry nodded. *That makes sense,* flickered through him. *The Martians [nonhumans; colonists by treaty arrangement in the time of the Commonwealth; glad to belong to it, but feeling betrayed when it broke down and the Troubles came; dragooned into the Empire] are still restless. Terra can best control them by removing the signs of Terran control. I suspect, after poor tottery Tetty is gone, Hans will buy out his heirs with a gimcrack title elsewhere and a lot of money and make a Martian the next Duke – who may not even know he's a puppet.*

At least, that's what I'd consider doing.

'But we're in grave danger o' seriousness,' Niccolini interrupted himself. 'Where've you been? Busy at what? Come, come, somethin' amusin' must've happened.'

'Oh, just knocking around with a friend.' Flandry didn't care to get specific. One reason why he had thus far declined promotion to admiral was that he'd be too conspicuous, too eagerly watched and sought after, while he remained near the Emperor. He liked his privacy. As a hanger-on who showed no further ambitions – and could therefore in time be expected to lose his energetic patron's goodwill – he drew scant attention.

'Or knockin' up a friend? Heh, heh, heh.' The Duke nudged him. 'I know your sort o' friends. How was she?'

'In the first place, she was a he,' Flandry said. Until he could escape, he might as well reconcile himself to humoring a man who had discovered the secret of perpetual adolescence. 'Of course, we explored. Found a new place on Ganymede which might interest your Grace, the Empress Wu in Celestial City.'

'No, no.' Niccolini waggled his head and free hand. 'Didn't y'know? I never go anywhere near Jupiter. Never. Not since the *La Reine Louise* disaster.'

Flandry cast his mind back. He couldn't identify— Oh, yes. It had happened five years ago, while he was out of the Solar System. Undeterred by civil war, a luxury liner was approaching Callisto when her screen field generators failed. The trapped radiation which seethes around the giant planet, engulfing its inner moons, killed everybody aboard; no treatment could restore a body burned by so much unfelt fire.

Nothing of the kind had happened for centuries of exploration and colonization thereabouts. Magnetohydrodynamic shields and their backups were supposed to be invulnerable to anything that wouldn't destroy a vehicle or a settlement anyway. Therefore, sabotage? The passenger list had included several powerful people. A court of inquiry had handed down the vaguest finding of 'cumulative negligence'.

'My poor young nephew, that I inherited the Dukedom from, was among the casualties,' Niccolini droned on. 'That roused the jolly old instinct o' self-preservation, I can tell you. Too blinkin' many hazards as is. Not that I flatter myself I'm a political bull's-eye. Still, one never knows, does one? So tell me 'bout this place you found. If it sounds intriguin', I'll see 'bout gettin' a sensie.'

Flandry was saved by a courier in Imperial livery who entered the arbor and bowed. 'A thousand pardons, your Grace,' she said. 'Sir Dominic, there is an urgent message for you. Will you please follow me?'

'With twofold pleasure,' Flandry responded, for she was young and well-formed. He couldn't quite place her accent, though he guessed she might be from some part of Hermes. Even when hiring humans, the majordomos of the new Emperor's various households were under orders to get as many non-Terrans as was politic.

Whoever the summons was from, and whether it was terrible or trivial, he was free of the Duke before he could otherwise have disengaged. The noble nodded a vague response to his apology and stood staring after him, all alone.

His Imperial Majesty, High Emperor Hans Friedrich Molitor, of his dynasty the first, Supreme Guardian of the Pax, Grand Director of the Stellar Council, Commander-in-Chief, Final Arbiter, acknowledged supreme on more worlds and honorary head of more organizations than any man could remember, sat by himself in a room at the top of a tower. It was sparsely furnished: a desk and communicator, a couch upholstered in worn but genuine horse-hide, a few straight-backed chairs and the big pneumatic that was his. The only personal items were a dolchzahn skin on the floor, from Germania; two portraits of his late wife, in her youth and her age, and one of a blond young man; a model of the corvette that had been his first command. A turret roof, beginning at waist height, was currently transparent, letting this eyrie overlook an illuminated complex of roofs, steeples, gardens, pools, outer walls, attendant rafts, and finally the night ocean.

The courier ushered Flandry through the door and vanished as it closed behind him. He saluted and snapped to attention. 'At ease,' the Emperor grunted. 'Sit. Smoke if you want.'

He was puffing a pipe whose foulness overcame the air 'fresher. In spite of the blue tunic, white trousers, and gold braid with nebula and three stars of a grand admiral, plus the pyrocrystal ring of Manuel the Great, he was not very impressive to see. Yet meditechnics could not account for so few traces of time. The short, stocky frame had grown a kettle belly, bags lay beneath the small dark eyes, the hair was thin and gray on the blocky head: nothing that could not easily be changed by the biocosmetics he scorned to use. Nor had he ever troubled about his face, low forehead, bushy brows, huge Roman nose, heavy jowls, gash of a mouth between deep creases, prow of a chin.

'Thank you, your Majesty.' Flandry settled his elegance opposite, flipped out a cigarette case which was a work of art and, at need, a weapon, and established a barrier against the reek around him.

'No foolish formalities,' growled the rusty, accented basso. 'I must make my grand appearance, and empty chatter will rattle for hours, and at last when I can go I'm afraid I'll be too tired for a nice new wench who's joined the collection, no matter how much I need a little fun.'

'A stim pill?' Flandry suggested.

'No. I take too many as is. The price to the body mounts, you know. And ... barely six years on the throne have I had. The first three, fighting to stay there. I need another twenty or thirty for carpentering this jerry-built, dry-rotted Empire into a thing that might last a few more generations, before I can lay down my tools.' Hans chuckled coarsely. 'Well, let the tool for pretty Thressa wait, recharging, till tomorrow night. You should see her, Dominic, my friend. But not to tell anybody. By herself she could cause a revolution.'

Flandry grinned. 'Yes, we humans are basically sexual beings, aren't we, sir? If we can't screw each other physically, we'll do it politically.'

Hans laughed aloud. He had never changed from a boy

who deserted a strait-laced colonial bourgeois home for several years of wild adventure in space, the youth who enlisted in the Navy, the man who rose through the ranks without connections or flexibility to ease his way.

But he had not changed either from the hero of Syrax, where the fleet he led flung back the Merseians and forced a negotiated end to a short undeclared war which had bidden fair to grow. Nor had he changed from the leader who let his personnel proclaim him Emperor – himself reluctantly, less from vainglory than a sense of workmanship, when the legitimate order of succession had dissolved in chaos and every rival claimant was a potential disaster.

A blunt pragmatist, uncultured and unashamed of it, shrewd rather than intelligent, he either appalled Manuel Argos or won a grudging approval, in whatever hypothetical hell or Valhalla the Founder dwelt. The question was academic. His hour was now. How long that hour would be, and what the consequences, were separate puzzles.

Mirth left. He leaned forward. The pipe smoldered between hairy hands clenched upon his knees. 'I talk too much,' he said, a curious admission from the curtest of the Emperors. Flandry understood, though. Few besides him were left, maybe none, with whom Hans dared talk freely. 'Let us come to business. What do you know about Dennitza?'

Inwardly taken aback, Flandry replied soft-voiced, 'Not much, sir. Not much about the whole Taurian Sector, in spite of having had the good luck to be there when Lady Megan needed help. Why ask me?'

Hans scowled. 'I suppose you do know how the Gospodar, my sector governor, is resisting my defense reorganization. Could be a simple difference of judgment, yes. But ... now information suggests he plans rebellion. And *that* – where he is – will involve the Merseians, unless he is already theirs.'

Flandry's backbone tingled. 'What are the facts, sir?'

'A wretched planet in Sector Arcturus. Diomedes, it's called. Natives who want to break away and babble of getting Ythrian help. Human agents among them. We would expect such humans would be from the Domain, likeliest Avalon – not true? But our best findings say the Ythrians hold no wish to make trouble for us. And our people discover those humans are Dennitzan. Only one was captured alive, and they had some problems with the hypnoprobing, but it does appear she went to Diomedes under secret official orders.'

Hans sighed. 'Not till yesterday did this reach me through the damned channels. It never would have before I left, did I not issue strictest orders about getting a direct look at whatever might possibly point to treason. And – *Gott in Himmel*, I am swamped, on top of all else! My computer screens out *lèse-majesté* cases and the rest of such piddle. Nevertheless—'

Flandry nodded. 'Aye, sir. You can't give any single item more than a glance. And even if you could pay full attention, you can't send the big clumsy Imperial machine barging into Tauria, disrupting our whole arrangement there, on the basis of a few accusations. Especially in your absence.'

'Yes. I must go. If we don't reorder Sector Spica, the barbarians will soon ruin it. But meanwhile Tauria may explode. You see how an uprising in Sector Arcturus would be the right distraction for a traitor Dennitzan before he rebels too.'

'Won't Intelligence mount a larger operation?'

'*Ja, ja, ja*. Though the Corps is still in poor shape, after wars and weedings. Also, it has much other business. And . . . Dominic, just the Corps by itself is too huge for me to know, for me to control as I should. I need – I am not sure what I need or if it can be had.'

Flandry foreknew: 'You want me to take a hand, sir?'

'Yes.' The wild boar eyes were sighted straight on him. 'In your olden style. A roving commission, and you report directly to me. Plenipotentiary authority.'

Flandry's pulse broke into a canter. He kept his tone level. 'Quite a solo, sir.'

'Co-opt. Hire. Bribe. Threaten. Whatever you see fit.'

'The odds will stay long against my finding out anything useful – at least, anything the Corps can't, quicker and better.'

'You are not good at modesty,' Hans said. 'Are you un-willing?'

'N-n-no, sir.' Surprised, Flandry realized he spoke truth. This could prove interesting. In fact, he knew damn well it would, for he had already involved himself in the affair. His motivation was half curiosity, half kindliness – he thought at the time – though probably, down underneath, the carnivore which had been asleep in him these past three years had roused, pricked up its ears, snuffed game scent on a night breeze. *Was that always my real desire? Not to chase down enemies of the Empire so I could go on having fun in it, but to have fun chasing them down?*

No matter. The blood surged. 'I'm happy to accept, sir, provided you don't expect much. Uh, my authority, access to funds and secret data and whatnot . . . better be kept secret itself.'

'Right.' Hans knocked the dottle from his pipe, a ringing noise through a moment's silence. 'Is this why you refused admiral's rank? You knew sneaking off someday on a mission would be easier for a mere captain.'

Flandry shrugged. 'If you'll tip the word to – better be none less than Kheraskov – I'll contact him as soon as may be and made arrangements.'

'Have you any idea how you will begin?' Hans asked, relaxing a trifle.

'Well, I don't know. Perhaps with that alleged Dennitzan agent. What became of . . . her, did you say?'

'How can I tell? I saw a précis of many reports, remember. What difference, after the 'probe wrung her dry?'

'Sometimes individuals count, sir.' Excitement in Flandry congealed to grimness. *I should think the fact she's a niece of the Gospodar – a fact available in the material on her that my son could freely scan from a data bank – would be worth mentioning to the Emperor. I should think such a hostage would not be sold for a slave, forced into whoredom except for the chance that I learned about her when she was offered for sale.*

Better not tell Hans. He'd only be distracted from the

41

million things he's got to do. And anyhow ... something strange here. I prefer to keep my mouth shut and my options open.

'Proceed as you wish,' the other said. 'I know you won't likely get far. But I can trust you will run a strong race.'

His glance went to the picture of the young man. His face sagged. Flandry could well-nigh read his mind: *Ach, Otto! If you had not been killed – if I could bring you back, yes, even though I must trade for you dull Dietrich and scheming Gerhart both – we would have an heir to trust.*

The Emperor straightened in his seat. 'Very well,' he rapped. 'Dismissed.'

The festival wore on. Toward morning, Flandry and Chunderban Desai found themselves alone.

The officer would have left sooner, were it not for his acquired job. Now he seemed wisest if he savored sumptuousness, admired the centuried treasures of static and fluid art which the palace housed, drank noble wines, nibbled on delicate foods, conversed with witty men, danced with delicious girls, finally brought one of these to a pergola he knew (unlocked, screened by jasmine vines) and made love. He might never get the chance again. After she bade him a sleepy goodbye, he felt like having a nightcap. The crowd had grown thin. He recognized Desai, fell into talk, ended in a small garden.

Its base was cantilevered from a wall, twenty meters above a courtyard where a fountain sprang. The waters, full of dissolved fluorescents, shone under ultraviolet illumination in colors more deep and pure than flame. Their tuned splashing resounded from catchbowls to make an eldritch music. Otherwise the two men on their bench had darkness and quiet. Flowers sweetened an air gone slightly cool. The moon was long down; Venus and a dwindling number of stars gleamed in a sky fading from black to purple, above an ocean coming all aglow.

'No, I am not convinced the Emperor does right to depart,' Desai said. The pudgy little old man's hair glimmered white

42

as his tunic; chocolate-hued face and hands were nearly invisible among shadows. He puffed on a cigarette in a long ivory holder. 'Contrariwise, the move invites catastrophe.'

'But to let the barbarians whoop around at will—' Flandry sipped his cognac and drew on his cigar, fragrances first rich, then pungent. He'd wanted to end on a relaxing topic. Desai, who had served the Imperium in many executive capacities on many different planets, owned a hoard of reminiscences which made him worth cultivating. He was on Terra for a year, teaching at the Diplomatic Academy, before he retired to Ramanujan, his birthworld.

The military situation – specifically, Hans' decision to go – evidently bothered him too much for pleasantries. 'Oh, yes, that entire frontier needs restructuring,' he said. 'Not simple reinforcement. New administrations, new laws, new economics : ideally, the foundations of an entire new society among the human inhabitants. However, his Majesty should leave that task to a competent viceroy and staff whom he grants extraordinary powers.'

'There's the problem,' Flandry pointed out. 'Who's both competent and trustworthy enough, aside from those who're already up to their armpits in alligators elsewhere?'

'If he has no better choice,' Desai said, 'his Majesty should let the Spican sector be ravaged – should even let it be lost, in hopes of regaining the territory afterward – anything, rather than absent himself for months. What ultimate good can he accomplish yonder if meanwhile the Imperium is taken from him? The best service he can render the Empire is simply to keep a grip on its heart. Else the civil wars begin again.'

'I fear you exaggerate,' Flandry said, though he recalled how Desai was always inclined to understate things. And Dennitzans on Diomedes ... 'We seem to've pacified ourselves fairly well. Besides, why refer to civil wars in the plural?'

'Have you forgotten McCormac's rebellion, Sir Dominic?'

Scarcely, seeing I was involved. Flandry winced at a memory. Lost Kathryn, as well as the irregular nature of his actions at the time, made him glad the details were still unpublic. 'No. But that was, uh, twenty-two years ago. And amounted to what? An admiral who revolted against Josip's sector governor for personal reasons. True, this meant he had to try for the crown. The Imperium could never have pardoned him. But he was beaten, and Josip died in bed.' *Probably poisoned, to be sure.*

'You consider the affair an isolated incident?' Desai challenged in his temperate fashion. 'Allow me to remind you, please – I know you know – shortly afterward I found myself the occupation commissioner of McCormac's home globe, Aeneas, which had spearheaded the uprising. We came within an ångström there of getting a messianic religion that might have burst into space and torn the Empire in half.'

Flandry took a hard swallow from his snifter and a hard pull on his cigar. Well had he studied the records of that business, after he encountered Aycharaych who had engineered it.

'The thirteen following years – seeming peace inside the Empire, till Josip's death – they are no large piece of history, are they?' Desai pursued. 'Especially if we bear in mind that conflicts have causes. A war, including a civil war, is the flower on a plant whose seed went into the ground long before ... and whose roots reach widely, and will send up fresh growths ... No, Sir Dominic, as a person who has read and reflected for most of a lifetime on this subject, I tell you we are well into our anarchic phase. The best we can do is minimize the damage, and hold outside enemies off until we win back to a scarred kind of unity.'

' "Our" anarchic phase?' Flandry questioned.

Desai misheard his emphasis. 'Or our interregnum, or whatever you wish to call it. Oh, we may not always fight over who shall be Emperor; we can find plenty of bones to contend about. And we may enjoy stretches of peace and relative prosperity. I hoped Hans would provide us such a respite.'

'No, wait, you speak as if this is something we have to go through, willy-nilly.'

'Yes. For about eighty more years, I think – though of

course modern technology, nonhuman influences, the sheer scale of interstellar dominion may affect the time-span. Basically, however, yes, a universal state – and the Terran Empire is the universal state of Technic civilization – only gives a respite from the wars and horrors which multiply after the original breakdown. Its Pax is no more than a subservience enforced at swordpoint, or today at blaster point. Its competent people become untrustworthy from their very competence; anyone who can make a decision may make one the Imperium does not like. Incompetence grows with the growing suspiciousness and centralization. Defense and civil functions alike begin to disintegrate. What can that provoke except rebellion? So this universal state of ours has ground along for a brace of generations, from bad to worse, until now—'

'The Long Night?' Flandry shivered a bit in the gentle air.

'I think not quite yet. If we follow precedent, the Empire will rise again ... if you can label as "rise" the centralized divine autocracy we have coming. To be sure, if the thought of such a government does not cheer you, then remember that that second peace of exhaustion will not last either. In due course will come the final collapse.'

'How do you know?' Flandry demanded.

'The cycle fills the history, yes, the archeology of this whole planet we are sitting on. Old China and older Egypt each went thrice through the whole sorry mess. The Western civilization to which ours is affiliated rose originally from the same kind of thing, that Roman Empire some of our rulers have liked to hark back to for examples of glory. Oh, we too shall have our Diocletian; but scarcely a hundred years after his reconstruction, the barbarians were camping in Rome itself and making emperors do their pleasure. My own ancestral homeland – but there is no need for a catalogue of forgotten nations. For a good dozen cases we have chronicles detailed to the point of nausea; all in all, we can find over fifty examples just in the dust of this one world.

'Growth, until wrong decisions bring breakdown; then ever more ferocious wars, until the Empire brings the Pax; then

45

the dissolution of that Pax, its reconstruction, its disintegration forever, and a dark age until a new society begins in the ruins. Technic civilization started on that road when the Polesotechnic League changed from a mutual-aid organization of free entrepreneurs to a set of cartels. Tonight we are far along the way.'

'You've discovered this yourself?' Flandry asked, not as skeptically as he could have wished he were able to.

'Oh, no, no,' Desai said. 'The basic analysis was made a thousand years ago. But it's not comfortable to live with. Prevention of breakdown, or recovery from it, calls for more thought, courage, sacrifice than humans have yet been capable of exercising for generation after generation. Much easier first to twist the doctrine around, use it for rationalization instead of rationality; then ignore it, finally suppress it. I found it in certain archives, but you realize I am talking to you in confidence. The Imperium would not take kindly to such a description of itself.'

'Well—' Flandry drank again. 'Well, you may be right. And total pessimism does have a certain bracing quality. If we're doomed to tread out the measure, we can try to do so gracefully.'

'There is no absolute inevitability.' Desai puffed for a minute, his cigarette end a tiny red pulsar. 'I suppose, even this late in the game, we could start afresh if we had the means – more importantly, the will. But in actuality, the development is often aborted by foreign conquest. An empire in the anarchic phase is especially tempting and especially prone to suffer invaders. Osmans, Afghans, Moguls, Manchus, Spaniards, British – they and those like them became overlords of cultures different from their own, in that same way.

'Beyond our borders, the Merseians are the true menace. Not a barbarian rabble merely filling a vacuum we have left by our own political machinations – not a realistic Ythri which sees us as its natural ally – not a pathetic Gorrazani remnant – but Merseia. We harass and thwart the Roidhunate everywhere, because we dare not let it grow too strong. Besides eliminating us as a hindrance to its dreams, think what a furtherance our conquest would be !

'That's why I dread the consequences of the Emperor's departure. Staying home, working to buttress the government and armed forces, ready to stamp fast on every attempt at insurrection, he might keep us united, uninvadable, for the rest of his life. Without his presence – I don't know.'

'The Merseians would have to be prepared to take quick advantage of any revolt,' Flandry argued. 'Assuming you're right about your historical pattern, are *they* aware of it? How common is it?'

'True, we don't have the knowledge to say how far it may apply to nonhumans, if at all,' Desai admitted. 'We should. In fact, it was Merseia, not ourselves, that set me on this resarch – for the Merseians too must have their private demons, and think what a weapon it would be for our diplomacy to have a generalized mechanic for them as well as us !'

'Hm?' said Flandry, surprised afresh. 'Are you implying perhaps they already are decadent? That's not what one usually hears.'

'No, it isn't. But what is decadence to a nonhuman? I hope to do more than read sutras in my retirement; I hope to apply my experience and my studies to thought about just such problems.' The old man sighed. 'Of necessity, this assumes the Empire will not fall prey to its foes before I've made some progress. That may be an unduly optimistic assumption ... considering what a head start they have in the Roidhunate where it comes to understanding us.'

'Are you implying they know this theory of human history which you've been outlining to me?'

'Yes, I fear that at least a few minds among them are all too familiar with it. For example, after considering the episode for many years, I think that when Aycharaych tried to kindle a holy war of man against man, starting on Aeneas, he knew precisely what he was doing.'

Aycharaych. The chill struck full into Flandry. He raised his eyes to the fading stars. Sol would soon drive sight away from them, but they would remain where they were, waiting.

'I have often wondered what makes him and his kind serve Merseia,' Desai mused. 'Genius can't really be conscripted. The Chereionites surely have something to win for themselves. But what – from an alien species, an alien culture?'

'Aycharaych's the only one of them I've ever actually met,' Flandry said. 'I've sometimes thought he's an artist.'

'An artist of espionage and sabotage, whose materials are living beings? Well, conceivably. If that's all, he is no more to be envied than you or I.'

'Why?'

'I'm not sure I can make the reason clear to you, or even very clear to myself. We have not had the good fortune to be born in an era when our society offers us something transcendental to live and die for.' Desai cleared his throat. 'I'm sorry. I didn't intend to read you a lecture.'

'No, I thank you,' Flandry said. 'Your ideas are quite interesting.'

CHAPTER FOUR

The *Hooligan* sprang from Terra, pierced the sky, and lined out for deep space. A steady standard gravity maintained by her interior fields gave no hint of furious acceleration toward regions sufficiently distant that she could go into hyperdrive and outpace light. Nor did her engine energies speak above an almost subliminal whisper and quiver through the hull. But standing in the saloon before its big viewscreen, Kossara watched the planet shrink, ever faster, a cloudy vastness, a gibbous globe of intricate blue and white, an agate in a diamondful jewel box.

At the back of her mind she wished she could appreciate this sight for which she had left the stateroom assigned her. Terra, Manhome, Maykasviyet; and sheer loveliness— But her heart knocked, her nails bit into wet palms though her tongue was dry and thick, she smelled her harsh sweat.

Yet when her owner entered, calm crystallized in her. By nature and training she met crises coolly, and here was the worst since— As far as she knew, nobody else was aboard but him and his servant. If she could, somehow, kill them – or hogtie the funny, kindly Shalmuan – maybe before he took her—

No. Not unless he grew altogether slack; and she sensed alertness beneath his relaxed manner. He was tall and well built and moved like a hunting vilya. Handsome too, she admitted to herself; then scorn added that anybody could be handsome who bought a biosculpture. A loose lace-trimmed blouse and flowing trousers gathered above sandals matched, in their sheen of expensive fabric, the knee-length gown she had chosen out of the wardrobe she found in her quarters.

'Good day, Donna Vymezal,' the man said, and bowed. What to do? She jerked a nod.

'Permit self-introduction,' he went on. 'Hardly to your surprise, I am Captain Sir Dominic Flandry, Intelligence

Corps of His Majesty's Navy.' He gestured at a bench curved around two sides of a table. 'Won't you be seated?'

She stood her ground.

Flandry smiled, placed hands on hips, and drawled: 'Please listen. I have no intention of compelling you. None. Not that you don't inspire certain daydreams, Donna. And not that I couldn't make you like it. Drugs, you know. But vanity forbids. I've never needed force or pharmacopoeia, even on those few young ladies I had occasion to buy in the past. Have you noticed your cabin door locks on the inside?'

Strength went from Kossara. She stumbled backward, fell to the bench, rested head in hands while whirling and darkness passed through her.

Presently she grew aware that Flandry stood above. His fingers kneaded her neck and shoulders. As she looked up, he stroked her hair. She gasped and drew aside.

He stepped back. 'No offense, Donna.' Sternly: 'See here, we've a bundle to discuss, none of it very amusing. Do you want a stim pill – or what, to make you operational?'

She shook her head. After two tries, she husked forth, 'Nothing, thank you. I am all right now.'

'Drink? The liquor cabinet is reasonably well stocked. I'm for Scotch.'

'Nothing,' she whispered, dreading in spite of his words what might be in a glass he gave her.

He seemed to guess that, for he said, 'You'll have to take from my galley in due course if not sooner. We've a long trip ahead of us.'

'What? ... Well, a little wine, please.'

He got busy, while she worked to loosen muscles and nerves. When he sat down, not too close, she could meet his eyes. She declined the cigarette he offered, but the claret was marvelous. He steamed smoke from his nostrils before saying, deliberately:

'You might recollect who else was bidding on you.' She felt her face blaze. 'And I didn't spend quite a lot of beer money out of chivalry. Your virtue is safe is long as you want it to be – while I'm your owner. But I need your cooperation in some rather larger matters. Understood?'

She gulped. 'If I can ... help you, sir—'

'In exchange for manumission and a ticket to Dennitza? Maybe. I haven't the legal right to free you, seeing what you were convicted of. I'd have to petition for a decree. Or I could simply order you to go back where you came from and enjoy yourself.' He saw her glance fall to the slave bracelet. 'Yes, now we're clear of Terra, I'm permitted to take that off you. But I haven't a key for it, and my tools would damage it, which'd put us through a certain amount of bureaucratic rain dance if we return there. Never mind. Beyond range of the comnet, it's inert.' Flandry grinned. 'If I were indeed a monster of lust, rather than a staid and hardworking monster, I'd still have taken you into space before commencing. The idea of an audience at any arbitrary time doesn't appeal. Let them invent their own techniques.'

Loathing tightened Kossara's throat. 'The Terran way of life.'

Flandry regarded her quizzically. 'You don't have a high opinion of the Empire, do you?'

'I hate it. I would die – be tortured – yes, go into a brothel, if I could pull the rotten thing down around me.' Kossara tossed off her wine.

Flandry refilled the glass. 'Better be less outspoken,' he advised. 'I don't mind, but various of my fellow Imperialists might.'

She stared. The real horror of her situation shocked home. 'Where are we bound?'

'Diomedes, for openers at any rate.' He nodded. 'Yes, I'm investigating what went on, what is going on, whether it threatens the Empire, and how to prevent same.'

Kossara rallied. 'You have the records of my ... arrest and interrogation, then,' she said fast. 'I have no further information. Less, actually, because the hypnoprobe blanked out related memories, including those from Dennitza. What's left is bits, blurry and jumbled together, like barely remembered dreams. So how can I help you – supposing I wanted to?'

'Oh, background and such.' Flandry's tone was casual. 'Give me the rest of your biography. Explain what your people have against the Imperium. I'll listen. Who knows, you may convert me. I won't hurry you. There's an unsanctified amount of information pumped into the data banks aboard, which I need to study en route. And we've time. Seventeen standard days to destination.'

'No more?' In spite of everything, astonishment touched her.

'This boat has legs, albeit not as well turned as yours. Do ease off, Donna. Your culture has a soldierly orientation, right? Consider me your honorable enemy, if nothing else, and the pair of us conducting a parley.'

She found little to say. He talked for two, mostly appealing to her xenological interests with tales of sophonts he had met. All were fascinating. A few eventually made her laugh.

Books, musical pieces, shows were available by the thousands, in playback or printout. Kossara grew restless anyhow. Flandry had withdrawn immediately after the first breakfast of the voyage (following a nightwatch wherein she slept unexpectedly well) to concentrate on his briefing material. Interstellar space, seen in the optical-compensating screens, was utter splendor; but however fast the *Hooligan* drove, those immensities changed too slowly for perception. She exercised, prowled around, tried out different hobby kits, at last sought Chives. He was in the galley fixing lunch. 'Can I help you?' she offered.

'I regret not, Donna,' the Shalmuan answered. 'While I have no wish to deprecate your culinary gifts, you can see that Sir Dominic does not willingly trust this excellent chef-machine to prepare his meals, let alone comparative strangers.'

She stared at the open-faced sandwiches growing beneath his fingers. Anchovies and pimientos lay across slices of hard-boiled egg on fresh-made mayonnaise, caviar and lemon peel complemented pâté de foie gras, cucumber and alfalfa sprouts revitalized cheddar cheese in the dignity of its age ... 'No, I couldn't do that,' she admitted. 'You must be a genius.'

'Thank you, Donna. I endeavor to give satisfaction. Although, in candor, Sir Dominic provided my initial training and the impetus to develop further.'

Kossara drew a long breath. A *chance to learn about him?* 'You were his slave, you said. How did that happen, if I may ask?'

Chives spoke imperturbably, never breaking the rhythm of his work. 'My planet of origin has no technologically advanced society, Donna. His late Majesty Josip appointed a sector governor who organized a slave trade in my people, chiefly selling to the barbarians beyond the *limes.* The charges against those captured for this purpose were, shall we say, arguable; but no one argued. When that governor met with misfortune, his successor attempted to right matters. However, this was impossible. Not even victims still within the Empire could be traced, across thousands of worlds. Sir Dominic merely chanced upon me in a provincial market.

'I was not prepossessing, Donna. My owner had put me up for sale because he doubted I could survive more labor in his mercury mine. Sir Dominic did not buy me. He instigated a game of poker which lasted several days and left him in possession of mine and workers alike.'

Chives clicked his tongue. 'My former master alleged cheating. Most discourteous of him, especially compared to Sir Dominic's urbanity in inviting him out. The funeral was well attended by the miners. Sir Dominic arranged for their repatriation, but kept me since this was far from Shalmu and, besides, I required a long course of chelating drugs to cleanse my system. Meanwhile he employed me in his service. I soon decided I had no wish to return to a society of ... natives ... and strove to make myself valuable to him.'

Head cocked, chin in hand, tail switching, Chives studied the lunch layout. 'Yes, I believe this will suffice. Akvavit and beer for beverages, needless to say. Since you wish occupation, Donna, you may assist me in setting the table.'

She scarcely heard. '*Moze,* if he's a decent man,' she blurted, 'how can he work for an Empire that lets things like, like your case happen?'

'I have oftener heard Sir Dominic described in such terms as – ah – for example, a slightly overexcited gentleman once called him a cream-stealing tomcat with his conscience in his balls, if you will pardon the expression, Donna. The fact is, he did cheat in that poker game. But as for the Empire, like the proverbial centenarian I suggest you consider the alternative. You will find tableware in yonder cabinet,'

Kossara bit her lip and took the hint.

'To the best of my admittedly circumscribed knowledge,' Chives said after silver, china, and glass (not vitryl) stood agleam upon snowy linen, 'your folk have, on the whole, benefited from the Empire. Perhaps I am misinformed. Would you care to summarize the history for me while the spiced meatballs are heating?'

His slim emerald form squatted down on the deck. Kossara took a bench, stared at her fists resting knotted on her lap, and said dully:

'I don't suppose the details, six hundred years of man on Dennitza, would interest anybody else. That is how long since Yovan Matavuly led the pioneers there. They were like other emigrant groups at the time, hoping not alone for opportunity, room to breathe, but to save traditions, customs, language, race – ethnos, identity, their souls if you like – everything they saw being swallowed up. They weren't many, nor had the means to buy much equipment. And Dennitza ... well, there are always problems in settling a new planet, physical environment, biochemistry, countless unknowns and surprises that can be lethal – but Dennitza was particularly hard. It's in an ice age. The habitable areas are limited. And in those days it was far from any trade routes, had nothing really to attract merchants of the League—'

Speaking of the ancestors heartened her. She raised head and voice. 'They didn't fall back to barbarism, no, no. But they did, for generations, have to put aside sophisticated technology. They lacked the capital, you see. Clan systems developed; feuding, I must admit; a spirit of local independence. The barons looked after their own. That social structure

54

persisted when industrialism began, and affected it.' Quickly:
'Don't think we were ever ignorant yokels. The Shkola –
university and research centrum – is nearly as old as the
colony. The toughest backwoodsman respects learning as
much as he does marksmanship or battle bravery.'

'Do you not have a Merseian element in the population?'
Chives asked.

'Yes. Merseian-descended, that is, from about four hundred
years ago. You probably know Merseia itself was starting to
modernize and move into space then, under fearful handicaps
because of that supernova nearby and because of the multi-
cornered struggle for power between Vachs, Gethfennu, and
separate nations. The young Dennitzan industries needed
labor. They welcomed strong, able, well-behaved displaced
persons.'

'Do such constitute a large part of your citizenry, Donna?'

'About ten percent of our thirty million. And twice as
many human Dennitzans live outsystem; since our industry
and trade got well underway, we've been everywhere in that
part of space. So what is this nonsense I hear about us being
Merseian-infiltrated?'

Yet we might be happier in the Roidhunate, Kossara added.

Chives recalled her: 'I have heard mention of the Gospodar. Does my lady care to define his functions? Is he like a
king?'

'M-m-m, what do you mean by "king"? The Gospodar is
elected out of the Miyatovich family by the plemichi, the
clan heads and barons. He has supreme executive authority
for life or good behavior, subject to the Grand Court ruling
on the constitutionality of what he does. A Court verdict
can be reversed by the Skuptshtina – Parliament, I suppose
you would say, though it has three chambers, for plemichi,
commons and ychani ... zmayi ... our nonhumans. Domestic government is mainly left to the different okruzhi –
baronies? prefectures? – which vary a lot. The head of one
of those may inherit office, or may be chosen by the resident
clans, or may be appointed by the Gospodar, depending on
ancient usage. He – such a nachalnik, I mean – he generally

lets townships and rural districts tend their own affairs through locally elected councillors.'

'The, ah, ychani are organized otherwise, I take it.'

Kossara gave Chives a look of heightened respect. 'Yes. Strictly by clans – or better say Vachs – subject only to planetary law unless there's some special fealty arrangement. And while you can find them anywhere on Dennitza, they concentrate on the eastern seaboard of Rodna, the main continent, in the northern hemisphere. Because they can stand cold better than humans, they do most of the fishing, pelagiculture, et cetera.'

'Nevertheless, I presume considerable cultural blending has taken place.'

'Certainly—'

Recollection rushed in of Trohdwyr, who died on Diomedes whither she was bound; of her father on horseback, a-gallop against a windy autumn forest, and the bugle call he blew which was an immemorial Merseian warsong; of her mother cuddling her while she sang an Eriau lullaby, '*Dwynafor, dwynafor, odhal tiv,*' and then laughing low, 'But you, little sleepyhead, you have no tail do you?'; of herself and Mihail in an ychan boat on the Black Ocean, snowfall, ice floes, a shout as a sea beast magnificently broached to starboard; moonlit gravbelt flight over woods, summer air streaming past her cheeks, a campfire glimpsed, a landing among great green hunters, their gruff welcome; and, 'I'm not hungry,' Kossara said, and left the saloon before Chives or, worse, Flandry should see her weep.

CHAPTER FIVE

Flandry's office, if that was the right name for it, seemed curiously spare amidst the sybaritic arrangements Kossara had observed elsewhere aboard. She wondered what his private quarters were like. *But don't ask. He might take that as an invitation.* Seated in front of the desk behind which he was, she made her gaze challenge his.

'I know this will be painful to you,' he said. 'You've had a few days to rest, though, and we must go through with it. You see, the team that 'probed you appears to have made every imaginable blunder and maybe created a few new ones.' She must have registered her startlement, for he continued, 'Do you know how a hypnoprobe works?'

Bitterness rose in her. 'Not really,' she said. 'We have no such vile thing on Dennitza.'

'I don't approve either. But sometimes desperation dictates.'

Flandry leaned back in his chair, ignited a cigarette, regarded her out of eyes whose changeable gray became the hue of a winter overcast. His tone remained soft: 'Let me explain from the ground up. Interrogation is an unavoidable part of police and military work. You can do it on several levels of intensity. First, simple questioning; if possible, questioning different subjects separately and comparing their stories. Next, browbeating of assorted kinds. Then torture, which can be the crude inflicting of pain or something like prolonged sleep deprivation. The trouble with these methods is, they aren't too dependable. The subject may hold out. He may lie. If he's had psychosomatic training, he can fool a lie detector; or, if he's clever, he can tell only a misleading part of the truth. At best, procedures are slow, especially when you have to cross-check whatever you get against whatever other information you can find.

'So we move on to narcoquiz, drugs that damp the will to

57

resist. Problem here is first, you often get idiosyncratic re-actions or nonreactions. People vary a lot in their body chemistry, especially these days when most of humanity has lived for generations or centuries on worlds that aren't Terra. And, of course, each nonhuman species is a whole separate bowl of spaghetti. Then, second, your subject may have been immunized against everything you have in your medicine chest. Or he may have been deep-conditioned, in which case no drug we know of will unlock his mind.'

Between the shoulderblades, Kossara's back hurt from tension. 'What about telepathy?' she snapped.

'Often useful but always limited,' Flandry said. 'Neural radiations have a low rate of information conveyance. And the receiver has to know the code the sender is using. For instance, if I were a telepath, and you concentrated on think-ing in Serbic, I'd be as baffled as if you spoke aloud. Or worse, because individual thought patterns vary tremendously, es-pecially in species like ours which don't normally employ telepathy. I might learn to read your mind – slowly, awk-wardly, incompletely at best – but find that everybody else's was transmitting gibberish as far as I was concerned. Inter-species telepathy involves still bigger difficulties. And we know tricks for combatting any sort of brain listener. A screen worn on the head will heterodyne the outgoing radia-tion in random fashion, make it absolutely undecipherable. Or, again, training, or deep conditioning, can be quite effec-tive.'

He paused. Wariness crossed his mobile countenance. 'There are exceptions to everything,' he murmured, 'includ-ing what I've said. Does the name Aycharach mean any-thing to you?'

'No,' she answered honestly. 'Why?'

'No matter now. Perhaps later.'

'I *am* a xenologist,' Kossara reminded him. 'You've told me nothing new.'

'Eh? Sorry. Unpredictable what somebody else does or does not know about the most elementary things, in a uni-verse where facts swarm like gnats. Why, I was thirty years old before I learned what the Empress Theodora used to complain about.'

She stared past his smile. 'You were going to describe the hypnoprobe.'

He sobered. 'Yes. The final recourse. Direct electronic attack on the brain. On a molecular level, bypassing drugs, conditionings, anything. Except – the subject can have been preconditioned, in his whole organism, to die when this happens. Shock reaction. If the interrogation team is prepared, it can hook him into machines that keep the vital processes going, and so have a fair chance of forcing a response. But his mind won't survive the damage.'

He ground his cigarette hard against the lip of an ashtaker before letting the stub be removed. 'You weren't in that state, obviously.' His voice roughened. 'In fact, you had no drug immunization. Why weren't you narcoed instead of 'probed? Or were you, to start with?'

'I don't remember—' Astounded, Kossara exclaimed, 'How do you know? About me and drugs, I mean? I didn't myself!'

'The slave dealer's catalogue. His medic ran complete cytological analyses. I put the data through a computer. It found you've had assorted treatments to resist exotic conditions, but none of the traces a psychimmune would show.'

Flandry shook his head, slowly back and forth. 'An overzealous interrogator might order an immediate 'probe, instead of as a last resort,' he said. 'But why carry it out in a way that wiped your associated memories? True, such things do happen occasionally. For instance, a particular subject might have a low threshold of tolerance; the power level might then be too high, and disrupt the RNA molecules as they come into play under questioning. As a rule, though, permanent psychological effects – beyond those which bad experiences generally leave – are rare. A competent team will test the subject beforehand and establish the parameters.'

He sighed. 'Well, the civil war and aftermath lopped a lot off the top, in my Corps too. Coprolite-brained characters who'd ordinarily have been left in safe routineering assignments were promoted to fill vacancies. Maybe you had the bad luck to encounter a bunch of them.'

'I am not altogether sorry to have forgotten,' Kossara mumbled.

Flandry stroked his mustache. 'Ah ... you don't think you've suffered harm otherwise?'

'I don't believe so. I can reason as well as ever. I remember my life in detail till shortly before I left for Diomedes, and I'm quite clear about everything since they put me aboard ship for Terra.'

'Good.' Flandry's warmth seemed genuine. 'There are enough unnecessary horrors around, without a young and beautiful woman getting annulled.'

He rescued me from the slime pit, she thought. *He has shown me every kindness and courtesy.*

Thus far. He admits – his purpose is to preserve the Empire.

'What pieces do you recall, Kossara?' Flandry had not used her first name before.

She strained fingers against each other. Her pulse beat like a trapped bird. *No. Don't bring them back. The fear, the hate, the beloved dead.*

'You see,' he went on, 'I'm puzzled as to why Dennitza should turn against us. Your Gospodar supported Hans, and was rewarded with authority over his entire sector. Granted, that's laid a terrible work load on him if he's conscientious. But it gives him – his people – a major say in the future of their region. A dispute about the defense mechanisms for your home system and its near neighbors ... well, that's only a dispute, isn't it, which he may still have some hope of winning. Can't you give me a better reason for him to make trouble? Isn't a compromise possible?'

'Not with the Imperium!' Kossara said out of upward-leaping rage.

'Between you and me, at least? Intellectually? Won't you give me your side of the story?'

Kossara's blood ebbed. 'I ... well, speaking for myself, the fighting cost me the man I was going to marry. What use an Empire that can't keep the Pax?'

'I'm sorry. But did any mortal institution ever work perfectly? Hans is trying to make repairs. Besides, think. Why would the Gospodar – if he did plan rebellion – why would he send you, a girl, his niece, to Diomedes?'

She summoned what will and strength she had left, closed her eyes, searched back through time.

[Bodin Miyatovich was a big man, trim and erect in middle age. He bore the broad, snub-nosed, good-looking family face, framed in graying dark-blond hair and close-cropped beard, tanned and creased by a lifetime of weather. His eyes were beryl. Today he wore a red cloak over brown tunic and breeks, gromatz leather boots, customary knife and sidearm sheathed on a silver-studded belt.

Dyavo-like, he paced the sun deck which jutted from the Zamok. In gray stone softened by blossoming creepers, that ancestral castle reared walls, gates, turrets, battlements, wind-blown banners (though the ulitmate fortress lay beneath, carved out of living rock) above steep tile roofs and pastel-tinted half-timbered stucco of Old Town houses. Thence Zorkagrad sloped downward; streets changed from twisty lanes to broad boulevards; traffic flitted around geometrical buildings raised in modern materials by later generations. Waterborne shipping crowded docks and bay. Lake Stoyan stretched westward over the horizon, deep blue dusted with glitter cast from a cloudless heaven. Elsewhere beyond the small city, Kossara could from this height see cultivated lands along the shores: green trees, hedges, grass, and yellowing grain of Terran stock; blue or purple where native foliage and pasture remained; homes, barns, sheds, sunpower towers, widely spaced; a glimpse of the Lyubisha River rolling from the north as if to bring greeting from her father's manse. Closer by, the Elena flowed eastward, oceanward; barges plodded and boats danced upon it. Here in the middle of the Kazan, she could not see the crater walls which those streams clove. But she had a sense of them, ramparts against glacier and desert, a chalice of warmth and fertility.

A breeze embraced her, scented by flowers, full of the sweet songs of guslars flitting ruddy to and from their nests in the vines. She sat back in her chair and thought, guilty at doing so, what a pity to spend such an hour on politics.

Her uncle's feet slammed the planks. 'Does Molitor imagine we'll never get another Olaf or Josip on the throne?' the Gospodar rumbled. 'A clown or a cancer ... and, once more, Policy Board, Admiralty, civil service bypassed, or terrorized, or corrupted. If we rely on the Navy for our whole defense, what defense will we have against future foolishness or tyranny? Let the foolishness go too far, and we'll have no defense at all.'

'Doesn't he speak about preventing any more civil wars?' Kossara ventured.

Bodin spat an oath. 'How much of a unified command is possible, in practical fact, on an interstellar scale? Every fleet admiral is a potential war lord. Shall we keep nothing to set against him?' He stopped. His fist thudded on a rail. 'Molitor trusts nobody. That's what's behind this. So why should I trust him?'

He turned about. His gaze smoldered at her. 'Besides,' he said, slowly, far down in his throat, 'the time may come ... the time may not be far off ... when we need another civil war.']

'No—' she whispered. 'I can't remember more than ... resentment among many. The Noradna Voyska has been a, a basic part of our society, ever since the Troubles. Squadron and regimental honors, rights, chapels, ceremonies – I'd stand formation on my unit's parade ground at sunset – us together, bugle calls, volley, pipes and drums, and while the flag came down, the litany for those of our dead we remembered that day – and often tears would run over my cheeks, even in winter when they froze.'

Flandry smiled lopsidedly. 'Yes, I was a cadet once.' He shook himself a bit. 'Well. No doubt your militia intertwines with a lot of civilian matters, social and economic. For instance, I'd guess it doubles as constabulary in some areas, and is responsible for various public works, and – yes. Disbanding it would disrupt a great deal of your lives, on a practical as well as emotional level. His Majesty may not appreciate this enough. Germania doesn't contain your kind of society, and though he's seen a good many others, between us, I wouldn't call him a terribly imaginative man.

'Still, I repeat, negotiations have not been closed. And whatever their upshot, don't you yourself have the imagination to see he means well? Why this fanatical hatred of yours? And how many Dennitzans share it?'

'I don't know,' Kossara said. 'But personally, after what men of the Empire did to, to people I care about – and later to me—'

'May I ask you to describe what you recall?' Flandry answered. She glared defiance. 'You see, if nothing else, maybe I'll find out, and be able to prove to their superiors, those donnickers rate punishment for aggravated stupidity.'

He picked up a sheaf of papers on his desk and riffled them. *The report on me must have violated my privacy more than I could ever do myself*, she thought in sudden weariness. *All right, let me tell him what little I can.*

[A cave in the mountains near Salmenbrok held the sparse gear which kept her and her fellows alive. They stood around her on a ledge outside, but except for Trohdwyr shadowy, no real faces or names upon them any more. Cliffs and crags loomed in darkling solidity, here and there a gnarled tree or a streak of snow tinged pink by a reddish sun high in a purple heaven. The wind thrust long, strong, chill; it had not only an odor but a taste like metal. A cataract, white and green half a kilometer away, boomed loud through thick air that also shifted the pitch and timbre of every sound. Huddled in her parka, she felt how Diomedes drew on her more heavily than Dennitza, nearly two kilograms added to every ten.

Eonan of the Lannachska poised almost clear in her mind. Yellow eyes aglow, wings unfurled for departure, he said in his shrill-accented Anglic: 'You understand, therefore, how

63

these things strike at the very life of my folk? And thus they touch our whole world. We thought the wars between Flock and Fleet were long buried. Now they stir again—'

(Both moons were aloft and near the full, copper-colored, twice the seeming size of Mesyatz (or Luna), one slow, one hasty across a sky where few stars blinked and those in alien constellations. The night cold gnawed. Flames sputtered and sparked. Their light fetched Trohdwyr from darkness, where he sat on feet and tail in the cave mouth, roasting meat from the ration box. The smoke bore a sharp aroma. He said to Kossara and her fellow humans: 'It's not for an old zmay to tell you wise heads how to handle a clutch of xenos. I'm here as naught but my lady's servant and bodyguard. However, if you want to keep peace among the natives, why not bring some Ythrians to explain Ythri really has no aim of backing any rebellion-minded faction?'

Steve Johnson – no! Stefan Ivanovich. Why in the name of madness should she think of him as Steve Johnson? – replied out of the face she could not give a shape: 'That'd have to be arranged officially. The resident can't on his own authority. He'd have to go through the sector governor. And I'm not sure if the sector governor wants Ythri – or Terra – to know how bad the situation is on Diomedes.'

'Besides,' added -?-, 'the effects aren't predictable, except they'd be far-reaching. We do have a full-scale cultural crisis here. Among nonhumans, at that.'

'Still,' said a third man (woman? And was his/her nose really flat, eyes oblique, complexion tawny?), 'whatever instincts and institutions they have, I think we can credit them – enough of them – with common sense. What we will need, however, is at least a partial solution to the Flock's difficulties. Otherwise, dashing their hopes of Ythrian help could drive them to . . . who knows what?' (If those features were not a mere trick of tattered memory, well, maybe this was a non-Dennitzan whom Uncle Bodin or his agents had engaged.)

'Yes,' Kossara opined, 'the trick will be to stay on top of events.'

Was that the very night when the Imperial marines stormed them?

[Or another night? Trohdwyr shouted, 'Let go of my lady!' In the gloom he snatched forth his knife. A stun pistol sent him staggering out onto the ledge, to collapse beneath the moons. After a minute, quite deliberately, the marine lieutenant gave him a low-powered blaster shot in the belly.

No surprise that Kossara didn't remember the fight which killed her companions. She knew only Trohdwyr, stirring awake again. His guts lay cooked below his ribs. After she tore loose from the grip upon her and fell to her knees beside him, she caught the smell. 'Trohdwyr, *dragan!*' He coughed, could not speak, maybe could not know her through the pain that blinded him. She raised his head, hugged it close, felt the blunt spines press into her breasts. '*Dwynafor, dwynafor, odhal tiv,*' she heard herself crazily croak.

A man dragged her away. 'Come along.' She turned on him, spitting, fingers rigid for a karate attack. Another man got a lock on her from behind. The first cuffed her till the world rocked. 'All that fuss over a xeno,' he complained, and booted Trohdwyr for a while. She couldn't tell whether the ychan felt the blows; but his body jerked like a dropped puppet.

[The office was cramped, its air stale. The commander of Intelligence said, 'Nothing slow and easy for you, Vymezal. Treason's too urgent a matter; and traitors deserve no careful handling.'

'I am not—'

'We'll soon find out. Take her away, O'Brien. I want her prepared for hypnoprobing.'

[Downward whirl through shrieks, thunders, flashes, pain and pain, down toward emptiness, but oh, she cannot reach blessed cool nothing; eternity has her.

The Golden Face, the cinnabar eyes, an indigo plume above, a voice of mercy: 'Rest, Kossara. Sleep. Forget.'

No more.

[She was still dazed, numb, when the drumhead court-martial condemned her to life enslavement.]

Flandry considered the papers in his hands. Her few dry words appeared to have turned him as impersonal, for he said in the same tone, expressionless, 'Thank you. Not much left in your mind, is there? No explanation of your hatred for the Empire.'

'What do you mean?' exploded from her. 'After what I told!'

'Please,' he said. 'You're a bright, educated, reasonably objective person. Taking your memories as correct – which they may not be; you could be recalling pieces of delirium – you should be able to entertain the possibility that you and your friends had the bad luck to meet fools and brutes such as infest every outfit. You should consider using established procedures to have them identified, traced, penalized. Unless, of course, you're so set in your attitude that this business seems typical, mere confirmation of what you already knew.'

He glanced up. 'Have you been told exactly what's in this report on you? The Intelligence report, that is.'

'No,' she got forth.

'I didn't expect you would. It's secret. Let me give you a summary.' His vision skimmed the sheets he flipped through as he recited:

'Overtly, you and your attendant Trohdwyr arrived at Thursday Landing for a duly approved xenological research project on behalf of your, um, Shkola, among the Diomedeans of the Sea of Achan area. The declared motivation was that Dennitzans have lately opened trade with a comparable species near home, and want an idea of what to expect from continued impact of high-technology civilization on them. Quite normal. The Imperial resident provided you the customary assistance. He and his household depose that you were a charming guest who gave them no hint of bad intentions. However, you were soon off for the field. They never saw you again.

'Meanwhile, Naval Intelligence was busy throughout that part of space. There was reason to suspect some kind of hostile operation, taking advantage of widespread disorganization caused by the war and not yet amended. Diomedes was certainly a trouble spot, secessionism steadily gaining strength in a principal society of the planet. Those revolutionaries seemed to hope for Ythrian support.

'But other, more reliable sources indicated Ythri had nothing to do with this. Then who were the humans known, from loyal native witnesses, to be active on Diomedes? If not Avalonians, working for the Domain they live in, who?

'With the help of informers, Intelligence agents tracked down a group of these subversives to a mountain hideout. Seeing what they took for a Merseian, they leaped to conclusions ... not unjustified, it turned out. The gang resisted arrest and, except for you, perished in the fire fight. Blasters in an enclosed space like a cave – the marines were wearing combat armor and your companions were not. The fact that the suspects fought, under those circumstances, seems to prove they were as fanatical as your psychograph says you are.

'Hypnoprobed, you revealed you were the deputy of your uncle the Gospodar, come to check on the progress. His idea was that Dennitzans posing as Avalonians could incite an uprising on Diomedes. This by itself would draw Imperial attention there. The apparent likelihood of Ythri being behind it would decoy considerable of our armed strength, too. Then at the right moment – you quoted your uncle simply as speaking of a "lever" to use on the Imperium, for getting concessions. But you spilled your belief – and you ought to know – that, if events broke favorably, he'd seize the chance to rebel. Depending on circumstances, he'd either try for the throne, or carry out the same plan as the late Duke Alfred was nursing along, to rip a sizable region loose from the Empire and place it under Merseian protection.

'Which, of course' – Flandry lifted his gaze again – 'would give the Roidhunate a bridgehead right in that frontier. Do you wonder that the treatment you got was rough?'

Kossara sprang from her chair. 'How crazy do you think we are?' she yelled.

'We're bound for Diomedes to find out,' he said.

'Why not straight to Dennitza like an honest man?'

'Others will, never fear. Detective work on an entire nation, or just on its leaders, takes personnel and patience. A single-ton like me does best *vis-à-vis* a small operation, as I suppose the one on Diomedes necessarily is.'

Flandry's eyes narrowed. 'If you want your liberty back, my dear, rather than being resold when I decide you're not worth your keep, you will cooperate,' he said. 'Think of it not as betraying your folk, but as helping save them from disastrously wrong-headed adventurers.

'We have a libraryful of material on Diomedes aboard. Study it. Ponder it. Something may jog your memory; a lot that you've forgotten is probably not irretrievably lost. Or you should be able to make deductions – you're a smart girl – deductions about likely rendezvous points remaining, where we can snare more agents. Or, better yet, I'd guess: Diome-deans involved in the movement, never identified by our people, they should recognize you, if you show yourself in the proper ways. They should make contact and – do you see?'

'Yes!' she screamed. 'And I won't!'

She fled.

The man sat quiet for a while before he said to the empty air, 'Very well, if you wish, Chives will bring you your meals in your cabin.'

CHAPTER SIX

As Flandry conned the *Hooligan*, Diomedes grew huge in the screens before him. Too heavily clouded for oceans and continents to show as anything but blurs, the dayside glowed amber-orange, with tinges of rose and violet, under the light of a dull sun. The nighted part gave pale whiteness back to moons and stars, reflections off ice and snow. When Kossara last came here, equinox was not long past; now absolute winter lay upon fully half the planet.

Flandry's attention was concentrated on piloting. Ordinarily he would have left that to the automatics, or to Chives if no ground-control facilities existed. But this time he must use both skill and the secret data he had commandeered back on Terra, to elude the Imperial space sentries.

Most were small detector-computer units in orbit, such as supervised traffic around any world of the Empire which got any appreciable amount of it, guarding against smugglers, hostiles, recklessness, or equipment failures. Flandry had long since rigged his speedster to evade them without much effort, given foreknowledge of their paths. But surely the unrest on Diomedes, the suspicion of outside interference, had caused spacecraft to be added. Sneaking past these required an artist. He enjoyed it.

Just the same, somewhere at the back of awareness, memory rehearsed what he had learned about his goal. Pictures and passages of text flickered by:

'Among the bodies which men have named Diomedes – among all the planets we know – in many respects, this one is unique.

'Though not unusually old, the system is metal-poor. To explain that, Montoya suggested chemical fractionation of the original cloud of dust and gas by the electromagnetic action of a passing neutron star ... As a result, while Diomedes has a mass of 4.75 Terra, the low net density gives it a surface gravity of only 1.10 standard. However, so large an object was bound to generate an extensive atmosphere. Between gravitational potential resulting from a diameter twice Terran, and low temperature and irradiation resulting from the G8 sun, much gas was retained. Life has modified it. Today mean sea-level pressure is 6.2 bars; the partial pressures of oxygen, nitrogen, and carbon dioxide are about the same as on Terra, the rest of the air consisting chiefly of neon ...

'Through some cosmic accident, the spin axis of Diomedes, like that of Uranus in the Solar System, lies nearly in the orbital plane. The arctic and antarctic circles thus almost coincide with the equator. In the course of a year 11 percent longer than Terra's, practically the whole of each hemisphere will be sunless for a period ranging from weeks to months. Chill even in summer, land and sea become so frigid in winter that all but highly specialized life-forms must either hibernate or migrate ...

'Progressive autochthonous cultures had brought Stone Age technology, the sole kind possible for them, to an astonishing sophistication. Once contacted by humans, they were eager to trade, originally for metals, subsequently for means to build modern industries of their own. Diomedes offers numerous organic substances, valuable for a variety of purposes, cheaper to buy from natives than to synthesize ...

'The biochemistry producing these compounds is only terrestroid in the most general sense. It consists of proteins in water solution, carbohydrates, lipids, etc. But few are nourishing to humans and many are toxic. They permeate the environment. A man cannot survive a drink of water or repeated breaths of air unless he has received thorough immunization beforehand. (Of course, that includes adaptation to the neon, which otherwise at this concentration would have ill effects too.) Short-term visitors prefer to rely on their basic antiallergen, helmets, protective clothing, and packaged rations.

'The Diomedean must be similarly careful about materials from offplanet. In particular most metals are poisonous to him. That he can use copper and iron anyway, as safely as we use beryllium or plutonium, is a tribute to his intelligence. But the precautions by themselves have inevitably joined those factors which force radical change upon ancient customs. Some cultures have adjusted without extreme stress. Others continue to suffer upheaval. Injustice and alienation bring dissension and violence . . .'

Although, Flandry thought, *if we Imperials packed up our toys and went home, everybody here would soon be a great deal worse off. There've been too many irreversible changes. You can't even sit still in this universe and not make waves.*

The sun was never down in summer; but Diomedes' 12½-hour rotation spun it through a circle. At the point in space and time where *Hooligan* landed, sharply rising mountains to the south concealed the disc.

The saloon was warm and scented. Nevertheless, what he saw in the screen made Flandry grimace and give an exaggerated shiver. 'Brrr! No wonder climes like this foster Spartan virtues. The inhabitants have to be in training before they can emigrate and dispossess whoever lives on desirable real estate.'

'You can't appreciate, can you, here is home for the Lannachska that they only want to keep unruined,' Kossara said.

Couldn't she recognize a joke? Maybe not. She'd held aloof since he interviewed her, studying as he urged but saying nothing about what meaning she drew from it.

What a waste, Flandry sighed. *We could have had a gorgeous voyage, you and I.*

His gaze lingered on her. A coverall did not hide the fullness of a tall and supple body. Blue-green eyes, mahogany locks, strongly sculptured countenance had begun to haunt his reveries, and in the last few nightwatches his dreams. Did she really speak in the exact husky contralto of Kathryn McCormac? . . .

She sensed his regard, flushed, and attacked: 'We *are* on Lannach, are we not? I think I recall several of these peaks.'

71

Flandry nodded and gave his attention back to the view. 'Yes. Not far south of Sagna Bay.' He hoped she'd admire how easily he'd found a particular site on the big island, nothing except maps and navigation to guide him down through the stormy atmosphere. But she registered unmixed anger. *Well, I suppose I shouldn't object to that, seeing how carefully I fueled it.*

Concealed by an overhanging cliff, the ship stood halfway up a mountain, with an overlook down rugged kilometers to a horizon-gleam which betokened sea. Clouds towered in amethyst heaven, washed by faint pink where lightning did not flicker in blue-black caverns. Crags, boulders, waterfalls reared above talus slopes and murky scarps. Thin grasslike growth, gray thornbushes, twisted low trees grew about; they became more abundant as sight descended toward misty valleys, until at last they made forest. Wings cruised on high, maybe upbearing brains that thought, maybe simple beasts of prey. Faint through the hull sounded a yowl of wind.

'Very well,' Kossara said grimly. 'I'll ask the question you want me to ask. Why are we here? Aren't you supposed to report in at Thursday Landing?'

'I exercised a special dispensation I have,' Flandry said. 'The Residency doesn't yet know we've come. In fact, unless my right hand has lost its cunning, nobody does.'

At least I get a human startlement out of her. He liked seeing expressions cross her face, like clouds and sunbeams on a gusty spring day. 'You see,' he explained, 'if subversive activities are going on, there's bound to be a spy or two around Imperial headquarters. News of your return would be just about impossible to suppress. And since you're in the custody of a Naval officer, it'd alarm the outfit we're after.

'Whereas if you suddenly reappear by yourself, right in this hotspot, you'll surprise them. They won't have time to get suspicious, I trust. They'll make you welcome—'

'Why should they?' Kossara interrupted. 'They'll wonder how I got back.'

'Ah, no. Because they won't know you were ever gone.'

She stared. Flandry explained: 'Your companions died. If

rebel observers learned that you lived, they learned nothing else. No matter how idiotically my colleagues behaved toward you, I'm sure they followed doctrine and let out no further information. You vanished into their building, and that was that. You were brought from there to the spaceship in a sealed vehicle, weren't you? ... Yes, I knew it ... The Corpsmen had no reason to announce you'd been condemned and deported, therefore they did not.

'Accordingly, the rest of the gang – human if any are left on Diomedes, and most certainly a lot of natives – have no reason to suppose you haven't just been held incommunicado. In fact, that would be a much more logical thing to do than shipping you off to Terra for purchase by any blabbermouth.'

She frowned, less in dislike of him than from being caught up, willy-nilly, by the intellectual problem which his planned deception presented. 'But wasn't it a special team that caught and, and processed me? They may well have left the planet by now.'

'If so, you can say they gave you in charge of the Intelligence agents stationed here semi-permanently. In fact, that's the safest thing for you to maintain in any event, and quite plausible. We'll work out a detailed story for you. I have an outline already, subject to your criticism. You wheedled a measure of freedom for yourself. That's plausible too, if you don't mind pretending you became the mistress of a bored, lonely commander. At last you managed to steal an aircar. I can supply that; we have two in the hold, one a standard civilian convertible we can set for Diomedean conditions. You fled back here, having enough memories left to know this is where your chances are best of being found by your organization.'

She tensed again, and stretched the words out: 'What will you do meanwhile?'

Flandry shrugged. 'Not having had your preventive-medical treatment, I'm limited in my scope. Let's consult. Tentatively, I've considered making an appearance in a *persona* I've used before, a harmlessly mad Cosmenosist missionary prospecting for customers on yet another globe. However,

I may do best to stay put aboard ship, following your adventures till the time looks ripe for whatever sort of action seems indicated.'

Her starkness deepened. 'How will you keep track of me?'

From his pocket Flandry took a ring. On its gold band sparkled what resembled a sapphire. 'Wear this. If anybody asks, say you got it from your jailer-lover. It's actually a portable transmitter, same as your bracelet was on Terra but with its own power source.'

'That little bit of a thing?' She sounded incredulous. 'Needing no electronic network around? Reaching beyond line-of-sight? And not detectable by those I spy on?'

Flandry nodded. 'It has all those admirable qualities.'

'I can't believe that.'

'I'm not at liberty to describe the principle. Anyway, nobody ever told me. I've indulged in idle speculations about modulated neutrino emission, but they're doubtless wildly wrong. What I do know is that the thing works.' Flandry paused. 'Kossara, I'm sorry, but under any circumstances ... before I can release you, before I can even land you again on a prime world like Terra, you'll have to have wiped from your memory the fact that such gadgets exist. The job will be painless and very carefully done.'

He held out the ring. She half reached for it, withdrew her hand, flickered her glance about till it came to rest on his, and asked most softly. 'Why do you think I'll help you?'

'To earn your liberty,' he answered. Each sentence wrenched at him. 'Defect, and you're outlaw. What chance would you have of getting home? The orbital watch, the surface hunt would be doubled. If you weren't caught, you'd starve to death after you used up your human-type food.

'And consider Dennitza. Your kin, your friends, small children in the millions, the past and present and future of your whole world. Should they be set at stake, in an era of planet-smasher weapons, for a political point at best, the vainglory of a few aristocrats at worst? You know better, Kossara.'

She stood still for a long while before she took the ring from him and put it on her bridal finger.

'Given the support of a dense atmosphere,' said a text, 'the evolution of large flying organisms was profuse. At last a particular species became fully intelligent.

'Typical of higher animals on Diomedes, it was migratory. Homeothermic, bisexual, viviparous, it originally followed the same reproductive pattern as its less developed cousins, and in most cultures still does. In fall a flock moves to the tropics, where it spends the winter. The exertion during so long a flight causes hormonal changes which stimulate the gonads. Upon arrival, there is an orgy of mating. In spring the flock returns home. Females give birth shortly before the next migration, and infants are carried by their parents. Mothers lactate like Terran mammals, and while they do, will not get pregnant. In their second year the young can fly independently, they have been weaned, their mothers are again ready to breed.

'This round formed the basis of a civilization centered on the islands around the Sea of Achan. The natives built towns, which they left every fall and reentered every spring. Here they carried on sedentary occupations, stoneworking, ceramics, carpentry, a limited amount of agriculture. The real foundation of their economy was, however, herding and hunting. Except for necessary spurts of activity, in their homelands they were an easygoing folk, indolent, artistic, ceremonious, matrilineal – since paternity was never certain – and loosely organized into what they called the Great Flock of Lannach.

'But elsewhere a different practice developed. Dwelling on large oceangoing rafts, fishers and seaweed harvesters, the Fleet of Drak'ho ceased migrating. Oars, sails, nets, windlasses, construction and maintenance work kept the body constantly exercised; year-round sexuality, season-free reproduction, was a direct consequence. Patriarchal monogamy ensued. The distances traveled annually were much less than for the Flock, and home was always nearby. It was possible to accumulate heavy paraphernalia, stores, machines, books. While civilization thus became more wealthy and complex than anywhere ashore, the old democratic organization gave way to authoritarian aristocracy.

'Histories roughly parallel to these have taken place elsewhere on the globe. But Lannach and Drak'ho remain the most advanced, populous, materially well-off representatives of these two strongly contrasted life-orderings. When they first made contact, they regarded each other with mutual horror. A measure of tolerance and cooperation evolved, encouraged by offplanet traders who naturally preferred peaceful conditions. Yet rivalry persisted, sporadically flaring into war, and of late has gained new dimensions.

'At the heart of the dilemma is this: that Lannachska culture cannot assimilate high-energy technology, in any important measure, and survive.

'The Drak'ho people have their difficulties, but no impossible choices. Few of them today are sailors. However, fixed abodes ashore are not altogether different from houses on rafts aforetime. Regular hours of work are a tradition, labor is still considered honorable, mechanical skills and a generally technophilic attitude are in the social atmosphere which members inhale from birth. Though machinery has lifted off most Drak'hoans the toil that once gave them a humanlike libido, they maintain it by systematic exercise (or, in increasingly many cases, by drugs), since the nuclear family continues to be the building block of their civilization.

'As producers, merchants, engineers, industrialists, even occasional spacefarers, they flourish, and are on the whole well content.

'But the cosmos of Lannach is crumbling. Either the Great Flock must remain primitive, poor, powerless, prey to storm and famine, pirates and pestilence, or it must modernize – with all that that implies, including earning the cost of the capital goods required. How shall a folk do this who spend half their lives migrating, mating, or living off nature's summertime bounty? Yet not only is their whole polity founded upon that immemorial cycle. Religion, morality, tradition, identity itself are. Imagine a group of humans, long resident in an unchanged part of Terra, devout churchgoers, for whom the price of progress was that they destroy every relic of the past, embrace atheism, and become homosexuals who reproduce by ectogenesis. For many if not all Lannachska, the situation is nearly that extreme.

'In endless variations around the planet, the same dream is being played. But precisely because the Great Flock has changed more than other nations of its kind, it feels the hurt most keenly, is most divided against itself and embittered at the outside universe.

'No wonder if revolutionary solutions are sought. Economic, social, spiritual secession, a return to the ways of the ancestors; shouts of protest against "discrimination", demands for "justice", help, subsidy, special consideration of every kind; political secession, no more taxes to the planetary peace authority or the Imperium, seizure of power over the whole sphere, establishment of a sovereign autarky – these are among the less unreasonable ideas afloat.

'There is also Alatanism. The Ythrians, not terribly far away as interstellar distances go, have wings. They should sympathize with their fellow flyers on Diomedes more than any biped ever can. They have their Domain, free alike of Empire and Roidhunate, equally foreign to both. Might it not, are its duty and destiny not to welcome Diomedes in?

'The fact that few Ythrian leaders have even heard of Diomedes, and none show the least interest in crusading, is ignored. Mystiques seldom respond to facts. They are instruments which can be played on . . .'

Twice had the sun come from the mountains and returned behind them.

'Goodbye, then,' Kossara said.

Flandry could find no better words than 'Goodbye. Good luck,' hoarse out of the grip upon his gullet.

She regarded him for a moment, in the entryroom where they stood. 'I do believe you mean that,' she whispered.

Abruptly she kissed him, a brief brush of lips which exploded in his heart. She drew back before he could respond. During another instant she poised, upon her face a look of bewilderment at her own action.

Turning, she twisted the handle on the inner airlock valve. He took a following step. 'No,' she said. 'You can't live out there, remember?' Her body prepared before she left Dennitza, she closed the portal on him. He stopped where he was. Pumps chugged until gauges told him the chamber beyond was now full of Diomedean air.

The outer valve opened. He bent over a viewscreen. Kossara's tiny image stepped forth onto the mountainside. A car awaited her. She bounded into it and shut its door. A minute later, it rose.

Flandry sought the control cabin, where were the terminals of his most powerful and sensitive devices. The car had vanished above clouds. 'Pip-ho, Chives,' he said tonelessly. A hatch swung wide. His Number Two atmospheric vehicle glided from the hold. It looked little different from the first, its engine, weapons, and special equipment being concealed in a teardrop fuselage. It disappeared more slowly, for the Shalmuan pilot wanted to stay unseen by the woman he stalked. But at last Flandry sat alone.

She promised she'd help me. What an inexperienced liar she is.

He felt no surprise when, after a few minutes, Chives' voice jumped at him: 'Sir! She is decending ... She has landed in the forest beside a river. I am observing through a haze by means of an infrared 'scope. Do you wish a relay?'

'Not from that,' Flandry said. Too small, too blurry. 'From her bracelet.'

A screen blossomed in leaves and hasty brown water. Her right hand entered. Off the left, which he could not see, she plucked the ring, which he glimpsed before she tossed it into the stream.

'She is running for cover beneath the trees sir,' Chives reported.

Of course, replied the emptiness in Flandry. *She thinks that, via the ring, I've seen what she's just done in the teeth*

78

of every pledge she gave me. She thinks that now, if she moves fast, she can vanish into the woods – make her own way afoot, find her people and not betray them, or else die striving.

Whereas in fact the ring was only intended to lull any fears of surveillance she might have after getting rid of it – only a circlet on her bridal finger – and Chives has a radio resonator along to activate her bracelet – the slave bracelet I told her would be blind and deaf outside of Terra.

'I do not recommend that I remain airborne, sir,' Chives said. 'Allow me to suggest that, as soon as the young lady has passed beyond observing me, I land likewise and follow her on the ground. I will leave a low-powered beacon to mark this site. You can flit here by grav-belt and retrieve the vehicles, sir. Permit me to remind you to wear proper protection against the unsalubrious ambience.'

'Same to you, old egg, and put knobs on yours.' Flandry's utterance shifted from dull to hard. 'I'll repeat your orders. Trail her, and call in to the recorder cum relay 'caster I'll leave here, in whatever way and at whatever times seem discreet. But "discretion" is your key word. If she appears to be in danger, getting her out of it – whether by bringing me in to help or by taking action yourself – that gets absolute priority. Understand?'

'Yes, sir.' Did the high, not quite human accent bear a hint of shared pain? 'Despite regrettable tactical necessities, Donna Vymezal must never be considered a mere counter in a game.' *That's for personnel and planets, the anonymous billions – and, savingly, for you and me, eh, Chives?* 'Will you proceed to the Technic settlement when your preparations are complete?'

'Yes,' Flandry said. 'Soon. I may as well.'

CHAPTER SEVEN

Where the equator crossed the eastern shoreline of a continent men called Centralia, Thursday Landing was founded. Though fertile by Diomedean standards, the country had few permanent residents. Rather, migration brought tides of travelers, northward and southward alternately, to their ancestral breeding grounds. At first, once the sharpest edge was off their sexual appetites, they had been glad to hunt and harvest those things the newcomers wanted from the wilderness, in exchange for portable trade goods. Later this business grew more systematized and extensive, especially after a large contingent of Drak'ho moved to these parts. Descending, Flandry saw a fair-sized town.

Most was man-built, blocky interconnected ferrocrete structures to preserve a human-suitable environment from monstrous rains and slow but ponderous winds. He glimpsed a park, vivid green beneath a vitryl dome, brightened by lamps that imitated Sol. Farther out, widely spaced in cultivated fields, stood native houses: tall and narrow, multiply balconied, graceful of line and hue, meant less to resist weather than to accept it, yielding enough to remain whole. Watercraft, ranging from boats to floating communities, crowded the harbor as wings did the sky.

Yet Flandry felt bleakness, as if the cold outside had reached in to enfold him. Beyond the fluorescents, half the world he saw was land, hills, meadows, dwarfish woods, dim in purple and black twilight, and half was bloodily glimmering ocean. For the sun stood barely above the northern horizon, amidst sulfur-colored clouds. At this place and season there was never true day or honest night.

Are you getting terracentric in your dotage? he gibed at himself. *Here's a perfectly amiable place for beings who belong in it.*

His mood would not go away. *Nevertheless it does feel*

80

unreal somehow, a scene from a bad dream. The whole mission has been like that. Everything shadowy, tangled, unstable, nothing what it seems to be ... nor anybody who doesn't carry secrets within secrets ...

Myself included. He straightened in the pilot chair. Well, that's what I'm paid for. I suppose these blue devils of mine come mainly from guilt about Kossara, fear of what may happen to her. O God Who is also unreal, a mask we put on emptiness, be gentle to her. She has been hurt so much.

Ground Control addressed him, in Anglic though not from a human mouth. He responded, and set Hooligan down on the spacefield as directed. The prospect of action heartened him. Since I can't trust the Almighty not to soldier on the job, let me start my share now.

He had slipped back into space from Lannach, then returned openly. The sentinel robots detected him, and an officer in a warship demanded identificaton before granting clearance, at a distance from the planet which showed a thoroughness seldom encountered around fifth-rate outpost worlds. No doubt alarm about prospective rebellion and infiltration had caused security to be tightened. Without the orbital information he possessed, not even a vessel as begimmicked as his could have neared Diomedes unbeknownst.

The image of the portmaster appeared in a comscreen. 'Welcome, sir,' he said. 'Am I correct that you are alone? The Imperial resident has been notified of your coming and invites you to be his house guest during your stay. If you will tell me where your accommodation lock is – frankly, I have never seen a model quite like yours – a car will be there for you in a few minutes.'

He was an autochthon, a handsome creature by any standards. The size of a short man, he stood on backward-bending, talon-footed legs. Brown-furred, the slim body ran out in a broad tail which ended in a fleshy rudder; at its middle, arms and hands were curiously anthropoid; above a massive chest, a long neck bore a round head – high, ridged brow, golden eyes with nictitating membranes, blunt-nosed, black-muzzled face with fangs and whiskers suggestive of a cat, no external ears but a crest of muscle on top of the skull. From his upper shoulders grew the bat wings, their six-meter span now folded. He wore a belt to support a pouch, a brassard of authority, and yes, a crucifix.

I'd better stay in character from the beginning. 'Many thanks, my dear chap,' Flandry replied in his most affected manner. 'I say, could you tell the chauffeur to come aboard and fetch my bags? Deuced lot of duffel on these extended trips, don't y'know.' He saw the crest rise and a ripple pass along the fur, perhaps from irritation at his rudeness in not asking the portmaster's name.

The driver obeyed, though. He was a husky young civilian who bowed at the sight of Flandry's gaudy version of dress uniform. 'Captain Ahab Whaling?'

'Right.' Flandry often ransacked ancient books. He had documentation aboard for several different aliases. Why risk alerting someone? The more everybody underestimated him, the better. Since he wanted to pump his fellow, he added, 'Ah, you are—?'

'Diego Rostovsky, sir, handyman to Distinguished Citizen Lagard. You mentioned baggage? ... Jumping comets, that much? ... Well, they'll have room at the Residency.'

'Nobody else staying there, what?'

'Not at the moment. We had a bunch for some while till about a month ago. But I daresay you know that already, seeing as how you're Intelligence yourself.' Rostovsky's glance at the eye insigne on Flandry's breast indicated doubt about the metaphorical truth of it.

However, curiosity kept him friendly. When airlocks had decoupled and the groundcar was moving along the road to town, he explained: 'We don't fly unnecessarily. This atmosphere plays too many tricks ... Uh, they'll be glad to meet you at the Residency. Those officers I mentioned were too busy to be very good company, except for—' He broke off. 'Um. And since they left, the isolation and tension ... My master and his staff have plenty to keep them occupied, but Donna Lagard always sees the same people, servants, guards, commercial personnel and their families. She's Terran-reared. She'll be happy for news and gossip.'

And you judge me the type to furnish them, Flandry knew. *Excellent.* His gaze drifted through the canopy, out over somber fields and tenebrous heaven. *But who was that exception whom you are obviously under orders not to mention?*

'Yes, I imagine things are a bit strained,' he said. 'Though really, you need have no personal fears, need you? I mean, after all, if some of the tribes revolted, an infernal nuisance, 'specially for trade, but surely Thursday Landing can hold out against primitives.'

'They aren't exactly that,' was the answer. 'They have industrial capabilities, and they do business directly with societies still further developed. We've good reason to believe a great many weapons are stashed around, tactical nukes among them. Oh, doubtless we could fend off an attack and stand siege. The garrison and defenses have been augmented. But trade would go completely to pieces – it wouldn't take many rebels to interdict traffic – which'd hurt the economy of more planets than Diomedes . . . And then, if outsiders really have been the, uh, the—'

'Agents *provocateurs*,' Flandry supplied. 'Or instigators, if y' prefer. Either way; I don't mind.'

Rostovsky scowled. 'Well, what might their bosses do?'

Martin Lagard was a small prim man in a large prim office. When he spoke, in Anglic still tinged by his Atheian childhood, both his goatee and the tip of his nose waggled. His tunic was of rich material but unfashionable cut, and he had done nothing about partial baldness.

Blinking across his desk at Flandry, who lounged behind a cigarette, the Imperial resident said in a scratchy voice, 'Well, I'm pleased to make your acquaintance, Captain Whaling, but frankly puzzled as to what may be the nature of your assignment. No courier brought me any advance word.' He sounded hurt.

I'd better soothe him. Flandry had met his kind by the

83

scores, career administrators, conscientious but rule-bound and inclined to self-importance. Innovators, or philosophers like Chunderban Desai, were rare in that service, distrusted by their fellows, destined either for greatness or for ruin. Lagard had advanced methodically, by the book, toward an eventual pension.

He was uncreative but not stupid, a vital cog of empire. How could a planetful of diverse nonhumans be closely governed by Terra, and why should it be? Lagard was here to assist Imperials in their businesses and their problems; to oversee continuous collection of information about this world and put it in proper form to feed the insatiable data banks at Home; to collect from the natives a modest tribute which paid for their share of the Pax; to give their leaders advice as occasion warranted, and not use his marines to see that they followed it unless he absolutely must; to speak on their behalf to those officials of the Crown with whom he dealt; to cope.

He had not done badly. It was not his fault that demons haunted the planet which were beyond his capability of exorcising, and might yet take possession of it.

'No, sir, they woudn't give notice. Seldom do. Abominably poor manners, but that's policy for you, what?' Flandry nodded at his credentials, where they lay on the desk. ' 'Fraid I can't be too explicit either. Let's say I'm on a special tour of inspection.'

Lagard gave him a close look. Flandry could guess the resident's thought: Was this drawling clothes horse really an Intelligence officer at work, or a pet relative put through a few motions to justify making an admiral of him? 'I will cooperate as far as possible, Captain.'

'Thanks. Knew y' would. See here, d'you mind if I bore you for a few ticks? Mean to say, I'd like to diagram the situation as I see it. You correct me where I'm wrong, fill in any gaps, that kind of thing, eh? You know how hard it is to get any proper overview of matters. And then, distances between stars, news stale before it arrives, *n'est-ce pas?*'

'Proceed,' Lagard said resignedly.

Flandry discarded his cigarette, crossed his legs and bridged fingers. No grav generator softened the pull of Diomedes. He let his added weight flow into the chair's crannies of softness, as if already wearied. (In actuality he did his calisthenics under two gees or more, because thus he shortened the dreary daily time he needed for keeping fit.) 'Troublemakers afoot,' he said. 'Distinct possibility of hostiles taking advantage of the disorganization left by the recent unpleasantness – whether those hostiles be Merseian, Ythrian, barbarian, Imperials who want to break away or even overthrow his Majesty – right? You got hints, various of those troublemakers were active here, fanning flames of discontent and all that sort of nonsense. How'd they get past your security?'

'Not my security, Captain,' Lagard corrected. 'I've barely had this post five years. I found the sentinel system in wretched condition – expectable, after the Empire's woes – and did my best to effect repairs. I also found our civil strife was doing much to heighten resentment, particularly in the Great Flock of Lannach. It disrupted offplanet commerce, you see. The migrant societies have become more dependent on that than the sedentary ones like Drak'ho which have industry to produce most of what they consume. But please realize, a new man on a strange world needs time to learn its ins and outs, and develop workable programs.'

'Oh, quite.' Flandry nodded. 'At first you'd see no reason to screen visitors from space. Rather, you'd welcome 'em. They might help restore trade, what? Very natural. No discredit to you. At last, however, clues started trickling in. Not every transient was spending his stay in the outback so benignly. Right?

'You asked my Corps to investigate. That likewise takes time. We too can't come cold onto a planet and hope for instant results, y' know. Ah, according to my briefing, it was sector HQ you approached. Terra just got your regular reports.'

'Of course,' Lagard said. 'Going through there would have meant a delay of months.'

'Right, right. No criticism intended, sir,' Flandry assured

him. 'Still, we do like to keep tabs at Home. That's what I'm here for, to find out what was done, in more detail than the official report' – *which was almighty sketchy* – 'could render. Or, you could say, my superiors want a feel of how the operation went.'

Lagard gave the least shrug.

'Well, then,' Flandry proceeded. 'The report does say a Commander Bruno Maspes brought an Intelligence team, set up shop in Thursday Landing, and got busy interrogating, collating data, sending people out into the field – the usual intensive job. They worked how long?'

'About six months.'

'Did you see much of them?'

'No. They were always occupied, often all away from here at once, sometimes away from the whole system. Personnel of theirs came and went. Even those who were my guests—' Lagard stopped. 'You'll forgive me, Captain, but I'm under security myself. My entire household is. We've been forbidden to reveal certain items. This clearance of yours does not give you power to override that.'

Ah-ha. It tingled in Flandry's veins. His muscles stayed relaxed. 'Yes, yes. Perfectly proper. You and yours were bound to spot details – f'r instance, a xenosophont with odd talents—' *Look at his face! Again, ah-ha.* – 'which ought not be babbled about. Never fret, I shan't pry.

'In essence, the team discovered it wasn't humans of Ythrian allegiance who were inciting to rebellion and giving technical advice about same. It was humans from Dennitza.'

'So I was told,' Lagard said.

'Ah ... during this period, didn't you entertain a Dennitzan scientist?'

'Yes. She and her companion soon left for the Sea of Achan, against my warnings. Later I was informed that they turned out to be subversives themselves.' Lagard sighed. 'Pity. She was a delightful person, in her intense fashion.'

'Any idea what became of her?'

'She was captured. I assume she's still detained.'

'Here?'

'Seems unlikely. Maspes and his team left weeks ago. Why leave her behind?'

What would I have done if they were around yet? Flandry wondered fleetingly. *Played that hand in style, I trust.* 'They might have decided that was the easiest way to keep the affair under wraps for a bit,' he suggested.

'The Intelligence personnel now on Diomedes are simply those few who've been stationed among us for years. I think I'd know if they were hiding anything from me. You're free to talk to them, Captain, but better not expect much.'

'Hm.' Flandry stroked his mustache. 'I s'pose, then, Maspes felt he'd cleaned out the traitors?'

'He said he had a new, more urgent task elsewhere. Doubtless a majority of agents escaped his net, and native sympathizers may well keep any humans among them fed. But, he claimed, if we monitor space traffic carefully, they shouldn't rouse more unrest than we can handle. I hope he was right.'

'You're trying to defuse local conflicts, eh?'

'What else?' Lagard sounded impatient. 'My staff and I, in consultation with loyal Diomedeans, are hard at work. A fair shake for the migrants is not impossible to achieve, if the damned extremists will let us alone. I'm afraid I'll be a poor host, Captain. Day after tomorrow – Terran, that is – I'm off for Lannach, to lay certain proposals before the Commander of the Great Flock and his councillors. They feel a telescreen is too impersonal.'

Flandry smiled. 'Don't apologize, sir. I'll be quite happy. And, I suspect, only on this planet a few days anyhow, before bouncing on to the next. You and Maspes seem offhand to've put on a jolly good show.'

Gratified, visions of bonuses presumably dancing through his head, the resident beamed at him. 'Thank you. I'll introduce you around tomorrow, and you can question or look through the files as you wish, within the limits of security I mentioned. But first I'm sure you'd like to rest. A servant will show you to your room. We'll have apéritifs in half an hour. My wife is eager to meet you.'

CHAPTER EIGHT

At dinner Flandry laid on the wit and sophistication he had programmed, until over the liqueurs Susette Kalehua Lagard sighed, 'Oh, my, Captain Whaling, how marvelous you're here! Nobody like you has visited us for ages – they've all been provincials, or if not, they've been so ghastly serious, no sensitivity in them either, except a single one and he wasn't human— Oh!' Her husband had frowned and nudged her. She raised fingers to lips. 'No, that was naughty of me. Please forget I said it.'

Flandry bowed in his chair. 'Impractical, I fear, Donna. How could I forget anything spoken by you? But I'll set the words aside in my mind and enjoy remembering the music.' Meanwhile alertness went electric through him. This warm, well-furnished, softly lighted room, where a recorded violin sang and from which a butler had just removed the dishes of an admirable rubyfruit soufflé, was a very frail bubble to huddle in. He rolled curaçao across his tongue and reached for a cigarette.

She fluttered her lashes. 'You're a darling.' She had had a good bit to drink. 'Isn't he, Martin? Must you really leave us in less than a week?'

Flandry shrugged. 'Looks as if Distinguished Citizen Lagard hasn't left me much excuse to linger, alas.'

'Maybe we can find something. I mean, you can exercise judgment in your mission, can't you? They wouldn't send a man like you out and keep a leash on him.'

'We'll see, Donna.' He gave a look of precisely gauged meaningfulness. She returned it in kind. The wine had not affected her control in that respect.

His inner excitement became half sardonicism, half a moderately interested anticipation. She was attractive in a buxom fashion, to which her low-cut shimmerlyn gown lent an emphasis that would have raised brows at today's Imperial court – the court she had never seen. Jewels glinted in black hair piled about a round brown countenace. Vivacity had increased in her throughout the meal, till her conversation sounded less platitudinous than it was.

Flandry knew her as he knew her husband, from uncounted encounters : the spouse of an official posted to a distant world of nonhumans. Occasionally such a pair made a team. But oftener the member who did not have the assignment was left to the dismal mercies of a tiny Imperial community, the same homes, bodies, words, games, petty intrigues and cat-fights for year after year. He or she might develop an interest in the natives, get into adventures and fascinations, even con-tribute a xenological study or a literary translation. Lady Susette lacked the gift for that. Since she had had no children when she arrived, there would be none for the rest of Lagard's ten-year hitch. The immunizations which let her walk freely outdoors on Diomedes were too deep-going for her organism to accept an embryo, and it would be too dangerous to have them reversed before she departed. What then was Susette Kalehua Lagard, daughter of prosperous and socially pro-minent Terrans, to do while she waited?

She could terminate the marriage. But a man who had gotten resident's rank was a fine catch. He could expect a subsequent commissionership on a prime human-colonized planet like Hermes, where plenty of glamor was available; in due course, he should become a functionary of some small importance on Terra itself, and perhaps receive a minor patent of nobility. She must feel this was worth her patience. Her eyes told Flandry she did have a hobby.

'Well, if our time's to be short, let's make it sweet,' she said. 'May I – we call you Ahab? We're Susette and Mar-tin.'

'I'm honored.' Flandry raised his glass in salute. 'And re-freshed. Folk on Terra have gotten stiffish these past few years, don't y' know. Example set by his Majesty and the inner circle.'

'Indeed?' Lagard asked. 'Nuances don't reach us here. I'd

have thought – with due reverence – the present Emperor would be quite informal.'

'Not in public,' Flandry said. 'Career Navy man of Germanian background, after all. I see us generally heading into a puritanical period.' *Which, if Desai is right, is not the end of decadence, but rather its next stage.* 'Luckily, we've plenty of nooks and crannies for carrying on in the grand old tradition. In fact, disapproval lends spice, what? I remember a while ago—'

His risqué reminiscence had happened to somebody else and the event had lacked several flourishes he supplied. He never let such nigglements hinder a story. It fetched a sour smile from Lagard but laughter and a blush down to the décolletage from Susette.

The staff, assistants, clerks, technical chiefs, Navy and marine personnel, were harried but cooperative, except when Flandry heard: 'Sorry sir. I'm not allowed to discuss that. If you want information, please apply at Sector HQ. I'm sure they'll oblige you there.'

Yes, they'll oblige me with the same skeleton account that Terra got. I could make a pest of myself, but I doubt if the secret files have ever contained any mention of what I'm really after. I could check on the whereabouts of Commander Maspes & Co., and make a long trip to find them – no, him, for probably the team's dispersed . . . ah, more probably yet, the files will show orders cut for them similar to those in Captain Whaling's papers, and the men have vanished . . . maybe to bob up again eventually, maybe never, depending on circumstances.

More deceptions, more phantoms.

He sauntered into the civilian part of town and was quickly on genial terms with factors and employees. Most of them found their work stimulating – they liked the Diomedeans – but were starved for new human contact. And none were under security. The trouble was, there had been no need for it. They knew a special Intelligence force came to search out the roots of the unrest which plagued them in their business.

They totally approved, and did not resent not being invited to meet the investigators save for interviews about what they themselves might know. None had seen the entire team together; when not in the field, it kept apart, officers in the Residency, enlisted men in a separate barrack. Yes, rumor said it included a xeno or two. What of that?

Otherwise the community had only heard of Lagard's brief announcement after the group was gone. '... I am not at liberty to say more than that human traitors have been trying to foment a rebellion among the Lannachska. Fortunately, the vast majority of the Great Flock stayed loyal and sensible. And now the key agents have been killed or captured. A few may still be at large, and information you may come upon concerning these should be reported immediately. But I don't expect they can do serious harm any longer, and I intend to proceed, with your cooperation, to remove the causes of discontent...'

The next Diomedean day, Flandry donned a heated coverall and a dome helmet with an air recycler, passed through the pressure change in a lock, and circulated among natives in their part of town. Most knew Anglic and were willing to talk; but none had further news. He wasn't surprised.

Finding a public phone booth, he took the opportunity to call Chives when nobody who chanced to observe him was likely to wonder what a solitary operative was doing there. He used a standard channel but a language he was sure had never been heard on this world. The nearest comsat bucked his words across the ocean to Lannach where, he having paid for the service, they were broadcast rather than beamed. The relay unit he had left under the cliff made contact with the Shalmuan's portable.

'Yes, sir, at present the young lady is eating rations taken from her car before she abandoned it. They should last her as far as the sea, for she is setting a hard pace despite the overgrowth and rugged topography. I must confess I have difficulty following, since I consider it inadvisable to go aloft on my gravbelt. I feel a certain concern for her safety. A fall down a declivity or a sudden tempest could have adverse effects, and she does not let caution delay her.'

'I think she can manage.' Flandry said. 'In any event, you can rescue her. What worries me is what may happen after she gets where she's going. Another twenty-four hours, did you estimate? I'd better try to act fast myself, here.'

Susette didn't wish to lose time either. Three hours after she and Flandry had seen Lagard off, she was snuggled against him whispering how wonderful he had been.

'You're no slouch on the couch yourself, m'love,' he said, quite honestly. 'More, I hope?'

'Yes. As soon and often as you want. And do please want.'

'Well, how about a breather first, and getting acquainted? A girl who keeps a bedside beer cooler is a girl whose sound mind I want to know as well as her delectable body.' Warm and wudgy, she caressed him while he leaned over to get bottles for them, and stayed in the circle of his free arm when they leaned back against the pillows.

Too bad this can't be a simple romp for me, he thought. *It deserves that. And by the way, so do I. Kossara was making chastity come hard.*

He savored the chill brisk flavor while his glance roved about. The resident's lady had a private suite where, she hinted, the resident was an infrequent caller. This room of it was plushly carpeted, draped, furnished, in rose and white. An incense stick joined its fragrance to her own. A dressing table stood crowded with perfumes and cosmetics. Her garments sheened above his, hastily tossed over a chair. In that richness, her souvenirs of Home – pictures, bric-à-brac, a stuffed toy such as she would have given to a child – seemed as oddly pathetic as the view in the window was grim. Hail dashed against vitryl, thicker and harder than ever fell on Terra, picked out athwart blue-black lightning-jumping violence by an ember sunbeam which stabbed through a rent in the clouds. Past every insulation and heaviness came a ghost of the wind's clamor.

Kossara ... Yes, Chives is right to fret about her while she struggles through yonder wildwood.

Susette stroked his cheek. 'Why do you look sad all of a sudden?' she asked.

'Eh?' He started. 'How ridiculous. "Pensive" is the word, my imp. Well, perhaps a drop of melancholy, recalling how I'll have to leave you and doubtless never see you again.'

She nodded. 'Me too. Though are you sure we won't – we can't?'

If I keep any control over events, yes, absolutely! Not that you aren't likable; but frankly, in public you're a bore. And what if Kossara found out?

Why should I care?

Well, she might accept my sporting as such. I get the impression hers is a double-standard society. But I don't believe she'd forgive my cuckolding a man whose salt I've eaten. To plead I was far from unique would get me nowhere. To plead military necessity wouldn't help either; I think she could see (those wave-colored eyes) that I'd have performed the same service free and enjoyed every microsecond.

Hm. The problem is not how to keep a peccadillo decently veiled in hypocrisy. The problem is what to do about the fact that I care whether or not Kossara Vymezal despises me.

'Can't we?' Susette persisted. 'The Empire's big, but people get around in it.'

Flandry pulled his attention back to the task on hand. He hugged her, smiled into her troubled gaze, and said, 'Your idea flatters me beyond reason. I'd s'posed I was a mere escapade.'

She flushed. 'I supposed the same. But – well—' Defiantly: 'I have others. I guess I always will, till I'm too old. Martin must suspect, and not care an awful lot. He's nice to me in a kind of absent-minded way, but he's overworked, and not young, and – you know what I mean. Diego, Diego Rostovsky, he's been the best. Except I know him inside out by now, what there is to know. You come in like a fresh breeze – straight from Home! – and you can talk about things, and make me laugh and feel good, and—' She leaned hard on him. Her own spare hand wandered. 'I'd never have thought . . .

93

you knew right away what I'd like most. Are you a telepath?'

No, just *experienced and imaginative. Aycharaych is the telepath.* 'Thank you for your commendation,' Flandry said, and clinked his bottle on hers.

'Then won't you stay a little while extra, Ahab, and return afterward?'

'I must go whither the vagaries of war and politics require, amorita. And believe me, they can be confoundedly vague.' Flandry took a long drink to gain a minute for assembling his next words. 'F'r instance, the secrecy Commander Maspes laid on you forces me to dash on to Sector HQ as soon's I've given Diomedes a fairly clean bill of health – which I've about completed. My task demands certain data, you see. Poor communications again. Maspes tucked you under a blanket prohibition because he'd no way of knowing I'd come here, and I didn't get a clearance to lift it because nobody back Home knew he'd been that ultracautious.' *If I produced the Imperial writ I do have, that might give too much away.*

Susette's palm stopped on his breast. 'Why, your heart's going like a hammer,' she said.

'You do that to a chap,' he answered, put down his bottle and gathered her to him for an elaborate kiss.

Breathlessly, she asked, 'You mean if you had the information you wouldn't be in such a hurry? You could stay longer?'

'I should jolly well hope so,' he said, running fingers through her hair. 'But what's the use?' He grinned. 'Never mind. In your presence, I am not prone to talk shop.'

'No, wait.' She fended him off, a push which was a caress. 'What do you need to know, Ahab?'

'Why—' He measured out his hesitation. 'Something you're not allowed to tell me.'

'But they'd tell you at HQ.'

'Oh, yes. This is a miserable technicality.'

'All right,' Susette said fast. 'What is it?'

'You might—' Flandry donned enthusiasm. 'Darling! You

wouldn't get in trouble, I swear. No, you'd be expediting the business of the Empire.'

She shook her head and giggled. 'Uh-uh. Remember, you've got to spend the time you gain here. Promise?'

'On my honor' *as a double agent.*

She leaned back again, her beer set aside, hands clasped behind her neck, enjoying her submission. 'Ask me anything.'

Flandry faced her, arms wrapped around drawn-up knees. 'Mainly, who was with Maspes? Nonhumans especi'lly. I'd better not spell out the reason. But consider. No mind can conceive, let alone remember, the planets and races we've discovered in this tiny offside corner of the solitary galaxy we've explored a little bit. Infiltration, espionage – such things have happened before.'

She stared. 'Wouldn't they check a memory bank?'

Memory banks can have lies put into them, whenever we get a government many of whose officials can be bought, and later during the confusion of disputed succession, civil war, and sweeping purges. Those lies can then wait, never called on and therefore never suspected, till somebody has need for one of them. 'Let's say no system is perfect, 'cept yours for lovemaking. Terra itself doesn't have a complete, fully updated file. Regional bitkeepers don't try; and checking back with Terra seldom seems worth the delay and trouble.'

'Golloo!' She was more titillated than alarmed. 'You mean we might've had an enemy spy right here?'

'That's what I'm s'posed to find out, sweetling.'

'Well, there was only a single xeno on the team.' She sighed. 'I'd hate to believe he was enemy. So beautiful a person. You know, I daydreamed about going to bed with him, though of course I don't imagine that'd have worked, even if he did look pretty much like a man.'

'Who was he? Where from?'

'Uh – his name, Ay ... Aycharaych.' She handled the dipthongs better than the open consonants. 'From, uh, he said his planet's called Chereion. Way off toward Betelgeuse.'

Further, Flandry thought amidst a thrumming.

This time he didn't bother to conceal his right name or his very origin. And why should he? Nobody would check on a duly accredited member of an Imperial Intelligence force — not that the files in Thursday Landing would help anyway — and he could read in their minds that none had ever heard of an obscure world within the Roidhunate — and the secrecy command would cover his trail as long as he needed, after he'd done his damage and was gone.

When at last, maybe, the truth came out: why, our people who do know a little something about Chereion would recognize that was where he glided from, as soon as they heard his description, regardless of whether he'd given a false origin or not. He might as well amuse himself by leaving his legal signature.

Which I'd already begun to think I saw in this whole affair. Dreams and shadows and flitting ghosts—

'He's about as tall as you are,' Susette was saying, 'skinny — no, I mean fine-boned and lean — except for wide shoulders and a kind of jutting chest. Six fingers to a hand, extra-jointed, ambery nails; but four claws to a foot and a spur behind, like a sort of bird. And he did say his race comes from a, uh, an analogue of flightless birds. I can't say a lot more about his body, because he always wore a long robe, though usually going barefoot. His face . . . well, I'd make him sound ugly if I spoke about a dome of a brow, big hook nose, thin lips, pointed ears, and of course all the, the shapes, angles, proportions different from ours. Actually, he's beautiful. I could've spent days looking into those huge red-brown whiteless eyes of his if he'd let me. His skin is deep gold color. He has no hair anywhere I saw, but a kind of shark-fin crest on the crown of his head, made from dark-blue feathers, and tiny feathers for eyebrows. His voice is low and . . . pure music.'

Flandry nodded. 'M-hm. He stayed in your house?'

'Yes. We and the servants were strictly forbidden to mention him anywhere outside. When he visited the building his team had taken over — or maybe left town altogether; I can't say — he'd put on boots, a cowl, a face mask, like he came from someplace where men cover up everything in public; and walking slow, he could make his gait pass for human.'

'Did you get any hints of what he did?'

'No. They called him a . . . consultant.' Susette sat upright. 'Was he really a spy?'

'I can identify him,' Flandry said, 'and the answer is no.' *Why should he spy on his own companions – subordinates? And he didn't bring them here to collect information, except incidentally. I'm pretty sure he came to kindle a war.*

'Oh, I'm glad.' Susette exclaimed. 'He was such a lovely guest. Even though I often couldn't follow his conversation. Martin did better, but he'd get lost too when Aycharaych started talking about art and history – of Terra! He made me ashamed I was that ignorant about my own planet. No, not ashamed; really interested, wanting to go right out and learn if only I knew how. And then he'd talk on my level, like mentioning little things I'd never much noticed or appreciated, and getting me to care about them, till this dull place seemed full of wonder and—'

She subsided. 'Have I told you enough?' she asked.

'I may have a few more questions later,' Flandry said, 'but for now, yes, I'm through.'

She held out her arms. 'Oh, no, you're not, you man, you! You've just begun. C'mere.'

Flandry did. But while he embraced her, he was mostly harking back to the last time he met Aycharaych.

CHAPTER NINE

[That was four years ago, in the planet-wide winter of eccentrically orbiting Talwin. Having landed simultaneously from the warships which brought them hither, Captain Sir Dominic Flandry and his opposite number, *Qanryf* Tachwyr the Dark, were received with painstaking correctness by the two commissioners of their respective races who administered the joint Merseian-Terran scientific base. After due ceremony, they expressed a wish to dine privately, that they might discuss the tasks ahead of them in frankness and at leisure.

The room for this was small, austerely outfitted as the entire outpost necessarily was. Talwin's system coursed through the Wilderness, that little explored buffer zone of stars between Empire and Roidhunate; it had no attraction for traders; the enterprise got a meager budget. A table, some chairs and stools, a sideboard, a phone were the whole furniture, unless you counted the dumbwaiter with sensors and extensible arms for serving people who might not wish a live attendant while they talked.

Flandry entered cheerily, 0.88 gee lending bounce to his gait. The Merseian officer waited, half dinosaurian despite a close-fitting silver-trimmed black uniform, bold against snowfields, frozen river, and shrunken sun in crystalline sky which filled a wall transparency behind him.

'Well, you old rascal, how are you?' The man held forth his hand in Terran wise. Tachwyr clasped it between warm dry fingers and leathery palm. They had no further amicable gesture to exchange, since Flandry lacked a tail.

'Thirsty,' Tachwyr rumbled. They sought the well-stocked sideboard. Tachwyr reached for Scotch and Flandry for telloch. They caught each other's glances and laughed, Merseian drumroll and human staccato. 'Been a long while for us both, *arrach?*'

Flandry noted the inference, that of recent years Tachwyr's work had brought him into little or no contact with Terrans, for whatever it might be worth. Likely that wasn't much. The Empire's mulish attitude toward the aggrandizement of the Roidhunate was by no means the sole problem which the latter faced. Still, Tachwyr was by way of being an expert on *Homo sapiens*; so if a more urgent matter had called him— To be sure, he might have planned his remark precisely to make his opponent think along these lines.

'I trust your wives and children enjoy good fortune,' Flandry said in polite Eriau.

'Yes, I thank the God.' The formula being completed, Tachwyr went on : 'Chydhwan's married, and Gelch has begun his cadetship. I presume you're still a bachelor?' He must ask that in Anglic, for his native equivalent would have been an insult. His jet eyes probed. 'Aren't you the gaudy one, though? What style is that?'

The man extended an arm to show off colors and embroideries of his mufti. The plumes bobbed which sprang from an emerald brooch holding his turban together. 'Latest fashion in Dehiwala – on Ramanujan, you know. I was there a while back. Garb at home has gotten positively drab.' He lifted his glass. 'Well, *tor ychwei.*'

'Here's to you,' the Merseian responded in Anglic. They drank. The telloch was thick and bitter-fiery.

Flandry looked outdoors. 'Brrr !' he said. 'I'm glad this time I won't need to tramp through that.'

'*Khraich?* I'd hoped we might go on a hunt.'

'Don't let me stop you. But if nothing else, my time here is limited. I must get back. Wouldn't have come at all except for your special invitation.'

Tachwyr studied Flandry. 'I never doubted you are busy these days,' he said.

'Yes, jumping around like a probability function in a high wind.'

'You do not seem discouraged.'

'N-no.' Flandry sipped, abruptly brought his gaze around, and stated : 'We're near the end of our troubles. What opposition is left has no real chance.'

'And Hans Molitor will be undisputed Emperor.' Tachwyr's relaxation evaporated. Flandry, who knew him from encounters both adversary and half friendly since they were fledglings in their services, had rather expected that. A big, faintly scaled hand clenched on the tumbler of whisky. 'My reason why I wanted this meeting.'

'Your reason?' Flandry arched his brows, though he knew Tachwyr felt it was a particularly grotesque expression.

'Yes. I persuaded my superiors to send your government – Molitor's – the proposal, and put me in charge of our side. However, if you had not come yourself, I imagine the conference would have proved as empty as my *datholch* claimed it would, when I broached the idea to him.'

I can't blame the good datholch, Flandry thought. It does seem ludicrous on the face of it: discussions between Intelligence officers of rank below admiral or fodaich, who can't make important commitments – discussions about how to 'resolve mutual difficulties' and assure the Imperium that the Roidhunate has never had any desire to interfere in domestic affairs of the Empire – when everybody knows how gleefully Merseian agents have swarmed through every one of our camps, trying their eternally damnedest to keep our family fight going.

Of course, Molitor's people couldn't refuse, because this is the first overt sign that Merseia will recognize him rather than some rival as our lord, and deal with his agents later on, about matters more real than this farce.

The intention is no surprise, when he's obviously winning. The surprise was the form the feeler took – and Tachwyr's note to me. Neither action felt quite Merseian.

Therefore I had to come.

'Let me guess,' Flandry said. 'You know I'm close to his Majesty and act as an odd-job man of his. You and your team hope to sound out me and mine about him.'

Tachwyr nodded. 'If he's to be your new leader, stronger than the past several, we want to know what to expect.'

'You must have collected more bits of information on him than there are stars in the galaxy. And he's not a complex man. And no individual can do more than throw a small extra vector or two in among the millions that whipsaw such a big and awkward thing as the Empire toward whatever destiny it's got.'

'He can order actions which have a multiplier effect, for war or peace between our folk.'

'Oh, come off it, chum! No Merseian has a talent for pious wormwords. He only sounds silly when he tries. As far as you are concerned vis-à-vis us, diplomacy is a continuation of war by other means.' Flandry tossed off his drink and poured a refill.

'Many Terrans disagree,' Tachwyr said slowly.

'My species also has more talent than yours for wishful thinking,' Flandry admitted. He waved at the cold landscape. 'Take this base itself. For two decades, through every clash and crisis, a beacon example of cooperation. Right?' He leered. 'You know better. Oh, doubtless most of the scientists who come here are sincere enough in just wanting to study a remarkable xenological development. Doubtless they're generally on good personal terms. But they're subsidized – they have their nice safe demilitarization – for no reason except that both sides find it convenient to keep a place for secret rendezvous. Neutral domains like Betelgeuse are so public, and their owners tend to be so nosy.'

He patted the Merseian's back. 'Now let's sit down to eat, and afterward serious drinking, like the cordial enemies we've always been,' he urged. 'I don't mind giving you anecdotes to pad out your report. Some of them may even be true.'

The heavy features flushed olive-green. 'Do you imply our attempt – not at final disengagement, granted, but at practical measures of mutual benefit – do you imply it is either idiotic or else false?'

Flandry sighed. 'You disappoint me, Tachwyr. I do believe you've grown stuffy in your middle age. Instead of continuing the charade, why not ring up your Chereionite and invite him to join us? I'll bet he and I are acquainted too.'

[The sun went down and night leaped forth in stars almost

space-bright, crowding the dark, making the winter world glow as if it had a moon. 'May I turn off the interior lights?' Aycharaych asked. 'The outside is too glorious for them.'

Flandry agreed. The hawk profile across the table from him grew indistinct, save for great starlight-catching eyes. The voice sang and purred onward, soft as the cognac they shared, in Anglic whose accent sounded less foreign than archaic.

'I could wish your turban did not cover a mindscreen and powerpack, my friend. Not merely does the field make an ugliness through my nerves amidst this frozen serenity; I would fain be in true communion with you.' Aycharaych's chuckle sounded wistful. 'That can scarcely be, I realize, unless you join my cause.'

'Or you mine,' Flandry said.

'And each of your men who might know something I would like to learn is likewise screened against me. Does not that apparatus on their heads make sleep difficult? I warn you in any case, wear the things not overmany days at a stretch. Even for a race like yours, it is ill to keep the brain walled off from those energies which inspirit the universe, behind a screen of forces that themselves must roil your dreams.'

'I see no reason for us to stay.'

Aycharaych inhaled from his glass. He had not touched the liquor yet. 'I would be happy for your company,' he said. 'But I understand. The consciousness that dreary death will in a few more decades fold this brightly checkered game board whereon you leap and capture – that keeps you ever in haste.'

He leaned back, gazed out at a tree turned into a jewel by icicles, and was quiet awhile. Flandry reached for a cigarette, remembered the Chereionite disliked tobacco smoke, and soothed himself with a swallow.

'It may be the root of your greatness as a race,' Aycharaych mused. 'Could a *St. Matthew Passion* have welled from an immortal Bach? Could a Rembrandt who knew naught of sorrow and had no need for steadfastness in it have brought those things alive by a few daubs of paint? Could a Tu Fu free of loss have been the poet of dead leaves flying amidst snow, cranes departing, or an old parrot shabby in its cage? What depth does the foreknowledge of doom give to your loves?'

He turned his head to face the man. His tone lightened: 'Well. Now that poor mortified Tachwyr is gone – most mightily had he looked forward to the sauce which gloating would put on his dinner! – we can talk freely. How did you deduce the truth?'

'Part hunch,' Flandry confessed. 'The more I thought about that message, the more suggestions of your style I found. Then logic took over. Plain to see, the Merseians had some ulterior motive in asking for a conference as nugatory *per se* as this. It could be just a signal to us, and an attempt at sounding out Molitor's prospective regime a bit. But for those purposes it was clumsy and inadequate. And why go to such trouble to bring *me* here?

'Well, I'm not privy to high strategic secrets, but I'm close enough to him that I must have a fair amount of critical information – the kind which'll be obsolete inside a year, but if used promptly could help Merseia keep our kettle longer on the boil, with that much more harm to us. And I have a freer hand than anybody else who's so well briefed; I could certainly come if I chose. And an invitation from Tachwyr could be counted on to pique my curiosity, if nothing else.

'The whole idea was yours, wasn't it?'

Aycharaych nodded, his crest a scimitar across the Milky Way. 'Yes,' he said. 'I already had business in these parts – *negotium perambulantem in tenebris*, if you like – and saw nothing to lose in this attempt. At least I have won the pleasure of a few hours with you.'

'Thanks. Although—' Flandry sought words. 'You know I put modesty in a class with virginity, both charming characteristics which should be gotten rid of as fast as puberty allows. However ... why me, Aycharaych? Do you relish the fact I'll kill you, regretfully but firmly, the instant a chance appears? In that respect, there are hundreds like me. True, I may be unusual in having come close, a time or two. And I can make more cultured noises than the average Navy man. But I'm no scholar, no esthete – a dilettante; you can do better than me.'

'Let us say I appreciate your total personality.' The smile, barely visible, resembled that upon the oldest stone gods of Greece. 'I admire your exploits. And since we have interacted again and again, a bond has formed between us. Deny not that you sense it.'

'I don't deny. You're the only Chereionite I've ever met—' Flandry stopped.

After a moment he proceeded: 'Are you the only Chereionite anybody has ever met?'

'Occasional Merseians have visited my planet, even resided there for periods of study,' Aycharaych pointed out.

Yes. Flandry remembered one such, who had endangered him there upon Talwin; how far in the past that seemed, and how immediately near! *I realize why the coordinates of your home are perhaps the best-kept secret in the Roidhunate. I doubt if a thousand beings from offworld know; and in most of them, the numbers have been buried deep in their unconsciousness, to be called forth by a key stimulus which is also secret.*

Secret, secret . . . What do we know about you that is substance and not shadow?

The data fled by, just behind his eyes.

Chereion's sun was dim, as Flandry himself had discovered when he noticed Aycharaych was blind in the blue end of the spectrum though seeing farther into the red than a man can. The planet was small, cold, dry – deduced from Aycharaych's build, walk, capabilities, preferences – not unlike human-settled Aeneas, because he could roam freely there and almost start a holy war to split the Empire, nineteen years ago.

In those days he had claimed that the enigmatic ruins found upon many worlds of that sort were relics of his own people, who ranged and ruled among the stars in an era geologically remote. He claimed . . . *He's as big a liar as I am, when either of us wants to be. If they did build and then withdraw, why? Where to? What are they upon this night?*

Dismiss the riddles. Imperial Intelligence knew for certain, with scars for reminders, he was a telepath of extraordinary power. Within a radius of x meters, he could read the thoughts of any being, no matter how alien, using any language, no matter how foreign to him. That had been theoretically impossible. Hence the theory was crudely modified (there is scant creativity in a waning civilization) to include suggestions of a brain which with computerlike speed and capacity analyzed the impulses it detected into basic units (binary?), compared this pattern with the one which its own senses and knowledge presented, and by some incredible process of trial and error synthesized in seconds a code which closely corresponded to the original.

It did not seem he could peer far below the surface thoughts, if at all. That mattered little. He could be patient; or in a direct confrontation, he had skill to evoke the memories he wanted. No wonder that the highest Merseian command paid heed to him. The Empire had never had a more dangerous single enemy.

Single—

Flandry grew aware of the other's luminous regard. ' 'Scuse me,' he said. 'I got thinking. Bad habit.'

'I can guess what.' Aycharaych's smile continued. 'You speculate whether I am your sole Chereionite colleague.'

'Yes. Not for the first time.' Flandry drank again. 'Well, are you? What few photographs or eyewitness accounts we've garnered, of a Chereionite among outsiders – never more than one. Were all of them you?'

'You don't expect me to tell you. I will agree to what's obvious, that partakers in ephemeral affairs, like myself, have been rare among my race. They laid such things aside before your kind were aught but apes.'

'Why haven't you?'

'In action I find an art; and every art is a philosophical tool, whereby we may seek to win an atom deeper into mystery.'

Flandry considered Aycharaych for a silent span before he murmured: 'I came on a poem once, in translation – it goes back a millennium or more – that's stayed with me. Tells how Pan – you know our Classical myths – Pan is at a riverside, splashing around, his goat hoofs breaking the lilies, till he plucks a reed and hollows it out, no matter the agony it feels; then the music he pipes forth enchants the whole forest. Is that what you think of yourself as doing?'

'Ah, yes,' Aycharaych answered, 'you have the last stanza in mind, I believe.' Low:

> 'Yet half a beast is the great god Pan,
>   To laugh as he sits by the river,
> Making a poet out of a man:
> The true gods sigh for the cost and pain, –
> For the reed which grows nevermore again
>   As a reed with the reeds in the river.'

Damn! Flandry thought. *I ought to stop letting him startle me.*

'My friend,' the other went on gently, 'you too play a satanic role. How many lives have you twisted or chopped short? How many will you? Would you protect me if the accidents of history had flung Empire rather than Roidhunate around my sun? Or if you had been born into those humans who serve Merseia? Indeed, then you might have lived more whole of heart.'

Anger flared. 'I know,' Flandry snapped. 'How often have I heard? Terra is old, tired, corrupt, Merseia is young, vigorous, pure. Thank you, to the extent that's true, I prefer my anomie, cynicism, and existential despair to counting my days in cadence and shouting huzza – worse, sincerely meaning it – when Glorious Leader rides by. Besides … the device every conqueror, yes, every altruistic liberator should be required to wear on his shield … is a little girl and her kitten, at ground zero.'

He knocked back his cognac and poured another. His temper cooled. 'I suspect,' he finished, 'down inside, you'd like to say the same.'

'Not in those terms,' Aycharaych replied. 'Sentimentality

ill becomes either of us. Or compassion. Forgive me, are you not drinking a trifle heavily?'

'Could be.'

'Since you won't get so drunk I can surreptitiously turn off your mindscreen, I would be grateful if you stay clear-headed. The time is long since last I relished discourse of Terra's former splendors, or even of her modern pleasures. Come, let us talk the stars to rest.']

In the morning, Flandry told Susette he must scout around the globe a few days, using certain ultrasensitive instruments, but thereafter he would return.

He doubted that very much.

CHAPTER TEN

Shadow and thunder of wings fell over Kossara. She looked up from the rolling, tawny-begrown down onto which she had come after stumbling from the forest. Against clouds and the plum-colored sky beyond, a Diomedean descended. She halted. Weariness shivered in her legs. Wind slithered around her. It smelled of damp earth and, somehow, of boulders.

An end to my search. Her heart slugged. *But what will I now find? Comrades and trust, or a return to my punishment?*

The native landed, a male, attired in crossbelts and armed with a knife and rifle. He must have been out hunting, when he saw the remarkable sight of a solitary human loose in the wilds, begrimed, footsore, mapless and compassless. He uttered gutturals of his own tongue.

'No, I don't speak that,' Kossara answered. The last water she had found was kilometers behind. Thirst roughened her throat. 'Do you know Anglic?'

'Some bit,' the native said. 'How you? Help?'

'Y-yes. But—' *But not from anybody who'll think he should call Thursday Landing and inquire about me.* During her trek she had sifted the fragments of memory, over and over. A name and nonhuman face remained. 'Eonan. Bring me Eonan.' She tried several different pronunciations, hoping one would be recognizable.

'*Gairath mochra.* Eonan? Wh ... what Eonan? Many Eonan.'

There would be, of course. She might as well have asked a random Dennitzan for Andrei. However, she had expected as much. 'Eonan who knows Kossara Vymezal,' she said, 'Find. Give Eonan this.' She handed him a note she had scrawled. 'Money.' She offered a ten-credit bill from the full wallet

Flandry had included in her gear. 'Bring Eonan, I give you more money.'

After repeated trials, she seemed to get the idea across, and an approximation of her name. The hunter took off northward. God willing, he'd ask around in the bayshore towns till he found the right person; and while this would make the dwellers curious, none should see reason to phone Imperial headquarters. God willing. She ought to kneel for a prayer, but she was too tired; Mary who fled to Egypt would understand. Kossara sat down on what resembled pale grass and wasn't, hugged herself against the bitter breeze and stared across treelessness beneath a wan sun.

Have I really won through?

If Eonan still had his life and liberty, he might have lost heart for his revolution – if, in truth, he had ever been involved; she had nothing more than a dream-vision from a cave. Or if he would still free his people from the Empire, he might be the last. Or if cabals and guerrillas remained, he might not know where they hid. Or if he brought her to them, what could she hope for?

She tossed her head. *A chance to fight. Maybe to win home in the end, likelier to die here: as a soldier does, and in freedom.*

Drowsiness overflowed. She curled herself as best she could on the ground. Heavy garments blunted its hardness, though she hated the sour smell they'd gotten. To be clean again ... Flandry had saved her from the soiling which could never be washed off. He had that much honor – and, yes, a diamond sort of mercy. If she'd done his bidding, tried her best to lead him to whatever was left of her fellows, he would surely have sent her back, manumitted – he'd have the prestige for such a favor to be granted him – unscathed— No! Not whole in her own honor! And release upon a Dennitza lashed to the Empire would be a cruel joke.

Then rest while you can, Kossara. Sleep comes not black, no, blue as a summer sky over the Kazan, blue as the cloak of Mary ... Pray for us, now and in the hour of our death.

A small callused hand shook her awake. Hunger said louder

than her watch what a time had passed while the sun brooded nightless. She stared into the yellow eyes above a blunt muzzle and quivering whiskers. Half open, bat wings made a stormcloud behind. He carried a blaster.

His face— She sat up, aware of ache, stiffness, cold. 'Eonan?'

'Torcha tracked me.' Apart from the piping accent, mostly due to the organs of speech, his Anglic came fluent. 'But you do not know him, do you?'

She struggled to her feet. 'I don't know you either, quite,' she got out. 'They made me forget.'

'*Ungn-n-n.*' He touched the butt of the gun, and his crest erected. Otherwise he stood in taut quietness. She saw he had arrived on a gravsled, no doubt to carry her.

Resolution unfroze him. 'I am Eonan Guntrasson, of the Wendru clan in the Great Flock of Lannach. And you are Kossara Vymezal, from the distant planet Dennitza.'

Gladness came galloping, and every weakness fled. 'I know that, *barem!* And you dared meet me? Then we are not finished yet!'

Eonan drew the membranes over his eyes. 'We?'

'The revolution. Yours and mine.' She leaned down to grip his upper shoulders. Beneath fur and warmth, the flight muscles stood like rock.

'I must be careful.' His tone underlined it. 'Torcha said you promised him a reward for fetching me. I paid him myself, not to have him along. Best we go aside and ... talk. First, in sign of good faith, let me search you.'

The place he chose was back in the highlands. Canyon walls rose darkly where a river rang; fog smoked and dripped till Kossara was soaked with chill; at moments when the swirling grayness parted, she glimpsed the black volcanic cone of Mount Oborch.

On the way, Eonan had fed her from a stock of preserved Terran food, and explained he was the factor for Nakamura & Malaysia in the area where he dwelt. This gave him wide contacts and sources of information, as well as an easy excuse to travel, disappearing into the hinterland or across the sea, whenever he wished. Thursday Landing had no suspicion of his clandestine activities. He would not speak about those until she related her story in full.

Then he breathed, 'E-e-e-ehhh,' and crouched in thought on the gravsled bench. Finally, sharply: 'Well, your Terran officer has likeliest concluded you slipped off in search of the cloudflyers – the, keh, the underground. A spacecraft was seen to lift from hereabouts not many sunspins ago. When I heard, I wondered what that meant.'

'I imagine he went to warn the resident and start a hunt for me,' Kossara said. 'He did threaten to, if I deserted.' Anxiety touched her. 'Yes, and a tightened space watch. Have I caused us trouble?'

'We shall see. It may have been worth it in all events. To learn about that spy device is no slight gain. We shall want your description of the place where you threw the ring away. Perhaps we can safely look for it and take it to study.'

'Chances are he's recovered it. But Eonan!' Kossara twisted around toward him. 'How are you doing here? How many survive? With what strength, what plans? How can I help?'

Again the third lids blurred his gaze. 'Best I keep still. I am just a link. They will answer you in the nest where I have decided to take you.'

The hideout was high in a mountainside. Approaching, Kossara felt her eardrums twinge from pressure change and cold strike deep. Snowpeaks, glaciers, ravines, cliffs, crags reached in monstrous confusion between a cloud ocean which drowned the lower slopes, and a sky whose emptiness the sun only seemed to darken. Silence dwelt here, save for air booming over the windshield and a mutter of native language as Eonan radioed ahead.

Why am I not happy? she wondered. *I am about to rejoin my comrades and regain my past – my purpose. What makes me afraid?*

Eonan finished. 'Everything will be ready,' he informed her. Was he as tense as he looked? She must have come to know Diomedeans well enough during her stay that she could tell; but that had been robbed from her. What had *he* to fear?

'I suppose,' she ventured, 'this is headquarters for the entire mission. They tucked it away here to make it undiscoverable.'

'Yes. They enlarged a cave.'

She recalled another cave, where she and Trohdwyr and a few more had huddled. 'Were we – those who died when I was captured – were we out in the field – liaison with freedom fighters whose homes were below timberline? Maybe we were betrayed by one of them' – she grimaced – 'who'd been caught at sabotage or whatever, and interrogated.'

'That sounds plausible.'

'But then nobody except us was destroyed! Am I right? Is the liberation movement still healthy?'

'Yes.'

Puzzlement: 'Why didn't I tell the Impies about our main base when they put me under hypnoprobe?'

'I do not know,' Eonan said impatiently. 'Please be quiet. I must bring us in on an exact course, or they will shoot.'

As the sled glided near, Kossara spied the defense, an energy cannon. It was camouflaged, but military training had enhanced her natural ability to notice things. A great steel door in the bluff behind it would go unseen from above, should anyone fly across this lofty desert. Instruments – infrared sensors, neutrino detectors, magnetometers, gravitometers, atmosphere sniffers, a hundred kinds of robot bloodhound – would expose the place at once. But who would think to come searching?

The door swung aside. The sled passed through and landed in a garage among several aircars. Here were warmth, echoes, a sudden brilliance of light better suited for eyes human or Merseian. Kossara shed her parka before she stepped off. Her pulse raced.

Four stood waiting. Three were men. She was not surprised to see the last was a big green heavy-tailed person, though

112

her heart said *O Trohdwyr* – and for an instant tears stung and blurred.

She rallied herself and walked toward them. Her boots thudded on the floor; Eonan's claws clicked. Those in front of her were simply clad, shirts, trousers, shoes on the men, a tunic on the zmay. She had expected them to be armed, as they were.

It flashed: *Why did I think zmay, not ychan?* And: *They aren't Dennitzans! None of them!*

She slammed to a halt. The men differed widely, genes from every breed of mankind scrambled in chance combinations. So they could be from Terra – or a colony within the Empire – or—

Eonan left her side. The Merseian drew his pistol. 'Hold,' he rapped. 'You are under arrest.'

He called himself Glydh of the Vach Rueth, nicknamed Far-Farer, an *afal* of his navy's Intelligence corps. His immediate assistant was a lanky, sallow, long-nosed man, introduced as Muhammad Snell but addressed by the superior officer as Kluwych. In the middle of wreck, Kossara could flickeringly wonder if the Eriau name had been given him by his parents, when he was born somewhere in the Roidhunate.

They took her to an office. On the way she passed through such space and among such personnel that she estimated the latter numbered about twenty, two or three of them Merseian by species, the rest human. That was probably all there were on Diomedes: sufficient to keep scores of native dupes like Eonan going, who in their turn led thousands.

Though are they dupes? she thought drearily. *Merseia would like to see them unchained from the Empire.*

No. That isn't true. Merseia doesn't give a curse. They're cheap, expendable tools.

The office was cramped and bleak. 'Sit,' Glydh ordered, pointing to a chair. He took a stool behind a desk. Snell settled on the left; his eyes licked her, centimeter by centimeter and back again.

'Khraich.' Glydh laid his hands flat on the desktop, broad and thick, strangler's hands. 'An astonishing turn of events. What shall we do with you?' His Anglic was excellent.

'Isn't this, uh, Captain Flandry more urgent, sir?' his subordinate asked.

'Not much, I believe,' Glydh said. 'True, from Vymezal's account via Eonon, he appears to be capable. But what can he know? That she defected, presumably joining a remnant of the underground if she didn't perish *en route*.' He pondered. 'Maybe he isn't capable, at that – since he let her go, trusting her mere self-interest to keep her on his side.'

Hoy? Chives said Flandry is famous ... No. How many light-years, how many millions of minds can fame cover before it spreads vanishingly thin?

'Of course, we will have our cell in Thursday Landing keep him under surveillance, and alert our agents globally if he leaves there,' Glydh continued. 'But I doubt he represents more than a blind stab on the part of somebody in the opposition. I don't think he is worth the risk of trying to kidnap, or even kill.'

'We may find out otherwise, sir, when we interrogate Vymezal in detail,' said the man. He moistened his lips.

'Maybe. I leave that to you. Co-opt what helpers you need.'

'Um-m-m ... procedures? Treatment? Final disposition?'

'No!' Kossara heard the yell and felt the leaping to her feet, as if from outside her body. This was not real, could not be, must not be, God and saints, no. 'I am not a, a Terran agent – I came here to – at least I'm a prisoner of war!'

'Sit!' Glydh's roar, and the gunshot slap of palm on desk, flung her back like a belly blow. She heard his basso through fever-dream distances and humming: 'Don't babble about military conventions. You are a slave, property we have acquired. If you do what you are told, there need not be pain. Else there will be, until you are broken to obedience. Do you hear me?'

Snell's fingers twisted together. He breathed fast. 'Sir,' he said, 'it could be a long while before we get a chance to send a report offplanet and ask for instructions about her. So we have to use our own judgment, don't we?'

'Yes,' Glydh answered.

'Well, considering what was originally intended for her, and the reason – sir, not a woman among us in this whole region—'

Glydh shrugged. His tone was faintly contemptuous. 'Quiz her out first under narco. Afterward do what you like, short of disfiguring damage. Remember, we may find use for her later, and the nearest biosculp laboratory is parsecs hence.'

I will make them kill me! Even as she plunged toward Snell, fingernails out to hook his eyeballs, Kossara knew Glydh would seize her and not let her die.

The explosion threw her against a wall. It made a drum of her skull. The floor heaved and cracked. Snell went over backward. Glydh flailed about to keep his balance.

Faintly through the brief deafness that followed, she heard screams, running, bang and hiss of firearms. Ozone drifted acrid to her nostrils, smoke, smells of roastedness.

She was already out of the office, into the central chamber beyond. At its far end, through the passageway which gave on the garage, she saw how the main door lay blown off its trunnions, crumpled and red-hot. Beyond was the ruin of the cannon. Men boiled around or sprawled unmoving.

Enormous shone the bulk of a suit of combat armor. Bullets whanged off it, blaster bolts fountained. The wearer stood where he was, and his own weapon scythed.

As she broke into view – 'Kossara!' Amplified from the helmet, his voice resounded like God's. His free hand reached beneath a plate that protected his gravbelt. He rose and moved slowly toward her. Survivors fled.

Fingers closed on her arm. Around her shoulder she saw Glydh. He swung her before his body. 'That's not nice,' the oncoming invader pealed. He spun his blaster nozzle to needle beam, aimed, and fired.

Glydh's brow spurted steam, brains, blood, shattered bone across Kossara. She knew a heartbeat's marvel at that kind of precision shooting. But then the heavy corpse bore her down. Her head struck the floor. Lightning filled the universe.

The armored man reached her, stood over her, shielded her. A spacecraft's flank appeared in the entry. It had sprouted a turret, whose gun sprayed every doorway where an enemy might lurk. Kossara let darkness flow free.

CHAPTER ELEVEN

A breath of air cool, pine-scented; all noises gone soft; a sense of muted energies everywhere around; a lessened weight – Kossara opened her eyes. She lay in bed, in her cabin aboard the *Hooligan*. Flandry sat alongside. He wore a plain coverall, his countenance was haggard and the gray gaze troubled. Nonetheless he smiled. 'Hello, there,' he murmured. 'How do you feel?'

Drowsy, altogether at ease, she asked, 'Have we left Diomedes?'

'Yes. We're bound for Dennitza.' He took her right hand between both of his. 'Now listen. Everything is all right. You weren't seriously harmed, but on examination we decided we'd better keep you under sleep induction awhile, with intravenous feeding and some medication. Look at your left wrist.' She did. It was bare. 'Yes, the bracelet is off. As far as I'm concerned, you're free, and I'll take care of the technicalities as soon as possible. You're going home, Kossara.'

Examination— She dropped her glance. A sheer nightgown covered her. 'I'm sorry I never thought to bring anything more decorous for you to sleep in,' Flandry said. He appeared to be summoning courage. 'Chives did the doctoring, the bathing, et cetera. Chives alone.' His mouth went wry. 'You may or may not believe that. It's true, but hell knows how much I've lied to you.'

And I to you, she thought.

He straightened in the chair and released her. 'Well,' he said, 'would you like a spot of tea and accompaniments? You should stay in bed for another watch cycle or two, till you get your strength back.'

'What happened . . . to us?'

'We'd better postpone that tale. First you should rest.' Flandry rose. Almost timidly, he gave her hair a stroke. 'I'll go now. Chives will bring the tea.'

Wakefulness returned. When the Shalmuan came to retrieve her tray, Kossara sat propped against pillows, ready for him. 'I hope the refreshments were satisfactory, Donna,' he said. 'Would you care for something more?'

'Yes,' she replied. 'Information.'

The slim form showed unease. 'Sir Dominic feels—'

'Sir Dominic is not me.' She spread her palms. 'Chives, how can I relax in a jigsaw puzzle? Tell me, or ask him to tell me, what went on in that den. How did you find me? What did you do after I lost consciousness? Why?'

Chives reached a decision. 'Well, Donna, we trust that in view of results obtained, you will pardon certain earlier modifications of strict veracity which Sir Dominic deemed essential. The ring he gave you was a mere ring; no such device exists as he described, at least within the purview of Technic civilization.' She choked. He continued: 'Sir Dominic, ah, has been known to indulge in what he describes as wistful fantasizing relevant to his occupation. Instead, the bracelet you wore was slave-driven from an external source of radiated power.'

'Slave-driven. A very good word.' And yet Kossara could feel no anger. She imitated it as a duty. Had they given her a tranquilizing drug which had not completely worn off?

'Your indignation is natural, Donna.' Chives' tail switched his ankles. 'Yet allow me to request you consider the total situation, including the fact that those whom you met were not noble liberators but Merseian operatives. Sir Dominic suspected this from the start. He believed that if you reappeared, they were sure to contact you, if only to find out what had transpired. He saw no method short of the empirical for convincing you. Furthermore, admiration for your honesty made him dubious of your ability knowingly to play a double role.

'Hence I trailed you at a discreet distance while he went to Thursday Landing to investigate other aspects of the case. Albeit my assignment had its vexations, I pinpointed the spot where you were brought and called Sir Dominic, who by then had returned to Lannach. Underground and surrounded by metal, your bracelet was blocked from us. We concluded immediate attack was the most prudent course – for your sake particularly, Donna. While Sir Dominic flitted down in armor, I blasted the cannon and entrance. Shortly afterward I landed to assist and, if you will excuse my immodesty, took the single prisoner we got. The rest were either dead or, ah, holed up sufficiently well that we decided to content ourselves with a nuclear missile dispatched through the entrance.

'The resultant landslide was somewhat spectacular. Perhaps later you will be interested to see the movie I took.

'Ah ... what he has learned has made Sir Dominic of the opinion that we must speed directly to Dennitza. Nevertheless, I assure you he would in all events have seen to your repatriation at the earliest feasible date.'

Chives lifted her tea tray. 'This is as much as I should tell you at the present stage, Donna. I trust you can screen whatever you wish in the way of literary, theatrical, or musical diversion. If you require assistance of any kind, please call on the intercom. I will return in two hours with a bowl of chicken soup. Is that satisfactory?'

Stars filled the saloon viewscreen behind Flandry's head. The ship went *hush-hush-hush*, on a voyage which, even at her pseudospeed, would take a Terran month. The whisky he had poured for them glowed across tongue and palate.

'It's a foul story,' he warned.

'Does evil go away just because we keep silent?' Kossara answered. Inwardly: *How evil are you, you claw of the Empire?* – but again without heat, a thought she felt obliged to think.

After all, his lean features looked so grim and unhappy, across the table from her. He shouldn't chain-smoke the way he did; anticancer shots, cardiovascular treatments, lung-flushes, and everything, it remained a flagellant habit. One could serve a bad cause without being a bad man. Couldn't one?

He sighed and drank. 'Very well. A sketch. I got a lot of details from a narcoquiz of our prisoner, but most are simply that, details, useful in hunting down the last of his outfit if and when that seems worthwhile. He did, though, confirm and amplify something much more scary.'

Memory prodded her with a cold finger. 'Where is he?'

'Oh I needled him and bunged him out an airlock.' Flandry observed her shock. His tone changed from casual to defensive. 'We were already in space; this business doesn't allow delays. As for turning him over to the authorities when we arrive – there may not be any authorities, or they may be in full revolt, Merseian-allied. At best, the fact he was alive could trickle across to enemy Intelligence, and give them valuable clues to what we know. This is how the game's played, Kossara.' He trailed out smoke before he added, 'Happens his name was Muhammad Snell.'

Blood beat in temples and cheeks. 'He had no chance – I don't need avengers.'

'Maybe your people will,' he said quietly.

After a second he leaned forward, locked eyes with her, and continued: 'Let's begin explanations from my viewpoint. I want you to follow my experiences and reasoning, in hopes you'll then accept my conclusions. You're an embittered woman, for more cause than you know right now. But I think you're also intelligent, fair-minded, yes, tough-minded enough to recognize truth, no matter what rags it wears.'

Kossara told herself she must be calm, watchful, like a cat – like Butterfeet when she was little . . . She drank. 'Go on.'

Flandry filled his lungs. 'The Gospodar, the Dennitzans in general are furious at Hans' scheme to disband their militia and make them wholly dependent on the Navy,' he said. 'After they supported him through the civil war, too! And we've other sources of friction, inevitable; and thoughts of breaking away or violently replacing the regnant Emperor are no longer unthinkable. Dennitza has its own culture, deep-rooted, virile, alien to Terra and rather contemptuous thereof – a culture influenced by Merseia, both directly and through the, uh, zmay element in your population.

'Aye, granted, you've long been in the forefront of resistance to the Roidhunate. However, such attitudes can change overnight. History's abulge with examples. For instance, England's rebellious North American colonies calling on the French they fought less than two decades before; or America a couple of centuries later, allied first with the Russians against the Germans, then turning straight around and—' He stopped. 'This doesn't mean anything to you, does it? No matter. You can see the workings in your own case, I'm sure. Dennitza is where your loyalties lie. What you do, whom you support, those depend on what you judge best for Dennitza. Right? Yes, entirely right and wholesome. But damnably misleadable.'

'Are you, then, a Terran loyalist?' she demanded.

He shook his head. 'A civilization loyalist. Which is a pretty thin, abstract thing to be; and I keep wondering whether we can preserve civilization or even should.

'Well. Conflict of interest is normal. Compromise is too, especially with as valuable a tributary as Dennitza – *provided* it stays tributary. Now we'd received strong accusations that Dennitzans were engineering revolt on Diomedes, presumably in preparation for something similar at home. His Majesty's government wasn't about to bull right in. That'd be sure to bring on trouble we can ill afford, perhaps quite unnecessarily. But the matter had to be investigated.

'And I, I learned a Dennitzan girl of ranking family had been caught at subversion on Diomedes. Her own statements out of partial recollections, her undisguised hatred of the Imperium, they seemed to confirm those accusations. Being asked to look into the questions, what would I do but bring you along?'

He sighed. 'A terrible mistake. We should've headed straight for Dennitza. Hindsight is always keen, isn't it, while foresight stays myopic, astigmatic, strabismic, and drunk. But I haven't even that excuse. I'd guessed at the truth from the first. Instead of going off to see if I could prove my hunch or not—' His fist smote the table. 'I should *never* have risked you the way I did, Kossara!'

She thought, amazed, *He is in pain about that. He truly is.*

'A-a-ah,' Flandry said. 'I'm a ruthless bastard. Better hunter than prey, and have we any third choice in these years? Or so I thought. You . . . were only another life.'

He ground out his cigarette, sprang from the bench, strode back and forth along the cabin. Sometimes his hands were gripped together behind him, sometimes knotted at his sides. His voice turned quick and impersonal:

'You looked like a significant pawn, though. Why such an incredibly bungled job on you? Including your enslavement on Terra. I'd have heard about you in time, but it was sheer luck I did before you'd been thrown into a whorehouse. And how would your uncle the Gospodar react to *that* news if it reached him?

'Might it be intended to reach him?

'Oh, our enemies couldn't be certain what'd happen; but you tilted the probabilities in their favor. They must've spent considerable time and effort locating you. Flandry's Law: "Given a sufficiently large population, at least one member will fit any desired set of specifications." The trick is to find that member.'

'What?' Kossara exclaimed. 'Do you mean – because I was who I was, in the position I was – that's why Dennitza—' She could speak no further.

'Well, let's say you were an important factor,' he replied. 'I'm not sure just how you came into play, though I can guess. On the basis of my own vague ideas, I made a decoy of you in the manner you've already heard about. That involved first deliberately antagonizing you on the voyage; then deliberately gambling your life, health, sanity—'

He halted in midstride. His shoulders slumped. She could barely hear him, though his look did not waver from hers: 'Every minute makes what I did hurt worse.'

She wanted to tell him he was forgiven, yes, go take his hand and tell him; but no, he had lied too often. With an effort, she said, 'I am surprised.'

His grin was wry. 'Less than I am.' Returning, he flopped back onto the bench, crossed ankle over thigh till he peered across his knee at her, swallowed a long draught from his glass, took out his cigarette case; and when the smoke was going he proceeded:

'Let's next assume the enemy's viewpoint, i.e. what I learned and deduced.

'They – a key one of them, anyhow – he realizes the Terran Empire is in an era when periods of civil war are as expectable as bouts of delirium in chronic umwi fever. I wasn't quite aware of the fact myself till lately. A conversation I had set me thinking and researching. But he knew right along, my opponent. At last I see what he's been basing his strategy on for the past couple of decades. Knowing him, if he believes the theory, I think I will. These days we're vulnerable to fractricide, Kossara. And what better for Merseia, especially if just the right conflict can be touched off at just the right moment?

'We've been infiltrated. They've had sleepers among us for ... maybe a lifetime ... notably in my own branch of service, where they can cover up for each other ... and notably during this past generation, when the chaos first of the Josip regime, then the succession struggle, made it easier to pass off their agents as legitimate colonial volunteers.

'The humans on Diomedes, brewing revolution with the help of a clever Alatanist pitch – thereby diverting some of our attention to Ythri – they weren't Dennitzans. They were creatures of the Roidhunate, posing as Dennitzans. Oh, not blatantly; that'd've been a giveaway. And they were sincerely pushing for an insurrection, since any trouble of ours is a gain for them. But a major objective of the whole operation was to drive yet another wedge between your people and mine, Kossara.'

Frost walked along her spine. She stared at him and whispered: 'Those men who caught me – murdered Trohdwyr – tortured and sentenced me – they were Merseians too?'

'They were human,' Flandry said flatly, while he unfolded himself into a more normal posture. 'They were sworn-in members of the Imperial Terran Naval Intelligence Corps. But, yes, they were serving Merseia. They arrived to "investigate" and thus add credence to the clues about Dennitza

123

which their earlier-landed fellows had already been spreading around.

'Let the Imperium get extremely suspicious of the Gospodar – d'you see? The Imperium will have to act against him. It dare not stall any longer. But this action forces the Gospodar to respond – he already having reason to doubt the goodwill of the Terrans—'

Flandry smashed his cigarette, drank, laid elbows on table and said most softly, his face near hers:

'He'd hear rumours, and send somebody he could trust to look into them. Aycharaych – I'll describe him later – Aycharaych of the Roidhunate knew that person would likeliest be you. He must make ready. Your incrimination, as far as Terra was concerned – your degradation, as far as Dennitza was concerned – d'you see? Inadequate by themselves to provoke war. Still, remind me and I'll tell you about Jenkins' Ear. Nations on the brink don't need a large push to send them toppling.

'I've learned something about how you were lured, after you reached Diomedes. The rest you can tell me, if you will. Because when he isn't weaving mirages, Aycharaych works on minds. He directed the blotting out of your memories. He implanted the false half-memories and that hate of the Empire you carry around. Given his uncanny telepathic capabilities, to let him monitor what drugs, electronics, hypnotism are doing to a brain, he can accomplish what nobody else is able to.

'But I don't think he totally wiped what was real. That'd have left you too unmistakably worked over. I think you keep most of the truth in you, disguised and buried.'

The air sucked between her teeth. Her fists clenched on the table. He laid a hand across them, big and gentle.

'I hope I can bring back what you've lost, Kossara.' The saying sounded difficult. 'And, and free you from those conditioned-reflex emotions. It's mainly a matter of psychotherapy. I don't insist. Ask yourself: Can you trust me that much?'

CHAPTER TWELVE

Sickbay was a single compartment, but astonishingly well equipped. Kossara entered with tightness in her gullet and dryness on her tongue. Flandry and Chives stood behind a surgical table. An electronic helmet, swiveled out above the pillow, crouched like an ugly arachnoid. The faint hum of driving energies, ventilation, service and life-support devices, seemed to her to have taken on a shrill note.

Flandry had left flamboyancy outside. Tall in a plain green coverall, he spoke unsmiling: 'Your decision isn't final yet. Before we go any further, let me explain. Chives and I have done this sort of thing before, and we aren't a bad team, but we're no professionals.'

This sort of thing— Muhammad Snell must lately have lain on that mattress, in the dream-bewildered helplessness of narco, while yonder man pumped him dry and injected the swift poison. *Shouldn't I fear the Imperialist? Dare I risk becoming the ally of one who treated a sentient being as we do a meat animal?*

I ought to feel indignation. I don't, though. Nor do I feel guilty that I don't.

Well, I'm not revengeful, either. At least, not very much. I do remember how Trohdwyr died because he was an inconvenience; I remember how Mihail Svetich died, in a war Flandry says our enemies want to kindle anew.

Flandry says— She heard him from afar, fast and pedantic. Had he rehearsed his speech?

'This is not a hypnoprobe here, of course. It puts a human straight into quasisleep and stimulates memory activity, after a drug has damped inhibitions and emotions. In effect, everything the organism has permanently recorded becomes accessible to a questioner – assuming no deep conditioning against it. The process takes more time and skill than an ordinary quiz, where all that's wanted is something the subject con-

125

sciously knows but isn't willing to tell. Psychiatrists use it to dig out key, repressed experiences in severely disturbed patients. I've mainly used it to get total accounts, generally from cooperative witnesses – significant items they may have noticed but forgotten. In your case, we'd best go in several fairly brief sessions, spaced three or four watches apart. That way you can assimilate your regained knowledge and avoid a crisis. The sessions will give you no pain and leave no recollection of themselves.'

She brought her whole attention to him. 'Do you play the tapes for me when I wake?' she asked.

'I could,' he replied, 'but wouldn't you prefer I wiped them? You see, when our questions have brought out a coherent framework of what was buried, a simple command will fix it in your normal memory. By association, that will recover everything else. You'll come to with full recall of whatever episode we concentrated on.'

His eyes dwelt gravely upon her. 'You must realize,' he continued, 'your whole life will be open to us. We'll try hard to direct our questioning so we don't intrude. However, there's no avoiding all related and heavily charged items. You'll blurt many of them out. Besides, we'll have to feel our way. Is such-and-such a scrap of information from your recent, bad past – or is it earlier, irrelevant? Often we'll need to develop a line of investigation for some distance before we can be sure.

'We're bound to learn things you'll wish we didn't. You'll simply have to take our word that we'll keep silence ever afterward . . . and, yes, pass no judgment, lest we be judged by ourselves.

'Do you really want that, Kossara?'

She nodded with a stiff neck. 'I want the truth.'

'You can doubtless learn enough for practical purposes by talking to the Gospodar, if he's alive and available when we reach Dennitza. And I make no bones: one hope of mine is gaining insight into the *modus operandi* of Merseian Intelligence, a few clear indentifications of their agents among us . . . for the benefit of the Empire.

'I won't compel you,' Flandry finished. 'Please think again before you decide.'

She squared her shoulders. 'I have thought.' Holding out her hand : 'Give me the medicine.'

The first eventide, her feet dragged her into the saloon. Flandry saw her disheveled, drably clad, signs of weeping upon her, against the stars. She had long been in her own room behind a closed door.

'You needn't eat here, you know,' he said in his gentlest tone.

'Thank you, but I will,' she answered.

'I admire your courage more than I have words to tell, dear. Come, sit down, take a drink or three before dinner.' Since he feared she might refuse, lest that seem to herself like running away from what was in her, he added, 'Trohdwyr would like a toast to his *manes*, wouldn't he?'

She followed the suggestion in a numb way. 'Will the whole job be this bad?' she asked.

'No.' He joined her, pouring Merseian telloch for them both though he really wanted a Mars-dry martini. 'I was afraid things might go as they went, the first time, but couldn't see any road around. You did witness Trohdwyr's murder, he suffered hideously, and he'd been your beloved mentor your whole life. The pain wasn't annulled just because your thalamus was temporarily anesthetized. Being your strongest lost memory, already half in consciousness, it came out ahead of any others. And it's still so isolated it feels like yesterday.'

She settled wearily back. 'Yes,' she said. 'Before, everything was blurred, even that. Now ... the faces, the whole betrayal—'

[Nobody died in the cave except Trohdwyr. The rest stood by when a mere couple of marines arrived to arrest her. 'You called them !' she screamed to the one who bore the name Steve Johnson, surely not his own. He grinned. Trohdwyr lunged, trying to get her free, win her a chance to scramble

127

down the slope and vanish. The lieutenant blasted him. The life in his tough old body had not ebbed out, under the red moons, when they pulled her away from him.

Afterward she overheard Johnson. 'Why'd you kill the servant? Why not take him along?'

And the lieutenant: 'He'd only be a nuisance. As is, when the Diomedeans find him, they won't get suspicious at your disappearance. They'll suppose the Terrans caught you. Which should make them handier material. For instance, if we want any of those who met you here to go guerrilla, our contact men can warn them they've been identified through data pulled out of you prisoners.'

'Hm, what about us four?'

'They'll decide at headquarters. I daresay they'll reassign you to a different region. Come on, now, let's haul mass.' The lieutenant's boot nudged Kossara, where she slumped wrist-bound against the cold cave wall. 'On your feet, bitch!']

'His death happened many weeks ago,' Flandry said. 'Once you get more memories back, you'll see it, feel it in perspective – including time perspective. You'll have done your grieving . . . which you did, down underneath; and you're too healthy to mourn forever.'

'I will always miss him,' she whispered.

Flandry regarded ghosts of his own. 'Yes, I know.'

She straightened. He saw her features harden, as if bones lent strength to flesh. The blue-green eyes turned arctic. 'Sir Dominic, you were right in what you did to Snell. Nobody in that gang was – is – fit to live.'

'Well, we're in a war, we and they, the nastier for being undeclared,' he said carefully. 'What you and I must do, if we can, is keep the sickness from infecting your planet. Or to the extent it has, if I may continue the metaphor, we've got to supply an antibiotic before the high fever takes hold and the eruptions begin.'

His brutal practicality worked as he had hoped, to divert her from both sorrow and rage. 'What do you plan?' The question held some of the crispness which ordinarily was hers.

'Before leaving Diomedes,' he said, 'I contacted Lagard's field office on Lannach, transmitted a coded message for him to record, and showed him my authority to command immediate courier service. The message is directly to the Emperor. The code will bypass channels. In summary, it says, "Hold off at Dennitza, no matter what you hear, till I've collected full information" – followed by a synopsis of all I've learned thus far.'

She began faintly to glow in her exhaustion. 'Why, wonderful.'

'M-m-m, not altogether, I'm afraid.' Flandry let the telloch savage his throat. 'Remember, by now his Majesty's barbarian-quelling on the Spican frontier. He'll move around a lot. The courier may not track him down for a while. Meantime – the Admiralty on Terra may get word which provokes it to emergency action, without consulting Emperor or Policy Board. It has that right, subject to a later court of inquiry. And I've no direct line there. Probably make no difference if I did. Maybe not even any difference what I counsel Hans. I'm a lone agent. They could easily decide I must be wrong.'

He forced a level look at her. 'Or Dennitza could in fact have exploded, giving Emperor and Admiralty no choice,' he declared. 'The Merseians are surely working that side of the street too.'

'You hope I – we can can get my uncle and the Skupshtina to stay their hands?' she asked.

'Yes,' Flandry said. 'This is a fast boat. However ... we'll be a month in transit, and Aycharaych & Co. have a long jump on us.'

[The resident and his lady made her welcome at Thursday Landing. They advised her against taking her research to the Sea of Achan countries. Unrest was particularly bad there. Indeed, she and her Merseian – pardon, her xenosophont companion – would do best to avoid migratory societies in general. Could they not gather sufficient data among the sedentary and maritime Diomedeans? Those were more intimate with modern civilization, more accustomed to dealing with off-worlders, therefore doubtless more relevant to the problem which had caused her planetary government to send her here.

Striving to mask her nervousness, she met Commander Maspes and a few junior officers of the Imperial Naval Intelligence team that was investigating the disturbances. He was polite but curt. His attitude evidently influenced the younger men, who must settle for stock words and sidelong stares. Yes, Maspes said, it was common knowledge that humans were partly responsible for the revolutionary agitation and organization on this planet. Most Diomedeans believed they were Avalonians, working for Ythri. Some native rebels, caught and interrogated, said they had actually been told so by the agents themselves. And indeed the Alatanist mystique was a potent recruiter ... Yet how could a naïve native distinguish one kind of human from another? Maybe Ythri was being maligned ... He should say no more at the present stage. Had Donna Vymezal had a pleasant journey? What was the news at her home?

Lagard apologized that he must bar her from a wing of the Residency. 'A team member, his work's confidential and – well, you are a civilian, you will be in the outback, and he's a xeno, distinctive appearance—'

Kossara smiled. 'I can dog my hatch,' she said; 'but since you wish, I'll leash my curiosity.' She gave the matter scant thought, amidst everything else.]

Flandry greeted her at breakfast: 'Dobar yutro, Dama.'

Startled, she asked, 'You are learning Serbic?'

'As fast as operant conditioning, electronics, and the pharmacopoeia can cram it into me.' He joined her at table. Orange juice shone above the cloth. Coffee made the air fragrant. He drank fast. She saw he was tired.

'I wondered why you are so seldom here when off duty,' she said.

'That's the reason.'

He gazed out at the stars. She considered him. After a while, during which her pulse accelerated, she said, 'No. I mean, if you're studying, there is no need. You must know most of us speak Anglic. You need an excuse to avoid me.'

It was his turn for surprise. 'Eh? Why in cosmos would I that?'

She drew breath, feeling cheeks, throat, breasts redden. 'You think I'm embarrassed at what you've learned of me.'

'No—' He swung back to look at her. 'Yes. Not that I— Well, I try not to, and what comes out regardless shows you clean as a ... knife blade – But of course you're full of life, you've been in love and—' Abruptly he flung his head back and laughed. 'Oh, hellflash! I was afraid you *would* make me stammer like a schoolboy.'

'I'm not angry. Haven't you saved me? Aren't you healing me?' She gathered resolution. 'I did have to think hard, till I saw how nothing about me could surprise you.'

'Oh, a lot could. Does.' Their eyes met fully.

'Maybe you can equalize us a little,' she said through a rising drumbeat. 'Tell me of your own past, what you really are under that flexmail you always wear.' She smiled. 'In exchange, I can help you in your language lessons, and tell you stories about Dennitza that can't be in your records. The time has been lonely for me, Dominic.'

'For us both,' he said as though dazed.

Chives brought in an omelet and fresh-baked bread.

[From a dealer in Thursday Landing, Kossara rented an aircamper and field equipment, bought rations and guide-books, requested advice. She needed information for its own sake as well as for cover. On the long voyage here – three changes of passenger-carrying freighter – she had absorbed what material on Diomedes the Shkola in Zorkagrad could supply. That wasn't much. It could well have been zero if the planet weren't unusual enough to be used as an interest-grabbing example in certain classes. She learned scraps of astronomy, physics, chemistry, topology, meteorology, bio-logy, ethnology, history, economics, politics; she acquired a

131

few phrases in several different languages, no real grasp of their grammar or semantics; her knowledge was a twig to which she clung above the windy chasm of her ignorance about an entire world.

After a few days getting the feel of conditions, she and Trohdwyr flew to Lannach. The resident had not actually forbidden them. In the towns along Sagna Bay, they went among the gaunt high dwellings of the winged folk, seeking those who understood Anglic and might talk somewhat freely. 'We are from a planet called Dennitza. We wish to find out how to make friends and stay friends with a people who resemble you—'

Eonan the factor proved helpful. Increasingly, Kossara tried to sound him out, and had an idea he was trying to do likewise to her. Whether or not he was involved in the subversive movement, he could well fear she came from Imperial Intelligence to entrap comrades of his. And yet the name 'Dennitza' unmistakably excited more than one individual, quick though the Diomedeans were to hide that reaction.

How far Dennitza felt, drowned in alien constellations! At night in their camper, she and Trohdwyr would talk long and long about old days and future days at home; he would sing his gruff ychan songs to her, and she would recite poems of Simich that he loved: until at last an inner peace came to them both, bearing its gift of sleep.]

Flandry always dressed for dinner. He liked being well turned out; it helped create an atmosphere which enhanced his appreciation of the food and wine; and Chives would raise polite hell if he didn't. Kossara slopped in wearing whatever she'd happened to don when she got out of bed. Not to mock her mourning, he settled for the blue tunic, red sash, white trousers, and soft half-boots that were a human officer's ordinary mess uniform.

When she entered the saloon in evening garb, he nearly dropped the cocktail pitcher. Amidst the subdued elegance around her, she suddenly outblazed a great blue star and multitudinously lacy nebula which dominated the view-

screen. Burgundy-hued velvyl sheathed each curve of her tall-
ness, from low on the bosom to silvery slippers. A necklace
of jet and turquoise, a bracelet of gold, gleamed against ivory
skin. Diamond-studded tiara and crystal earrings framed the
ruddy hair; but a few freckles across the snub nose redeemed
that high-cheeked, full-mouthed, large-eyed face from queen-
liness.

'Nom de Dieu!' he gasped, and there sang through him,
*Yes, God, Whom the believers say made all triumphant
beauty. She breaks on me and takes me like a wave of sunlit
surf.* 'Woman, that's not fair! You should have sent a
trumpeter to announce you.'

She chuckled. 'I decided it was past time I do Chives the
courtesy of honoring his cuisine. He fitted me yesterday and
promised to exceed himself in the galley.'

Flandry shook head and clicked tongue. 'Pity I won't be pay-
ing his dishes much attention.' Underneath, he hurt for joy.

'You will. I know you, Dominic. And I will too.' She
pirouetted. 'This gown is lovely, isn't it? Being a woman
again—' The air sent him an insinuation of her perfume,
while it lilted with violins.

'Then you feel recovered?'

'Yes.' She sobered. 'I felt strength coming back, the strength
to be glad, more and more these past few days.' A stride
brought her to him. He had set the pitcher down. She took
both his hands – the touch radiated through him – and said
gravely: 'Oh, I've not forgotten what happened, nor what
may soon happen. But life is good. I want to celebrate its
goodness ... with you, who brought me home to it. I can
never rightly thank you for that, Dominic.'

Nor can I rightly thank you for existing, Kossara. In spite
of what she had let slip beneath the machine, she remained
too mysterious for him to hazard kissing her. He took refuge: 'Yes, you can. You can throw off your frontier steadfastness, foresight, common sense, devotion to principle, et
cetera, and be frivolous. If you don't know how to frivol,
watch me. Later you may disapprove to your heart's con-
tempt, but tonight let's cast caution to the winds, give three-

point-one-four-one-six cheers, and speak disrespectfully of the Lesser Magellanic Cloud.'

Laughing, she released him. 'Do you truly think we Dennitzans are so stiff? I'd call us quite jolly. Wait till you've been to a festival, or till I show you how to dance the luka.'

'Why not now? Work up an appetite.'

She shook her head. The tiara flung glitter which he noticed only peripherally because of her eyes. 'No, I'd rip this dress, or else pop out of it like a cork. Our dances are all lively. Some people say they have to be.'

'The prospect of watching you demonstrate makes me admit there's considerable to be said for an ice age.'

Actually, the summers where she lived were warm. Farther south, the Pustinya desert was often hot. A planet is too big, to many-sided for a single idea like 'glacial era' to encompass.

Through Flandry passed the facts he had read, a parched obbligato to the vividness breathing before him. He would not truly know her till he knew the land, sea, sky, which had given her to creation; but the data were a beginning.

Zoria was an F8 sun, a third again as luminous as Sol. Dennitza, slightly smaller than Terra, orbiting at barely more than Terran distance from the primary, should have been warmer – and had been for most of its existence. Loss of water through ultraviolet cracking had brought about that just half the surface was ocean-covered. This, an axial tilt of $32\frac{1}{2}°$, and an 18.8-hour rotation period led to extremes of weather and climate. Basically terrestroid, organisms adapted as they evolved in a diversity of environments.

That stood them in good stead when the catastrophe came. Less than a million years ago, a shower of giant meteoroids struck, or perhaps an asteroid shattered in the atmosphere. Whirled around the globe by enormous forces, the stones cratered dry land – devastated by impact, concussion, radiation, fire which followed – cast up dust which dimmed the sun for years afterward. Worse were the ocean strikes. The tsunamis they raised merely ruined every coast on the planet; life soon returned. But the thousands of cubic kilometers of water they evaporated became a cloud cover that endured for millennia. The energy balance shifted. Ice caps formed at the poles, grew, begot glaciers reaching halfway to the equator. Species, genera, families died; fossil beds left hints that among them had been a kind starting to make tools. New forms arose, winterhardy in the temperate zones, desperately contentious in the tropics.

Then piece by piece the heavens cleared, sunlight grew brilliant again, glaciers melted back. The retreat of the ice that men found when they arrived, six hundred years later, was a rout. The Great Spring brought woes of its own, storms, floods, massive extinctions and migrations to overthrow whole ecologies. In her own brief lifespan, Kossara had seen coastal towns abandoned before a rising sea.

Her birth country lay not far inland, though sheltered from northerly winds and easterly waters – the Kazan, Cauldron, huge astrobleme on the continent Rodna, a bowl filled with woods, farmlands, rivers, at its middle Lake Stoyan and the capital Zorkagrad. Her father was voivode of Dubina Dolyina province, named for the gorge that the Lyubisha River had cut through the ringwall on its way south from the dying snows. Thus she grew up child of a lord close to the people he guided, wilderness child who was often in town, knowing the stars both as other suns and as elven friends to lead her home after dark . . .

Flandry took her arm. 'Come, my lady,' he said. 'Be seated. This evening we shall not eat, we shall dine.'

[At last Eonan told Kossara about a person in the mountain community Salmenbrok who could give her some useful tidings. If she liked, he would take her and Trohdwyr on his gravsled – he didn't trust her vehicle in these airs – and introduce them. More he would not yet say. They accepted eagerly.

Aloft he shifted course. 'I bespoke one in Salmenbrok because I feared spies overhearing,' he explained. 'The truth is, they are four in a cave whom we will visit. I have asked them about you, and they will have you as guests while you explore each other's intents.'

She thought in unease that when the Diomedean went back, she and her companion would be left flightless, having brought no gravbelts along. The ychan got the same realization and growled. She plucked up the nerve to shush him and say, 'Fine.'

The two men and two women she met were not her kind. Racial types, accents, manners, their very gaits belied it. Eonan talked to them and her passionately, as if they really were Dennitzans who had come to prepare the liberation of his folk. She bided in chill and tension, speaking little and nothing to contradict, until he departed. Then she turned on them and cried, 'What's this about?' Her hand rested on her sidearm. Trohdwyr bulked close, ready to attack with pistol, knife, tail, foot-claws if they threatened her.

Steve Johnson smiled, spread empty fingers, and replied, 'Of course you're puzzled. Please come inside where it's warmer and we'll tell you.' The rest behaved in equally friendly wise.

Their story was simple in outline. They too were Imperial subjects, from Esperance. That planet wasn't immensely remote from here. True to its pacifistic tradition, it had stayed neutral during the succession fight, declaring it would pledge allegiance to whoever gave the Empire peace and law again. (Kossara nodded. She had heard of Esperance.) But this policy required a certain amount of armed might and a great deal of politicking and intriguing abroad, to prevent forcible recruitment by some or other pretender. The Esperancians thus got into the habit of taking a more active role than hitherto. Conditions remained sufficiently turbulent after Hans was crowned to keep the habit in tune.

When their Intelligence heard rumors of Ythrian attempts to foment revolution on Diomedes, their government was immediately concerned. Esperance was near the border of Empire and Domain. Agents were smuggled onto Diomedes to spy out the truth – discreetly, since God alone knew what the effect of premature revelations might be. Johnson's party was such a band.

'Predecessors of ours learned Dennitzans were responsible,'

136

he said. 'Not Avalonian humans serving Ythri, but Dennit-zan humans serving their war lord!'

'No!' Kossara interrupted, horrified. 'That isn't true! And he's not a war lord!'

'It was what the natives claimed, Mademoiselle Vymezal,' the Asian-looking woman said mildly. 'We decided to try posing as Dennitzans. Our project had learned enough about the underground – names of various members, for instance – that it seemed possible, granted the autochthons couldn't spot the difference. Their reaction to us does indicate they ... well, they have reason to believe Dennitzans are sparking their movement. We've been, ah, leading them on, collecting information without actually helping them develop para-military capabilities. When Eonan told us an important Den-nitzan had arrived, openly but with hints she could be more than a straightforward scientist – naturally, we grew interested.'

'Well, you've been fooled,' burst from Kossara. 'I'm here to, to disprove those exact same charges against us. The Gos-podar, our head of state, he's my uncle and he sent me as his personal agent. I should know, shouldn't I? And I tell you, he's loyal. We are!'

'Why doesn't he proclaim it?' Johnson asked.

'Oh, he is making official representations. But what are they worth? Across four hundred light-years— We need proof. We need to learn who's been blackening us and why.' Kossara paused for a sad smile. 'I don't pretend I can find out much. I'm here as a, a forerunner, a scout. Maybe that special Navy team working out of Thursday Landing – have you heard about them? – maybe they'll exonerate us without our doing anything. Maybe they already have. The com-mander didn't act suspicious of me.'

Johnson patted her head. 'I believe you're honest, Mademoiselle,' he said. 'And you may well be correct, too. Let's exchange what we've discovered – and, in between, give you some outdoor recreation. You look space-worn.'

The next three darkling springtime days were pleasant.

Kossara and Trohdwyr stopped wearing weapons in the cave.]

Flandry sighed. 'Aycharaych.' He had told her something of his old antagonist. 'Who else? Masks within masks, shadows that cast shadows ... Merseian operatives posing as Esperancians posing as Dennitzans whose comrades had formerly posed as Avalonians, while other Merseian creatures are in fact the Terran personnel they claim to be ... Yes, I'll bet my chance of a peaceful death that Aycharaych is the engineer of the whole diablerie.'

He drew on a cigarette, rolled acridity over his tongue and streamed it out his nostrils, as if this mordant would give reality a fast hold on him. He and she sat side by side on a saloon bench. Before them was the table, where stood glasses and a bottle of Demerara rum. Beyond was the viewscreen, full of night and stars. They had left the shining nebula behind; an unlit mass of cosmic dust reared thunderhead tall across the Milky Way. The ship's clocks declared the hour was late. Likewise did the silence around, above the hum which had gone so deep into their bones that they heard it no more.

Kossara wore a housedress whose brevity made him all too aware of long legs, broad bosom, a vein lifting blue from the dearest hollow that her shoulderblades made at the base of her throat. She shivered a trifle and leaned near him, unperfumed now except for a sunny odor of woman. 'Monstrous,' she mumbled.

'N-no ... well, I can't say.' *Why do I defend him?* Flandry wondered, and knew: *I see in my mirror the specter of him. Though who of us is flesh and who image?* 'I'll admit I can't hate him, even for what he did to you and will do to your people and mine if he can. I'll kill him the instant I'm able, but – Hm, I suppose you never saw or heard of a coral snake. It's venomous but very beautiful, and strikes without malice ... Not that I really know what drives Aycharaych. Maybe he's an artist of overriding genius. That's a kind of monster, isn't it?'

She reached for her glass, withdrew her hand – she was a light drinker – and gripped the table edge instead, till the ends of her nails turned white. 'Can such a labyrinth of a scheme work? Aren't there hopelessly many chances for something to go wrong?'

Flandry found solace in a return to pragmatics, regardless of what bitterness lay behind. 'If the whole thing collapses, Merseia hasn't lost much. Not Hans nor any Emperor can make the Terran aristocrats give up their luxuries – first and foremost, their credo that eventual accommodation is possible – and go after the root of the menace. He couldn't manage anything more than a note of protest and perhaps the suspension of a few negotiations about trade and the like. His underlings would depose him before they allowed serious talk about singeing the beard the Roidhun hasn't got.'

His cigarette butt scorched his fingers. He tossed it away and took a drink of his own. The piratical pungency heartened him till he could speak in detachment, almost amusement: 'Any plotter must allow for his machine losing occasional nuts and bolts. You're an example. Your likely fate as a slave was meant to outrage every man on Dennitza when the news arrived there. By chance, I heard about you in the well-known and deservedly popular nick of time – I, not someone less cautious—'

'Less noble,' She stroked his arm. It shone inside.

Nonetheless he grinned and said, 'True, I may lack scruples, but not warm blood. I'm a truncated romantic. A mystery, a lovely girl, an exotic planet – could I resist hallooing off—'

It jarred through him: – *off into whatever trap was set by a person who knew me?* His tongue went on. 'However, prudence, not virtue, was what made me careful to do nothing irrevocable' *to you, darling; I praise the Void that nothing irrevocable happened to you.* 'And we did luck out, we did destroy the main Merseian wart on Diomedes.' *Was the luck poor silly Susette and her husband's convenient absence? Otherwise I'd have stayed longer at Thursday Landing, playing sleuth – long enough to give an assassin, who was expecting me specifically, a chance at me.*

No! This is fantastic! Forget it!

'Wasn't that a disaster to the enemy?' Kossara asked.

' 'Fraid not. I don't imagine they'll get their Diomedean insurgency. But that's a minor disappointment. I'm sure the whole operation was chiefly a means to the end of maneuvering Terra into forcing Dennitza to revolt. And those false clues have long since been planted and let sprout; the false authoritative report has been filed; in short, about as much damage has been done on the planet as they could reasonably expect.'

Anguish: 'Do you think . . . we will find civil war?'

He laid an arm around her. She leaned into the curve of it, against his side. 'The Empire seldom bumbles fast,' he comforted her. 'Remember, Hans himself didn't want to move without more information. He saw no grounds for doubting the Maspes report – that Dennitzans were involved – but he realized they weren't necessarily the Gospodar's Dennitzans. That's why I got recruited, to check further. In addition, plain old bureaucratic inertia works in our favor. Yes, as far as the problems created on Diomedes are concerned, I'm pretty sure we'll get you home in time.'

'Thanks to you, Dominic.' Her murmur trembled. 'To none but you.'

He did not remind her that Diomedes was not, could never have been the only world on which the enemy had worked, and that events on Dennitza would not have been frozen. This was no moment for reminders, when she kissed him.

Her shyness in it made him afraid to pursue. But they sat together a spell, mute before the stars, until she bade him goodnight.

[On the tundra far north of the Kazan, Bodin Miyatovich kept a hunting lodge. Thence he rode forth on horseback, hounds clamorous around him, in quest of gromatz, yegyupka, or ice troll. At other times he and his guests boated on wild waters, skied on glacier slopes, sat indoors by a giant hearthfire talking, drinking, playing chess, playing music, harking to blizzard winds outside. Since her father bore her cradle from aircar to door, Kossara had loved coming here.

Though this visit was harshly for business, she felt pleasure at what surrounded her. She and her uncle stood on a slate terrace that jutted blue-black from the granite blocks of the house. Zoria wheeled dazzling through cloudless heaven, ringed with sun dogs. Left, right, and rearward the land reached endless, red-purple mahovina turf, widespaced clumps of firebush and stands of windblown plume, here and there a pool ablink. Forward, growth yielded to tumbled boulders where water coursed. In these parts, the barrens were a mere strip; she could see the ice beyond them. Two kilometers high, its cliff stood over the horizon, a worldwall, at its distance not dusty white but shimmering, streaked with blue crevasses. The river which ran from its melting was still swift when it passed near the lodge, a deep brawl beneath the lonesome tone of wind, the remote cries of a sheerwing flock. The air was cold, dry, altogether pure. The fur lining of her parka hood was soft and tickly on her cheeks.

The big man beside her growled, 'Yes, too many ears in Zorkagrad. Damnation! I thought if we put Molitor on the throne, we'd again know who was friend and who was foe. But things only get more tangled. How many faithful are left? I can't tell. And that's fouler than men becoming outright turncoats.'

'You trust me, don't you?' Kossara answered in pride.

'Yes,' Miyatovich said. 'I trust you beyond your fidelity. You're strong and quick-witted. And your xenological background ... qualifies you and gives you a cover story ... for a mission I hope you'll undertake.'

'To Diomedes? My father's told me rumors.'

'Worse. Accusations. Not public yet. I actually had bloody hard work finding out, myself, why Imperial Intelligence agents have been snooping amongst us in such numbers. I sent men to inquire elsewhere and— Well, the upshot is, the Impies know revolt is brewing on Diomedes and think Dennitzans are the yeast. The natural conclusion is that a cabal of mine sent them, to keep the Imperium amused while we prepare a revolt of our own.'

'You've denied it, I'm sure.'

'In a way. Nobody's overtly charged me. I've sent the Emperor a memorandum, deploring the affair and offering to cooperate in a full-dress investigation. But guilty or not, I'd do that. How to prove innocence? As thin as his corps is spread, we could mobilize – on desert planets, for instance, without positive clues for them to find.'

The Gospodar gusted a sigh. 'And appearances are against us. There *is* a lot of sentiment for independence, for turning this sector into a confederacy free of an Empire that failed us and wants to sap the strength we survived by. Those *could* be Dennitzans yonder, working for a faction who plot to get us committed – who'll overthrow me if they must—'

'I'm to go search out the truth if I can,' she knew. 'Uncle, I'm honored. But me alone? Won't that be like trying to catch water in a net?'

'Maybe. Though at the bare least, you can bring me back … um … a feel of what's going on, better than anybody else. And you may well do more. I've watched you from baby-hood. You're abler than you think, Kossara.'

Miyatovich took her by the shoulders. Breath smoked white from his mouth, leaving frost in his beard, as he spoke: 'I've never had a harder task than this, asking you to put your life on the line. You're like a daughter to me. I sorrowed nearly as much as you did when Mihail died, but told myself you'd find another good man who'd give you sound children. Now I can only say – go in Mihail's name, that your next man needn't die in another war.'

'Than you think we should stay in the Empire?'

'Yes. I've made remarks that suggested different. But you know me, how I talk rashly in anger but try to act in calm. The Empire would have to get so bad that chaos was better, before I'd willingly break it. Terra, the Troubles, or the tyranny of Merseia – and those racists wouldn't just subject us, they'd tame us – I don't believe we have a fourth choice, and I'll pick Terra.'

She felt he was right.]

A part of the *Hooligan*'s hold had been converted to a gymnasium. Outbound, and at first on the flight from Diomedes, Flandry and Kossara used it at separate hours. Soon after her therapy commenced, she proposed they exercise together. 'Absolutely!' he caroled. 'It'll make calisthenics themselves fun, whether or not that violates the second law of thermodynamics.'

In truth, it wasn't fun – when she was there in shorts and halter, sweat, laughter, herself – it was glory.

Halfway to Dennitza, he told her: 'Let's end our psychosessions. You've regained everything you need. The rest would be in detail, not worth further invasion of your privacy.'

'No invasion,' she said low. Her eyes dropped, her blood mounted. 'You were welcome.'

'Chives!' Flandry bellowed. 'Get busy! Tonight we do not dine, we feast!'

'Very good, sir,' the Shalmuan replied, appearing in the saloon as if his master had rubbed a lamp. 'I suggest luncheon consist of a small salad and tea to drink.'

'You're the boss,' Flandry said. 'Me, I can't sit still. How about a game of tennis, Kossara? Then after our rabbit repast we can snooze, in preparation for sitting up the whole nightwatch popping champagne.'

She agreed eagerly. They changed into gym briefs and met below. The room was elastic matting, sunlamp fluorescence, gray-painted sides. In its bareness, she flamed.

The ball thudded back and forth, caromed, bounced, made them leap, for half an hour. At last, panting, they called time out and sought a water tap.

'Do you feel well?' She sounded anxious. 'You missed an awful lot of serves.' They were closely matched, her youth against his muscles.

'If I felt any better, you could turn off the ship's powerplant and hook me into the circuits,' he replied.

'But why – ?'

'I was distracted.' He wiped the back of a hand across the salt dampness in his mustache, ran those fingers through his hair and recalled how it was turning gray. Decision came. He prepared a light tone before going on: 'Kossara, you're a beautiful woman, and not just because you're the only woman for quite a few light-years around. Never fear, I can mind my manners. But I hope it won't bother you overmuch if I keep looking your way.'

She stood quiet awhile, except for the rise and fall of her breasts. Her skin gleamed. A lock of hair clung bronzy to her right cheekbone. The beryl eyes gazed beyond him.

Suddenly they returned, focused, met his as sabers meet in a fencing match between near friends. Her husky voice grew hoarse and, without her noticing, stammered Serbic: 'Do you mean – Dominic, do you mean you never learned, while I was under . . . I love you?'

Meteorstruck, he heard himself croak, 'No. I did try to avoid – as far as possible, I let Chives question you, in my absence—'

'I resisted,' she said in wonder, 'because I knew you would be kind but dared not imagine you might be for always.'

'I'd lost hope of getting anybody who'd make me want to be.'

She came to him.

Presently: 'Dominic, darling, please, no. Not yet.'

'– Do you want a marriage ceremony first?'

'Yes. If you don't mind too much. I know you don't care, but, well, did you know I still say my prayers every night? Does that make you laugh?'

'Never. All right, we'll be married, and in style !'

'Could we really be? In St. Clement's Cathedral, by Father Smed who christened and confirmed me – ?'

'If he's game, I am. It won't be easy, waiting, but how can I refuse a wish of yours? Forgive these hands. They're not used to holding something sacred.'

'Dominic. you star-fool, stop babbling ! Do you think it will be easy for me?'

CHAPTER THIRTEEN

The earliest signs of trouble reached them faintly across distance. Fifty astronomical units from Zoria and well off the ecliptic plane, the *Hooligan* phased out of hyperdrive into normal state. Engines idle, she drifted at low kinetic velocity among stars, her destination sun only the brightest; and instruments strained after traces.

Flandry took readings and made computations. His lips tightened. 'A substantial space fleet, including what's got to be a Nova-class dreadnought,' he told Kossara and Chives. 'In orbits or under accelerations that fit the pattern of a battle-ready naval force.'

The girl clenched her fists. 'What can have happened?'

'We'll sneak in and eavesdrop.'

Faster-than-light pseudospeed would give them away to detectors. (Their Schrödinger 'wake' must already have registered, but no commander was likely to order interception of a single small vessel which he could assume would proceed until routinely checked by a picket craft.) However, in these far regions they could drive hard on force-thrust without anybody observing or wondering why. Nearing the inner system, where ships and meters were thick. Flandry plotted a roundabout course. It brought him in behind the jovian planet Svarog, whose gravitational, magnetic, and radiation fields screened the emissions of *Hooligan*. Amidst all fears for home and kin, Kossara exclaimed at the majestic sight as they passed within three million kilometers – amber-glowing disc, swarming moons – and at the neatness wherewith the planet swung them, their power again turned off, into the orbit Flandry wanted, between its own and that of Perun to sunward.

'With every system aboard at zero or minimum, we should pass for a rock if a radar or whatever sweeps us,' he explained.

'And we'll catch transmissions from Dennitza – maybe

intercept a few messages between ships, though I expect those'll be pretty boring.'

'How I hope you are right,' Kossara said with a forlorn chuckle.

He regarded her, beside him in the control cabin. Interior illumination was doused, heating, weight generator, anything which might betray. They hung loosely harnessed in their seats, bodies if not minds enjoying the fantasy state of free fall. As yet, cold was no more than a nip in the air Chives kept circulating by a creaky hand-cranked fan. Against the clear canopy, stars crowned her head. On the opposite side, still small at this remove, Zoria blazed between outspread wings of zodiacal light.

'They're definitely Technic warcraft,' he said, while wishing to speak her praises. 'The neutrino patterns alone prove it. From what we've now learned, closer in, about their numbers and types, they seem to match your description of the Dennitzan fleet, though there're some I think must belong to the Imperium. My guess is, the Gospodar has gathered Dennitza's own in entirety, plus such units of the regular Navy as he felt he could rely on. In short, he's reached a dangerous brink, though I don't believe anything catastrophic has happened yet.'

'We are in time, then?' she asked gladly.

He could not but lean over and kiss her. 'Luck willing, yes. We may need patience before we're certain.'

Fortune spared them that. Within an hour, they received the basic information. Transmitters on Dennitza sent broad-beam rather than precisely lased 'casts to the telsats for relay, wasting some cheap energy to avoid the cost of building and maintaining a more exact system. By the time the pulses got as far as *Hooligan*, their dispersal guaranteed they would touch her; and they were not too weak for a good receiver-amplifier-analyzer to reconstruct a signal. The windfall program Flandry tuned in was a well-organized commentary on the background of the crisis.

It broke two weeks ago. (*Maybe just when Kossara and I found out about each other?* he wondered. *No; meaningless;*

146

simultaneity doesn't exist for interstellar distances.) Before a tumultuous parliament, Bodin Miyatovich announced full mobilization of the Narodna Voyska, recall of units from outsystem duty, his directing the Imperial Navy command for Tauria to maintain the Pax within the sector, his ordering specific ships and flotillas belonging to it to report here for assignment, and his placing Dennitzan society on a stand-by war footing.

A replay from his speech showed him at the wooden lectern, carved with vines and leaves beneath outward-sweeping yelen horns, from which Gospodar had addressed Skupshtina since the days of the Founders. In the gray tunic and red cloak of a militia officer, knife and pistol on hips, he appeared still larger than he was. His words boomed across crowded tiers in the great stone hall, seemed almost to make the stained-glass windows shiver.

'– Intelligence reports have grown more and more disquieting over the past few months. I can here tell you little beyond this naked fact – you will understand the need not to compromise sources – but our General Staff takes as grave a view of the news as I do. Scouts dispatched into the Roidhunate have brought back data on Merseian naval movements which indicate preparations for action ... Diplomatic inquiries both official and unofficial have gotten only assurances for response, unproved and vaguely phrased. After centuries, we know what Merseian assurances are worth ...

'Thus far I have no reply to my latest message to the Emperor, and can't tell if my courier has even caught up with him on the Spicon frontier ... High Terran authorities whom I've been able to contact have denied there is a Merseian danger at the present time. They've challenged the validity of the information given me, have insisted their own is different and is correct ...

'They question our motives. Fleet Admiral Sandberg told me to my face, when I visited his command post, he believes our government has manufactured an excuse to marshal strength, not against foreign enemies but against the Imperium. He cited charges of treasonous Dennitzan activity elsewhere in the Empire. He forbade me to act. When I reminded him that I am the sector viceroy, he declared he would see about getting me removed. I think he would have had me arrested then and there' – a bleak half-smile – 'if I'd not taken the precaution of bringing along more firepower than he had on hand . . .

'He revealed my niece, Kossara Vymezal, whom I sent forth to track down the origin of those lies – he claimed she'd been caught at subversion, had confessed under their damnable mind-twisting interrogation – I asked why I was not informed at once, I demanded she be brought home, and learned—' He smote the lectern. Tears burst from his eyes. 'She has been sold for a slave on Terra.'

The assembly roared.

'*Uyak* Bodin, *Uyak* Bodin,' Kossara herself wept. She lifted her hands to the screen as if to try touching him.

'Sssh,' Flandry said. 'This is past, remember. We've got to find out what's happening today and what brought it on.'

She gulped, mastered her sobs, and gave him cool help. He had a fair grasp of Serbic, and the news analyst was competent, but as always, much was taken for granted of which a stranger was ignorant.

Ostensibly the Merseian trouble sprang from incidents accumulated and ongoing in the Wilderness. Disputes between traders, prospectors, and voortrekkers from the two realms had repeatedly brought on armed clashes. Dennitzans didn't react to overbearingness as meekly as citizens of the inner Empire were wont to. They overbore right back, or took the initiative from the beginning. Several actions were doubtless in a legal sense piracy by crews of one side or the other. Matters had sharpened during the civil war, when there was no effective Imperial control over humans.

Flandry had known about this, and known too that the Roidhunate had asked for negotiations aimed at solving the problem, negotiations to which Emperor Hans agreed on the principle that law and order were always worth establishing even with the cooperation of an enemy. The delegates had wrangled for months.

In recent weeks Merseia had changed its tack and made totally unacceptable demands – for example, that civilian craft must be cleared by its inspectors before entering the Wilderness. 'They know that's ridiculous,' Flandry remarked. 'Without fail, in politics that kind of claim has an ulterior purpose. It may be as little as a propaganda ploy for domestic consumption, or as much as the spark put to a bomb fuse.'

'A reason to bring their strength to bear – while most of the Empire's is tied up at Spica – and maybe denounce the Covenant of Alfzar and occupy a key system in the Wilderness?' Kossara wondered.

'Could be ... *if* Merseia is dispatching warships in this direction,' Flandry said. 'The Imperium thinks not – thinks Dennitza concocted the whole business to justify mobilization. The Merseians would've been delighted to co-conspire, a behind-the-scenes arrangement with your uncle whereby they play intransigent at the conference. Any split among us is pure gain for them. From the Imperium's viewpoint, Dennitza has done this either to put pressure on it – to get the disbanding decree rescinded and other grievances settled – or else to start an out-and-out rebellion.'

He puffed on his cigarette, latest of a chain. 'From your uncle's viewpoint – I assume he was honest with you about his opinions and desires – if he believes Merseia may be readying for combat, he dare not fail to respond. Terra can think in terms of settling border disputes by negotiation, even after several battles. Dennitza, though, will be under attack. A tough, proud people won't sit still for being made pawns of. And given the accusations against them, the horrible word about you – how alienated must they not feel?'

The commentator had said: 'Is it possible the connivance is between Emperor and Roidhun? Might part of a secret bargain be that Merseia rids the Imperium of troublesomely independent subjects? It would like to destroy us. To it, we are worse than a nuisance, we are the potential igniters of a new spirit within the Empire, whose future leadership may actually come from among us. On the Terran side, the shock of such an event would tend to unite the Empire behind the present bearer of the crown, securing it for him and his posterity ...'

Flandry said: 'I'm pretty sure that by now, throughout the Dennitzan sphere of influence, a majority favors revolution. The Gospodar's stalling, trying to bide his time in hopes the crisis will slack off before fighting starts. Wouldn't you guess so, love? I suspect, however, if it turns out he doesn't have to resist Merseia, he will then use his assembled power to try squeezing concessions from Terra. His citizens won't let him abstain – and I doubt if he wants to. And ... any wrong action on the part of the Imperium or its Navy, or any wrong inaction, anywhere along the line, will touch off rebellion.'

'We'll go straight to him—' she began.

Flandry shook his head. 'Uh-uh. Most reckless thing we could do. Who supplied those Intelligence reports that scared Miyatovich and his staff – reports contradicted by findings of my Corps in separate operations? If the Merseian fleet is making ominous motions, is this a mere show for the Dennitzan scouts they knew would sneak into their space? How did the news about you get here so speedily, when the sale of one obscure slave never rated a word on any Terran newscast? Could barbarian activity in Sector Spica have been encouraged from outside, precisely to draw the Emperor there and leave his officers on this frontier to respond as awkwardly as they've done?'

He sighed. 'Masks and mirages again, Kossara. The program we heard showed us only the skin across the situation. We can't tell what's underneath, except that it's surely explosive, probably poisonous. Zorkagrad must be acrawl with Merseian undercover men. I'd be astonished if some of them aren't high and trusted in the Gospodar's councils, fending off any information they prefer he doesn't get. Aycharaych's been at work for a long time.'

'What shall we do?' she asked steadily.

Flandry's glance sought for Dennitza. It should be visible here, soft blue against black. But the brightnesses which burned were too many. 'Suppose you and I pay a covert visit on your parents,' he said. 'From there we can send a house-hold servant, seemingly on an ordinary errand, who can find a chance to slip your uncle a word. Meanwhile Chives lands at Zorkagrad port and takes quarters to be our contact in the city. Shalmuan spacers aren't common but they do exist – not that the average person hereabouts ever heard of Shalmu – and I'll modify one of our spare documentations to support his story of being an innocent entrepreneur just back from a long exploration, out of touch, in the Wilderness.'

'It seems terribly roundabout.' Kossara said.

'Everything is on this mission.'

She smiled. 'Well, you have the experience, Dominic. And it will give us a little time alone together.'

CHAPTER FOURTEEN

First the planet loomed immense in heaven, clouds and ice lending it a more than Terran whiteness against which the glimpsed oceans became a dazzlingly deep azure. Then it was no longer ahead, it was land and sea far below. When Flandry and Kossara bailed out, it became a roar of night winds.

They rode their gravbelts down as fast as they dared, while the *Hooligan* vanished southward. The chance of their being detected was maybe slight, but not nonexistent. They need have no great fear of being shot at; as a folk who lived with firearms, the Dennitzans were not trigger-happy. However, two who arrived like this, in time of emergency, would be detained, and the matter reported to military headquarters. Hence Kossara had proposed descending on the unpeopled taiga north of the Kazan. The voivode of Dubina Dolyina must have patrols and instruments active throughout his district.

Even at their present distance from it, she and Flandry could not have left the vessel secretly in an aircraft. The captain of the picket ship which contacted Chives had settled for a telecom inspection of his papers, without boarding, and had cleared him for a path through atmosphere which was a reasonable one in view of his kinetic vector. Yet orbital optics and electronics must be keeping close watch until ground-based equipment could take over.

Hoar in moonlight, treetops rushed upward. The forest was not dense, though, and impact quickly thudded through soles. At once the humans removed their spacesuits, stopping only for a kiss when heads emerged from helmets. Flandry used a trenching tool to bury the outfits while Kossara re-stowed their packs. In outdoor coveralls and hiking boots, they should pass for a couple who had spent a furlough on a trip afoot. Before they established camp for what remained of the night, they'd better get several kilometers clear of any evidence to the contrary.

Flandry bowed. 'Now we're down, I'm in your hands,' he said. 'I can scarcely imagine a nicer place to be.'

Kossara looked around, filled her lungs full of chill sweet-scented air, breathed out, 'Domovina' – home – and began striding.

The ground was soft and springy underfoot, mahovina turf and woodland duff. A gravity seven percent less than Terran eased the burden on backs. Trees stood three or four meters apart, low, gnarly, branches plumed blue-black, an equivalent of evergreens. Shrubs grew in between, but there was no real underbrush; moonlight and shadow dappled open sod. A full Mesyatz turned the sky nearly violet, leaving few stars and sheening off a great halo. Smaller but closer in than Luna, it looked much the same save for brilliance and haste. No matter countless differences, the entire scene had a familiarity eerie and wistful, as if the ghosts of mammoth hunters remembered an age when Terra too was innocent.

'Austere but lovely,' the man said into silence. His breath smoked, though the season, late summer, brought no deep cold. 'Like you. Tell me, what do Dennitzans see in the markings on their moon? Terrans usually find a face in theirs.'

'Why ... our humans call the pattern an orlik. That's a winged theroid; this planet has no ornithoids.' A sad smile flickered over Kossara's night-ivory lips. 'But I've oftener thought of it as Ri. He's the hero of some funny ychan fairy tales, who went to live on Mesaytz. I used to beg Trohdwyr for stories about Ri when I was a child. Why do you ask?'

'Hoping to learn more about you and yours. We talked a lot in space, but we've our lifetimes, and six hundred years before them, to explain if we can.'

'We'll have the rest of them for that.' She crossed herself. 'If God wills.'

They were laconic thereafter, until they had chosen a sleeping place and spread their bags. By then the crater wall showed dream-blue to south, and the short night of the planet was near an end. Rime glimmered. Flandry went behind a tree to change into pyjamas. When he came back, Kossara was doing so. 'I'm sorry!' he apologized, and wheeled about. 'I forgot you'd say prayers.'

She was quiet an instant before she laughed, unsteadily but honestly. 'I was forgetful too. Well, look if you wish, darling. What harm? You must have seen the holograms . . .' She lifted her arms and made a slow turn before his eyes. 'Do you like what you're getting?'

'Sun and stars—'

She stopped to regard him, as if unaware of chill. He barely heard her : 'Would it be wrong? Here in these clean spaces, under heaven?'

He took a step in her direction, halted, and grinned his most rueful. 'It would not be very practical, I'm afraid. You deserve better.'

She sighed. 'You are too kind to me, Dominic.' She put on her bedclothes. They kissed more carefully than had been their way of late, and got into the bags that lay side by side in the heavy shadow of a furbark tree.

'I'm not sleepy,' she told him after a few minutes.

'How could I be?' he answered.

'Was I wanton just now? Or unfair? That would be much worse.'

'I was the Fabian this time, not you.'

'The what? . . . Never mind.' She lay watching the final stars and the first silvery flush before daybreak. Her voice stumbled. 'Yes, I must explain. You could have had me if you'd touched me with a fingertip. You can whenever you ask, beloved. Chastity is harder than I thought.'

'But it does mean a great deal to you, doesn't it? You're young and eager. I can wait awhile.'

'Yes – I suppose that is part of what I feel, the wanting to know – to know you. You've had many women, haven't you? I'm afraid there's no mystery left for me to offer.'

'On the contrary,' he said, 'you have the greatest of all. What's it like to be man and wife? I think you'll teach me more about that than I can teach you about anything else.'

154

She was mute until she could muster the shy words: 'Why have you never married, Dominic?'

'Nobody came along whom I couldn't be happy without – what passes for happy in an Imperial Terran.'

'Nobody? Out of hundreds to choose from?'

'You exaggerate ... Well, once, many years ago. But she was another man's, and left with him when he had to flee the Empire. I can only hope they found a good home at some star too far away for us to see from here.'

'And you have longed for her ever since?'

'No, I can't say that I have in any romantic sense, though you are a lot like her.' Flandry hesitated. 'Earlier, I'd gotten a different woman angry at me. She had a peculiar psionic power, not telepathy but – beings tended to do what she desired. She wished on me that I never get the one I wanted in my heart. I'm not superstitious, I take no more stock in curses or spooks than I do in the beneficence of governments. Still, an unconscious compulsion— Bah! If there was any such thing, which I positively do not think, then you've lifted it off me, Kossara, and I refuse to pursue this morbid subject when I could be chattering about how beautiful you are.'

At glaciation's midwinter, a colter of ice opened a gap in the Kazan ringwall. Melt-begotten, the Lyubisha River later enlarged this to a canyon. Weathering of mostly soft crater material lowered and blurred the heights. But Flandry found his third campsite enchanting.

He squatted on a narrow beach. Before him flowed the broad brown stream, quiet except where it chuckled around a boulder or a sandbar near its banks. Beyond, and at his back, the gorge rose in braes, bluffs, coombs where brooks flashed and sang, to ocherous palisades maned with forest. The same deep bluish-green and plum-colored leaves covered the lower slopes, borne on trees which grew taller than the taiga granted. Here and there, stone outcrops thrust them aside to make room for wildflower-studded glades. A mild breeze, full of growth and soil odors, rustled through the woods till light and shadow danced. That light slanted from a sun a third again as bright as Sol is to Terra, ardent rather than harsh, an evoker of infinite hues.

Guslars trilled on boughs, other wings flew over in their hundreds, a herd of yelen led by a marvelously horned bull passed along the opposite shore, a riba hooked from the water sputtered in Flandry's frying pan while a heap of cloud apples waited to be dessert – no dismally predictable field rations in this meal. He gestured. 'How well a planet does if left to its own devices,' he remarked.

'Nature could take a few billion years for R & D,' Kossara pointed out. 'We mortals are always in a hurry.'

He gave her a sharp look. 'Is something wrong?' she asked.

'N-no. You echoed an idea I've heard before – coincidence, surely.' He relaxed, threw a couple of sticks on the fire, turned the fillets over. 'I am surprised your people haven't long since trampled this area dead. Such restraint seems downright inhuman.'

'Well, the Dolyina has belonged to the Vymezals from olden time, and without forbidding visitors, we've never encouraged them. You've seen there are no amenities, and we ban vehicles. Besides, it's less reachable than many wild lands elsewhere – though most of those are more closely controlled.'

Kossara hugged knees to chin. Her tone grew slow and thoughtful. 'We Dennitzans are ... are conservationists by tradition. For generations after the Founding, our ancestors had to take great care. They could not live entirely off native life, but what they brought in could too easily ruin the whole little-understood ecology. The ... *zemlyoradnik* ... the landsman learned reverence for the land, because otherwise he might not survive. Today we could, uh, get away with more; and in some parts of the planet we do, where the new industries are. Even there, law and public opinion enforce carefulness – yes, even Dennitzans who live in neighboring systems, the majority by now, even they generally frown on bad practices. And as for the Kazan, the cradle of mankind out here, haven't heartlands often in history kept old ways that the outer dominions forgot?'

Flandry nodded. 'I daresay it helps that wealth flows in

from outside, to support your barons and yeomen in the style to which they are accustomed.' He patted her hand. 'No offense, darling. They're obviously progressive as well as conservative, and less apt than most people to confuse the two. I don't believe in Arcadian utopias, if only because any that might appear would shortly be gobbled up by somebody else. But I do think you here have kept a balance, a kind of inner sanity – or found it anew – long after Terra lost it.'

She smiled. 'I suspect you're prejudiced.'

'Of course. Common sense dictates acquiring a good strong prejudice in favor of the people you're going to live among.'

Her eyes widened. She unfolded herself, leaned on her knuckles toward him, and cried, 'Do you mean you'll stay?'

'Wouldn't you prefer that?'

'Yes, yes. But I'd taken for granted – you're a Terran – where you go, I go.'

Flandry said straight to her flushed countenance: 'At the very least, I'd expect us to spend considerable time on Dennitza. Then why not all, or most? I can wangle a permanent posting if events work out well. Otherwise I'll resign my commission.'

'Can you really settle down to a squire's life, a stormbird like you?'

He laughed and chucked her under the chin. 'Never fear. I don't imagine you're ambitious either to rise every dawn, hog the slops, corn the shuck, and for excitement discuss with your neighbors the scandalous behavior of Uncle Vanya when he lurched through the village, red-eyed and reeling from liter after liter of buttermilk. No, we'll make a topnotch team for xenology, and for Intelligence when need arises.' Soberly: 'Need will keep arising.'

Graveness took her too. 'Imagine the worst, Dominic. Civil war again, Dennitza against Terra.'

'I think then the two of us could best be messengers between Emperor and Gospodar. And if Dennitza does tear loose ... it still won't be the enemy. It'll still deserve whatever we can do to help it survive. I'm not that fond of Terra anyway. Here is much more hope.'

Flandry broke off. 'Enough,' he said. 'We've had our minimum adult daily requirement of apocalypse and dinner grows impatient.'

The Vymezal estate lay sufficiently far inside the crater that the ringwall cut off little sky – but on high ground just the same, to overlook the river and great reaches of farm and forest. Conducted from an outer gate, on a driveway which curved through gardens and parkscape, Flandry saw first the tile roof of the manor above shading trees, then its half-timbered brick bulk, at last its outbuildings. Situated around a rear court, they made a complete hamlet: servants' cottages, garages, sheds, tables, kennels, mews, workshops, bakery, brewery, armory, recreation hall, school, chapel. For centuries the demesne must have brawled with life.

On this day it felt more silent and deserted than it was. While many of the younger adults were gone to their militia units, many folk of every other age remained. Most of them, though, went about their tasks curt-spoken; chatter, japes, laughter, song or whistling were so rare as to resound ghostly between walls; energy turned inward on itself and became tension. Dogs snuffed the air and walked stiff-legged, ready to growl.

At a portico, the gamekeeper who accompanied Flandry explained to a sentry: 'We met this fellow on the riverside lumber road. He won't talk except to insist he has to see the voivode alone. How he got here unbeknownst I couldn't well guess. He *claims* he's friendly.'

The soldier used an intercom. Flandry offered cigarettes around. Both men looked tempted but refused. 'Why not?' he asked. 'They aren't drugged. Nothing awful has happened since mobilization, right?' Radio news received on his minicom had been meager during the seven planetary days of march; entering inhabited country, he and Kossara had shunned its dwellers.

'We haven't been told,' the ranger grated. 'Nobody tells us a thing. They must be waiting – for what?'

'I'm lately back from an errand in the city,' the guardsman

added. 'I heard, over and over— Well, can we trust those Impies the Gospodar called in along with our own ships? Why did he? If we've got to fight Terra, what keeps them from turning on us, right here in the Zorian System? They sure throw their weight around in town. What're you up to, Impie?'

A voice from the loudspeaker ended the exchange. Danilo Vymezal would see the stranger as requested. Let him be brought under armed escort to the Gray Chamber.

Darkly wainscoted and heavily furnished like most of the interior, smaller than average, that room must draw its name from rugs and drapes. An open window let in cool air, a glimpse of sunlight golden through the wings of a hovering chiropteroid. Kossara's father stood beside, arms folded, big in the embroidered, high-collared shirt and baggy trousers of his home territory. She resembled her uncle more, doubtless through her mother, but Flandry found traces of her in those weather-darkened craggy features. Her gaze could be as stern.

'Zdravo, stranac,' Vymezal said, formal greeting, tone barely polite. 'I am he you seek, voivode and nachalnik.' Local aristocrat by inheritance, provincial governor by choice of Gospodar and popular assembly. 'Who are you and what is your business?'

'Are we safe from eavesdroppers, sir?' Flandry responded.

'None here would betray.' Scorn: 'This isn't Zorkagrad, let alone Archopolis.'

'Nevertheless, you don't want some well-intentioned retainer shouting forth what I'll say. Believe me, you don't.'

Vymezal studied Flandry for seconds. A little wariness left him, a little eagerness came in. 'Yes, we are safe. Three floors aloft, double-thick door, for hearing confidences.' A haunted smile touched his lips. 'A cook who wants me to get the father of her child to marry her has as much right to privacy as an admiral discussing plans for regional defense. Speak.'

The Terran gave his name and rank. 'My first news – your daughter Kossara is unharmed. I've brought her back.'

Vymezal croaked a word that might be oath or prayer, and caught a table to brace himself.

He rallied fast. The next half-hour was furiously paced talk, while neither man sat down.

Flandry's immediate declaration was simple. He and the girl lacked accurate knowledge of how matters stood, of what might happen if her return was announced. She waited in the woods for him to fetch her, or guide Vymezal to her, depending on what was decided. Flandry favored the latter course – the voivode only, and a secret word to the Gospodar.

He must spell out his reasons for that at length. Finally the Dennitzan nodded. 'Aye,' he growled .'I hate to keep the tidings from her mother ... from all who love her ... but if she truly is witness to a galaxy-sized trick played on us – we'll need care, oh, very great care' – he clapped hand on sidearm – 'till we're ready to kill those vermin.'

'Then you agree Zorkagrad, the planet's government and armed service, must be infested with them?'

'Yes.' Vymezal gnawed his mustache. 'If things are as you say – you realize I'll see Kossara first, out of your earshot, Captain – but I've small doubt you're honest. The story meshes too well with too much else. Why is our crisis hanging fire? Why— Ha, no more gabble. Tomorrow dawn I'll send ... him, yes, Milosh Tesar, he's trusty, quick of wit and slow of mouth – I'll send him on a "family matter" as you suggest. Let me see ... my wife's dowry includes property wherein her brother also has an interest – something like that.'

'Kossara will have to lie low,' Flandry reminded. 'Me too. You can call me an Imperial officer who stopped off on his liberty to give you a minor message. Nobody will think or talk much about that. But you'd better squirrel me away.'

' "Squirrel"?' Vymezal dismissed the question. 'I understand. Well, I've a cabin in the Northrim, stocked and equipped for times when I want to be unpestered a while. Includes a car. I'll flit you there, telling the houshold I'm lending it to you. They can't see us land at Kossara's hideout, can they?'

'No. We foresaw—' Flandry stopped, aware of how intent

the stare was upon him. 'Sir, I've told you she and I aim to get married.'

'And aren't yet – and nobody wants a hedge-wedding, not I myself when I don't know you.' The voivode sketched a grin. 'Thanks, Captain. But if you've told me truth, she needs a marksman more than a chaperone. Anyhow whatever's between you two must already have happened or not happened. Come, let's go.'

CHAPTER FIFTEEN

The year wanes rapidly on Dennitza. On the morning after Danilo Vymezal had shaken Flandry's hand, kissed Kossara's brow, and left them, they woke to frost on the windows and icy clearness outside. They spent much of the day scrambling around wooded steeps begun to flaunt hues that recalled fall upon ancient Manhome. Flocks of southbound yegyupka made heaven clangorous. Once they heard the cry of a vilya, and savage though the beast was, its voice sang wonderfully sweet. Firebush, spontaneously burning to ripen and scatter its seeds, spread faint pungency through the air. By a waterfall whose spray stung their skins with cold, they gathered feral walnuts. Regardless of what spun around the world beyond its frail blue roof, they often laughed like children.

At dusk they returned to the log building, cooked dinner together, sated huge appetites, and took brandy-laced coffee to the hearth, where they settled down on a shaggy rug, content to let the blaze they had kindled light the room for them. Red flames crackled jokelets of green and blue and yellow, sent warmth in waves, made shadows leap. The humans looked at each other, at the fire, back again, and talked about their tomorrows.

'— we'd better stay around the house hereafter,' Flandry said. 'Your father's man could scarcely have gotten an appointment today, but he should soon. Your uncle's aides can't all be traitors, assuming I'm right that some are. Two or three, in critical posts, are the most I'd guess possible. And they themselves will see no reason to stall his brother-in-law's personal business. In fact, that'd look too queer. So I expect we'll get word shortly; and Miyatovich may want us to move fast.'

Highlights crossed Kossara's face above her cheekbones, shone in eyes, glowed in hair. 'What do you think he'll do, Dominic?'

'Well, he's tough, smart, and experienced; he may have better ideas than I. But in his place, I'd manufacture an excuse to put myself somewhere more or less impregnable. Like your Nova-class warship; she's the biggest around, Dennitzan or Imperial, and the pride of your fleet damn well ought to have a solidly loyal crew. I'd get the most important persons, including us, there with me. And, oh, yes, a copy of the microfiles on everybody who might be involved in the plot, Imperial officers and locals who've worked themselves close to the Gospodar's hand in the past several years. A clever, widely traveled captain of Naval Intelligence, such as – ahem – could help me get a shrewd notion of whom to suspect. I'd order fleet dispositions modified accordingly, again on an unalarming pretext. When this was done, I'd have the appropriate arrests made, then broadcast a "hold everything" to the populace, then wait on the *qui vive* to see what the interrogators dig out.'

Memory made Kossara wince. Flandry laid an arm about her shoulder. 'We've a stiff way yet to go,' he said, 'but we should be home safe by blossom time.'

She thawed, flowed into his embrace, and whispered, 'Thanks to you.'

'No, you. If you'd lacked courage to visit Diomedes, the strength to stay sane and fight on— Why quibble? We're both magnificent. The species has need of our chromosomes.'

'Lots and lots of fat babies,' she agreed. 'But do you mean it about spring . . . we may have to wait that long?'

'I hope not. The creaking sound you hear is my gentlemanliness. I'm sitting on its safety valve, which is blistering hot.'

She touched a corner of his smile. Her own look became wholly serious. 'Are your jests always armor?' The question trembled. 'Dominic, we may not live till spring.'

'We'll take no chances, heart of mine. None. I plan for us to scandalize our respectable grandchildren.'

'We'll have to take chances.' She drew breath. 'I can't become pregnant till my immunity treatment's reversed. Tonight— We'll not deceive Father and Mother. The first chaplain we find can marry us.'

163

'But, uh, your cathedral wedding—'

'I've come to see how little it matters, how little the universe does, next to having you while I can. Tonight, Dominic. Now.'

He seized her to him.

A flash went blue-white in the front windows.

They sprang up. The light had not been blinding, but they knew its color.

Flandry flung the door wide and himself out onto the porch. Cold poured over him, sharp liquid in his nostrils. Stars glinted countless. Between shadow-masses that were trees, he saw the craterside shelve away downward into the murk which brimmed its bowl. Distance-dwindled, a fireball yonder lifted and faded. The cloud pillar following appeared against a constellation just as the thunder rumbled faintly in his skull.

'That was home,' Kossara said out of numbness.

'A tactical nuke, doubtless fired from an aircraft,' responded a machine within Flandry.

The danger to her flogged him aware. He grabbed her arm. 'Inside!' She staggered after him. He slammed the door and drew her against his breast. She clung, beginning to shudder.

'My love, my love, my love, we've got to get away from here,' he said in a frantic chant. 'They must have been after us.'

'After you—' She tautened, freed herself, snapped at steadiness and caught it. Her eyes gleamed steel-dry. 'Yes. But we'll take a few minutes to pack. Food, clothes, weapons.'

Defiant, he also tried phoning the manor. Emptiness hummed reply. They trotted to the shed where the car was, stowed survival gear within, trotted back for more, boarded.

The cabin tumbled from sight. Flandry swept radar around the encompassing darkness. Nothing registered. A traffic safety unit wasn't much use here, of course, but at least this bubble carrying them had a prayer of crawling to safety before the military vessel that did the murder could find it.

If – 'Wait a second,' Flandry said.

'What?' Kossara asked dully.

He glanced at her, dim in star-glow and wanness off the control panel. She sat hunched into her parka, staring ahead through the canopy. The heater had not yet taken hold and the chill here was no honest outside freeze, but dank. Air muttered around the car body.

He dropped near treetop level and activated the optical amplifier. Its screen showed the wilderness as a gray jumble, above which he zigzagged in search of a secure hiding place. Though belike they had no immediate need of any – 'I'll take for granted we were a principal target,' he said, quick and toneless. 'Snatching us from the household would be too revealing. But if the killers knew where we were, why not come directly to our lodge? If they even suspected we might be there, why not try it first? My guess is, they don't know it exists. However, we're safer in motion regardless.'

She bit a knuckle till blood came forth, before she could say : 'Everybody died on our account?'

'No, I think not. Your father, at least, had to be gotten rid of, since he knew the truth. And there was no being sure he hadn't told somebody else. I dare hope the enemy thinks we went out with him.'

'How did they learn, Dominic?' Through the curbed hardness of her voice, he sensed dread. 'Is Aycharaych in Zorkagrad?'

'Conceivable.' Flandry's words fell one by one. 'But not probable. Remember, we did consider the possibility. If we were to land on the taiga, Chives must proceed to the spaceport, simply to maintain our fiction. Wearing his mindscreen would make him overly conspicuous. Anyhow, Aycharaych wouldn't fail to check on each newcomer, and he knows both Chives and *Hooligan* by sight. I decided the odds were he went to Dennitza from Diomedes, but having made sure the mischief he'd started was proceeding along the lines he wanted, didn't linger. He's no coward, but he knows he's too valuable to risk in a merely warlike action – which this affair has to bring, and soon, or else his efforts have gone for naught. My guess was, he's hanging around Zoria in a wide orbit known only to a few of his most trusted chessmen.'

'Yes, I remember now. Talk on. Please, Dominic. I have to be nothing except practical for a while, or I'll fall apart.'

'Me too. Well, I still believe my assessment was confirmed when we made such trouble-free contact with your father. Chives had been in Zorkagrad for days. Aycharaych would have found him, read him, and prepared a trap to spring on us the minute we arrived. Anything else would have been an unnecessary gamble.' Bleakness softened: 'You know, I went into the manor house using every psychotrick they ever drilled into me to keep my knowledge of where you were out of conscious thought, and ready to swallow the old poison pill on the spot should matters go awry.'

'What?' She turned her head toward him. 'Why, you ... you told me to leave the rendezvous if you didn't return by sunset – but – Oh, Dominic, no!'

Then she did weep. He comforted her as best he could. Meanwhile he found a place to stop, a grove on the rim beneath which he could taxi and be sheltered from the sky.

She gasped back to self-mastery and made him tell her the rest of his thoughts. 'I feel certain what caused the attack tonight was the capture of your father's courier,' he said. 'He must have been interrogated hastily. Aycharaych would have found out about our cabin, whether or not your father explicitly told his man. But a quick narcoquiz by nontelepaths—' He scowled into murk. 'The problem is, what made the enemy suspicious of him? He wasn't carrying any written message, and his cover story was plausible. Unless—'

He leaned forward, snapped a switch. 'Let's try for news.'

'The next regular 'cast is in about half an hour,' Kossara said in a tiny voice, 'if that hasn't changed too.'

He tuned in the station she named. Ballet dancers moved to cruelly happy music. He held her close and murmured.

A woman's countenance threw the program out. Terror distorted it. 'Attention!' she screeched. 'Special broadcast! Emergency! We have just received word from a spokesman of the Zamok – officers of the Imperial Navy have arrested Gospodar Miyatovich for high treason. Citizens are required to remain calm and orderly. Those who disobey can be shot.

166

And ... and weather satellites report a nuclear explosion in the Dubina Dolyina area – neighborhood of the voivode's residence – attempts to phone there have failed. The voivode was, is ... the Gospodar's brother-in-law ... No announcement about whether he was trying to rebel or— Stay calm! Don't move till we know more! Ex-except ... the city police office just called in – blast shelters will be open to those who wish to enter. I repeat, blast shelters will be open—'

Repetition raved on for minutes. Beneath it, Flandry snarled, 'If ever they hope to provoke their war, they've reckoned this is their last and maybe their best chance.'

The newsroom vanished. 'Important recorded announcement,' said a man in Dennitzan uniform. 'A dangerous agent of Merseia is at large in Zorkagrad or vicinity.' What must be a portrait from some xenological archive, since it was not of Chives, flashed onto the screen. 'He landed eight days ago, posing as a peaceful traveler. Four days ago' (the computer must redub every 18.8 hours) 'he was identified, but fought his way free of arrest and disappeared. He is of this species, generally known as Shalmuan. When last seen he wore a white kilt and had taken a blaster from a patrolman after injuring the entire squad. I repeat, your government identifies him as a Merseian secret agent, extremely dangerous because of his mission as well as his person. If you see him, do not take risks. Above all, do not try talking with him. If he cannot safely be killed, report the sighting to your nearest military post. A reward of 10,000 gold dinars is offered for information leading to his death or capture. Dead or alive, he himself is worth a reward of 50,000—'

Air hissed between Kossara's teeth. Flandry sat moveless for minutes before he said stonily, 'That's how. Somebody, in some fashion, recognized Chives. That meant I was around, and most likely you. That meant – any contact between your family and the Gospodar – yes.'

Kossara wept anew, in sorrow and in rage.

Yet at the end it was she who lifted her head and said, hoarse but level-toned, 'I've thought of where we might go, Dominic, and what we might try to do.'

167

CHAPTER SIXTEEN

Clouds and a loud raw wind had blown in across the ocean. Morning along the Obala, the east coast of Rodna, was winterlike, sky the color of lead, sea the colors of iron and gunmetal. But neither sky nor sea was quiet. Beneath the overcast a thin smoky wrack went flying; surf cannonaded and exploded on reefs and beaches.

All Nanteiwon boats were in, big solid hulls moored behind the jetty or tied at the wharf. Above the dunes the fisher village huddled. Each house was long and wide as an ychan family needed, timbers tarred black, pillars that upheld the porch carved and brightly painted with ancestral symbols, blue-begrown sod roof cable-anchored against hurricanes, a spacious and sturdy sight. But there were not many houses. Beyond them reached the flatlands the dwellers cultivated, fields harvested bare and brown, trees a-toss by roadsides, on the horizon a vague darkening which betokened the ringwall of the Kazan. The air smelled of salt and distances.

Inside the home of Ywodh were warmth, sun-imitating fluorescents, musky odor of bodies, growls to drown out the piping at the windows. Some forty males had crowded between the frescoed walls of the mootroom, while more spilled throughout the building. They wore their common garb, tunic in bright colors thrown over sinewy green frame and secured by a belt which held the knuckleduster knife. But this was no common occasion. Perched on tails and feet, muscles knotted, they stared at the three on the honor-dais.

Two were human. One they knew well, Kossara Vymezal. She used to come here often with Trohdwyr, brother to Khwent, Yffal, drowned Qythwy . . . How weary she looked. The other was a tall man who bore a mustache, frosted brown hair, eyes the hue of today's heaven.

Ywodh, Hand of the Vach Anochrin, steadcaptain of Nanteiwon, raised his arms. 'Silence !' he called. 'Hark.' When he had his desire, he brought his gaunt, scarred head forward and told them:

'You have now heard of the outrages done and the lies proclaimed. Between dawn, when I asked you to keep ashore today, and our meeting here, I was in phonetalk up and down the Obala. Not an ychan leader but swore us aid. We know what Merseian rule would bring.

'Let us know, too, how empty of hope is a mere rebellion against rebellion. We have boats, civilian aircars, sporting guns; a revolutionary government would have military flyers and armored groundcars, spacecraft, missiles, energy weapons, gases, combat shielding. The plotters have ignored us partly because they took for granted we care little about a change of human overlords and might welcome Merseians – untrue – but mainly because they see us as well-nigh powerless against their crews – true.

'Can we then do aught? These two have made me believe it. Rebellion can be forestalled. Yet we've netted a flailfish. We need care as much as courage.

'To most of us, what's gone on of late in Zorkagrad and in space has been troubling, even frightening, and not understandable, like an evil dream. Therefore we went about our work, trusting Gospodar Miyatovich and his councillors to do what was right for Dennitza. Last night's tale of his arrest as a traitor stunned us. We'd have stood bewildered until too late for anything – this was intended – had not Kossara Vymezal and Dominic Flandry come to us in our darkness.

'The whole planet must be in the same clubbed state, and likewise its fighting forces. What to do? Where is truth? Who is friend and who is foe? Everyone will think best he wait a few days, till he has more knowledge.

'In that brief span, a small band of well-placed illwishers, who know exactly what they are at, can put us on the tack they want, too hard over to come about: unless, in the same span, we go up against them, knowing what we do.

'This day, leaders will meet in Novi Aferoch and decide on a course for us. This morning along the Obala, other meetings hear what I tell you : Stand fast with your weapons, speak to no outsiders, keep ready to move.'

Father. Mother. Ivan. Gyorgye. Little, little Natalie.

Mihail. Trohdwyr. And every soul who perished in our home, every living thing that did.

Father of Creation, receive them. Jesus, absolve them. Mary, comfort them. Light of the Holy Spirit, shine upon them forever.

I dare not ask for more. Amen.

Kossara signed herself and rose. The boulder behind which she had knelt no longer hid Nanteiwon. It looked very small, far down the beach between gray sea and gray sky. Lutka her doll and Butterfeet her cat might take shelter in those houses from the wind that blew so cold, so cold.

Strange she should think of them when their loss belonged to her childhood and most of her dead were not a day old. She turned from the village and walked on over the strand. It gritted beneath her boots. Often an empty shell crunched, or she passed a tangle of weed torn from the depths and left to dry out. On her right, a hedge of cane barred sight of autumn fields, rattling and clicking. Waves thundered in, rushed out, trundled hollowly back again. Wind shrilled, thrust, smacked her cheeks and laid bitterness across her lips.

Do I comprehend that they are gone?

If only things would move. They had hours to wait, safest here, before the ychan chiefs could be gathered together. Flandry had offered her medicines from his kit, for sleep, for calm and freedom from pain, but when she declined, he said, 'I knew you would. You'll always earn your way,' and when she told him she would like to go out for a while, he saw she needed aloneness. He saw deeper than most, did her Dominic, and covered the hurt of it with a jape. If only he did not see right past God.

In time? I'll never preach at him, nor admit outright that I pray for him. But if we are given time—

They had had no end to their plans. A house in the Dubina Dolyina country, an apartment in Zorkagrad; they could afford both, and children should have elbow room for body and mind alike. Quests among the stars, wild beauties, heart-soaring moment of a new truth discovered, then return to the dear well-known. Service, oh, nothing too hazardous any more, staff rather than field Intelligence – nonetheless, sword-play of wits in the glad knowledge that this was for the future, not the poor wayworn Empire but a world he too could believe in, the world of their own blood. Ideas, invest-ments, enterprises to start; the things they might undertake had sparkled from them like fireworks . . .

It had all gone flat and blurred, unreal. What she could still hold whole in her daze were the small hopes. She shows him an overlook she knows in the Vysochina highlands. He teaches her the fine points of winetasting. She reads aloud to him from Simich, he to her from *Genji*. They attend the opera in Zorkagrad. They join in the dances at a land festival. They sail a boat across Lake Stoyan to a café beneath flower-ing viyenatz trees on Garlandmakers' Island. They take their children to the zoo and the merrypark.

If we prevail.

She stopped. Her body ached, but she straightened, faced into the wind, and told it, *We will. We will. I can borrow strength and clarity from his medicines. The repayment afterward will simply be a time of sleep, a time of peace.* She wheeled and started back. As she fared, her stride lengthened.

Novi Aferoch climbed from the docks at the Elena River mouth, up a hill from whose top might be spied the ruins of Stari Aferoch when they jutted from the sea at low tide. There stood Council Hall, slate-roofed, heavy-timbered, colon-naded with carven water monsters. In the main chamber was a table made three hundred years ago from timbers out of Gwyth's ship. Around it perched the steadcaptains of the Obala. At its head stood their moot-lord Kyrwedhin, Hand of the Vach Mannoch, and the two humans.

A storm hooted and dashed rain on windowpanes. Inside, the air was blue and acrid from the pipes whereon many had been puffing. Anger smoldered behind obsidian eyes, but the leathery visages were moveless and not a tailtip twitched. These males had heard what the voivode's daughter had to tell, and roared their curses. The hour had come to think.

Kyrwedhin addressed them in quick, precise words. He was short for an ychan, though when he was younger it had not been wise to fight him. He was the wealthy owner of seareaping and merchant fleets. And ... he held a degree from the Shkola, a seat in the Skupshtina, a close experience of great affairs.

'For myself I will merely say this,' he declared in Eriau. (Flitting from Zorkagrad after receiving Ywodh's urgent, argot-phrased call, he had been pleased to learn Flandry was fluent in the language, at least its modern Merseian version. His own Serbic was excellent, his Anglic not bad, but that wasn't true of everybody here.) 'The ideas of our Terran guest feel right. We in the House of the Zmayi have doubtless been too parochial where the Empire was concerned, too narrowly aimed at Dennitzan matters – much like the House of the Folk. However, we have always kept a special interest in our mother world, many of us have gone there to visit, some to study, and the inhabitants are our species. Thus we have a certain sense for what the Roidhunate may or may not do. And, while I never doubted its masters wish us harm, what news and clues have reached me do not suggest current preparations for outright war. For instance, I've corresponded for years with Korvash, who lately became Hand of the Vach Rueth there. If an attack on us were to be mounted soon, he would know, and he must be more cunning than I believe for this not to change the tone of his letters.

'No proof, I agree. A single bit of flotsam in the maelstrom. I will give you just one more out of many, given me by Lazar Ristich, voivode of Kom Kutchki. Like most members of the House of the Lords, he takes close interest in Imperial business and is familiar with several prime parts of the inner Empire; he has friends on Terra itself, where he's spent considerable time. He told me the story we heard about Kossara Vymezal could not be right. Whether truly accused because she belonged to an overzealous faction among us, or falsely accused for a twisted political reason elsewhere, a person of her rank would not be shipped off to shame like any common criminal. That could only happen through monumental incompetence – which he felt sure was unlikely – or as a deliberate provocation – which he felt sure the present Imperium itself would not give us, though a cabal within it might. He wanted to discuss this with her uncle. The Zamok kept putting him off, claiming the Gospodar was too busy during the crisis.

'Well, both Ristich and I know Bodin Miyatovich of old. Such was not his way. It had to be the doing of his staff. Expecting we'd get a chance at him somehow, soon – since he was never one to closet himself in an office – we did not press too hard. We should have. For now he is captive.'

Kyrwedhin halted. The wind shrilled. Finally Kossara said, tone as uncertain as words, 'I can't find out what's really happened to him. Do you know?'

'Nobody does except the doers,' he answered. 'There are – were – Imperial liaison officers about, and their aides. Bodin had explained publicly why he, as sector governor, called in chosen craft that serve the Emperor directly, as well as those of the Voyska. Besides their guns, should Merseia attack, he wanted to demonstrate our reluctance to break with Terra.

'Spokesmen for the Zamok – the Castle,' he added to Flandry; 'the executive center and those who work there – spokesmen for the Zamok have said they aren't sure either. Apparently a party of Imperials got Bodin alone, took him prisoner, and spirited him away to a ship of theirs. Which vessel is not revealed. None have responded to beamed inquiries.'

'They wouldn't,' Flandry observed.

Kyrwedhin nodded his serrated head. 'Naturally not. Imperial personnel still on the ground deny any knowledge. Thus far we have nothing except the statement that a high Terran officer contacted Milutin Protich, informed him Bodin Miyatovich was under arrest for treason, and demanded Dennitza and its armed forces give immediate total obedience to Admiral da Costa. He's the ranking Imperial in the Zorian

System at the moment, therefore can be considered the Emperor's representative.'

'And who is, m-m, Milutin Protich?'

'A special assistant to the Gospodar. According to the announcement, he was the first important man in the Zamok whom the Terrans managed to get in touch with.' Kyrwedhin pondered. 'Yes-s-s. He isn't Dennitzan-born – from a nearby system where many families from here have settled. He arrived several years back, entered administrative service, did brilliantly, rose fast and far. Bodin had much faith in him.'

Flandry drew forth a cigarette. 'I take it everybody's been pretty well paralyzed throughout today,' he said.

'Aye. We must decide what to do. And we've fiendish little information to go on, half of it contradicting the other half. Were the Imperialists essentially right to seize our Gospodar, or was this their next step in subjugating us, or even getting us destroyed? Should we declare independence – when Merseia lurks in the wings? The Imperials can't prevent that; our ships vastly outnumber theirs hereabouts. But if fighting starts, they could make us pay heavily.'

'You Dennitzans, human and zmay – ychan – you don't strike me as hesitant people,' Flandry remarked. 'As we say in Anglic, "He who dithers is diddled." The newscasts have been forgivably confused. But am I right in my impression that your parliament – Skupshtina – meets tomorrow?'

'Yes. In the Gospodar's absence, the Chief Justice will preside.'

'Do you think the vote will go for secession?'

'I had no doubt of it . . . until I heard from Dama Vymezal and yourself.'

The captains gripped their pipes, knife handles, the edge of the table, hard. They would have their own words to say later on; but what they heard in the next few minutes would be their compass.

'If you rise and tell them—' Flandry began.

Kossara cut him off. 'No, dear. That's impossible.'

'What?' He blinked at her.

She spoke carefully, clearly. The stim she had taken made

174

vigor shine pale through flesh and eyes. 'The Skupshtina's no controlled inner-Empire congress. It's about five hundred different proud individuals, speaking for as many different proud sections of land or walks of life. It's often turbulent – fights have happened, yes, a few killings – and tomorrow it'll be wild. Do you think our enemy hasn't prepared for the climax of his work? I know the Chief Justice; he's honest but aged. He can be swayed about whom he recognizes. And if somebody did get the floor, started telling the whole truth – do you imagine he'd live to finish?'

'She's right,' Kyrwedhin said.

Flandry drew on his cigarette till his face creased before he replied, 'Yes, I'd supposed something like that must be the case. Assassination's easy. A few concealed needle guns, spotted around – and as a backup, maybe, some thoroughly armed bully boys hidden away in buildings near the Capitol. If necessary, they seize it, proclaim themselves the Revolutionary Committee ... and, given the spadework the enemy's done over the years, they can probably raise enough popular support to commit your people beyond any chance of turning back.'

'If you have thought of this and not despaired,' Kyrwedhin said, 'you must have a plan.'

Flandry frowned. 'I'd rather hear what you have in mind. You know your establishment.'

'But I am taken by surprise.'

Kossara spoke against storm-noise: 'I know. If you and I, Dominic – especially I – if we appear before them, suddenly, in person – why, killing us would be worse than useless.'

Kyrwedhin's tail smacked the floor. 'Yes!' he cried, 'My thoughts were headed your same way. Though you can't simply walk in from Constitution Square. You'd never pass the Iron Portal alive. What you need is an escort, bodies both shielding and concealing you, on your way right into the Union Chamber.'

'How?' snapped from a village chief.

Kossara had the answer: 'Ychani have always been the Peculiar People of Dennitza. The House of the Zmayi has

175

never entirely spoken for them; it's a human invention. If, in a desperate hour, several hundred Obala fishers enter Zorkagrad, march through Square and Portal into the Chamber, demanding their leaders be heard – it won't be the first time in history. The enemy will see no politic way to halt that kind of demonstration. They may well expect it'll turn to their advantage; outsiders would naturally think Merseian-descended Dennitzans are anti-Terran, right? Then too late—' She flung her hands wide, her voice aloft. 'Too late, they see who came along !'

Beneath the surf of agreement, Flandry murmured to her : 'My idea also. I kept hoping somebody would have a better one.'

CHAPTER SEVENTEEN

Just before their car set down, Flandry protested to Kossara, 'God damn it, why does your parliament have to meet in person? You've got holocom systems. Your politicians could send and receive images ... and we could've rigged untraceable methods to call them and give them the facts last night.'

'Hush, darling.' She laid a hand across his fist. 'You know why. Electronics will do for ornamental relics. The Skupshtina is alive, it debates and decides real things, the members need intimacies, subtleties, surprises.'

'But you, you have to go among murderers to reach them.'

'And I fear for you,' she said quietly. 'We should both stop.'

He looked long at her, and she at him, in the seat they shared. Beryl eyes under wide brow and bronze hair, strong fair features though her smile quivered the least bit, height, ranginess, fullness, the warmth of her clasp and the summery fragrance of herself: had she ever been more beautiful? The vitality that surged in her, the serenity beneath, were no work of a drug; it had simply let her put aside shock, exhaustion, grief for this while and be altogether Kossara.

'If there is danger today,' she said, 'I thank God He lets me be in it with you.'

He prevented himself from telling her he felt no gratitude. They kissed, very briefly and lightly because the car was crammed with ychans.

It landed in a parking lot at the edge of Zorkagrad. None farther in could have accommodated the swarm of battered vehicles which was arriving. Besides, a sudden appearance downtown might have provoked alarm and a quick reaction by the enemy. A march ought to have a calming effect. Flandry and Kossara donned cowled cloaks, which should hide their species from a cursory glance when they were surrounded by hemianthropoid xenos, and stepped outside.

A west wind skirled against the sun, whose blaze seemed paled in a pale heaven. Clouds were brighter; they scudded in flocks, blinding white, their shadows sweeping chill across the world, off, on, off, on. Winged animals wheeled and thinly cried. Trees around the lot and along the street that ran from it – mostly Terran, oak, elm, beech, maple – cast their outer branches about, creaked, soughed Delphic utterances though tongue after firetongue ripped loose to scrittle off over the pavement. Rainpuddles wandered and wandered. All nature was saying farewell.

The ychans closed in around the humans. They numbered a good four hundred, chosen by their steadcaptains as bold, cool-headed, skilled with the knives, tridents, harpoons, and firearms they bore. Ywodh of Nanteiwon, appointed their leader by Kyrwedhin before the parliamentarian returned here, put them in battle-ready order. They spoke little and showed scant outward excitement, at least to human eyes or nostrils; such was the way of the Obala. They did not know the ins and outs of what had happened, nor greatly care. It was enough that their Gospodar had been betrayed by the enemy of their forefathers, that his niece had come home to speak truth, and that they were her soldiers. The wind snapped two standards in their van, star white on blue of Yovan Matavuly, ax red on gold of Gwyth.

'All set,' Ywodh reported. A shout: 'Forward!' He took the lead. Flandry and Kossara would fain have clasped hands as they walked, but even surrounded must clutch their cloaks tight against this tricksy air. The thud of their boots was lost amidst digitigrade slither and click.

At first it was predictable they would encounter nobody. Here was a new district of private homes and clustered condominium units, beyond the scope of forcefield generators that offered the inner city some protection. Residents had sought safe quarters. An occasional militia squad, on patrol to prevent looting, observed the procession from a distance but did not interfere.

Farther on, buildings were older, higher, close-packed on streets which had narrowed and went snakily uphill: red tile roofs, stucco walls of time-faded gaudiness, signs and emblems hung above doorways, tenements, offices, midget factories, restaurants, taverns, amusements, a bulbous-domed parish church, a few big stores and tiny eccentric shops by the score, the kind of place that ought to have pulsed with traffic of vehicles and foot, been lively with movement, colors, gestures broad or sly, words, laughter, whistling, song, sorrow, an accordion or a fiddle somewhere, pungencies of roast corn and nuts for sale to keep the passerby warm, oddments in display windows, city men, landmen, offworlders, vagabonds, students, soldiers, children, grannies, the unforgettably gorgeous woman whom you know you will never glimpse again ... A few walkers stepped aside, a few standers poised in doorways or leaned on upper-story sills, warily staring. Now and then a groundcar detoured. A civilian policeman in brown uniform and high-crowned hat joined Ywodh; they talked; he consulted his superiors via minicom, stayed till an aircar had made inspection from above, and departed.

'This is downright creepy,' Flandry murmured to Kossara. 'Has everybody evacuated, or what?'

She passed the question on. Untrained humans could not have conveyed information accurately in that wise; but soon she told Flandry from Ywodh: 'Early this morning – the organizers must have worked the whole night – an *ispravka* started against Imperial personnel. That's when ordinary citizens take direct action. Not a riot or lynching. The people move under discipline, often in their regular Voyska units; remember, every able-bodied adult is a reservist. Such affairs seldom get out of control, and may have no violence at all. Offenders may simply be expelled from an area. Or they may be held prisoner while spokesmen of the people demand the authorities take steps to punish them. A few *ispravkai* have brought down governments. In this case, what's happened is that Terrans and others who serve the Imperium were rounded up into certain buildings: hostages for the Gospodar's release and the good behavior of their Navy ships. The Zamok denounced the action as illegal and bound to increase tension, demanded the crowds disperse, and sent police. The people stand fast around those buildings. The police haven't charged them; no shots have yet been fired on either side.'

'I've heard of worse customs,' Flandry said.

Puzzled, she asked, 'Shouldn't the plotters be pleased?'

Flandry shrugged. 'I daresay they are. Still, don't forget the vast majority of your officials must be patriotic, and whether or not they prefer independence, consider civil war to be the final recourse. The top man among them issued that cease-and-desist order.' He frowned. 'But, um, you know, this nails down a lot of our possible helpers, both citizens and police. The enemy isn't expecting us. However, if too many parliament members refuse to board the secession railroad, he'll have a clear field for attempting a *coup d'état*. Maybe the firebrand who instigated that, uh, *ispravka* is a Merseian himself, in human skin.'

The wind boomed between walls.

A minor commotion occurred on the fringes of the troop. Word flew back and forth. 'Chives!' Kossara gasped.

The ychans let him through. He also went cloaked to muffle the fact of his race from any quick glance. Emerald features were eroded from spare to gaunt; eyes were more fallow than amber; but when Flandry whooped and took him by the shoulders, Chives said crisply, 'Thank you, sir. Donna Vymezal, will you allow me the liberty of expressing my sympathy at your loss?'

'Oh, you dear clown!' She hugged him. Her lashes gleamed wet. Chives suffered the gesture in embarrassed silence. Flandry sensed within him a deeper trouble.

They continued through hollow streets. A fighter craft passed low above chimneys. Air whined and snarled in its wake. 'What've you been doing?' Flandry asked. 'How'd you find us?'

'If you have no immediate statement or directive for me, sir,' the precise voice replied, 'I will report chronologically. Pursuant to instructions, I landed at the spaceport and submitted to inspection. My cover story was approved and I given license, under police registry, to remain here for a stated period as per my declared business. Interested in exotics, many townspeople conversed with me while I circulated among them in the next few planetary days. By pretending to less familiarity with *Homo sapiens* than is the case, I gathered impressions of their individual feelings as respects the present imbroglio. At a more convenient time, sir, if you wish, I will give you the statistical breakdown.

'I must confess it was a complete surprise when a Naval patrol entered my lodgings and declared an intention to take me in custody. Under the circumstances, sir, I felt conformity would be imprudent. I endeavored not to damage irreparably men who wore his Majesty's uniform, and in due course will return the borrowed blaster you observe me wearing. Thereupon I took refuge with a gentleman I suspected of vehement anti-Terran sentiments. May I respectfully request his name and the names of his associates be omitted from your official cognizance? Besides their hospitality and helpfulness toward me, they exhibited no more than a misguided zeal for the welfare of this planet, and indeed I was the occasion of their first overt unlawful act. They sheltered me only after I had convinced them I was a revolutionary for my own society, and that my public designation as a Merseian agent was a calumny which the Imperialists could be expected to employ against their kind too. They were persuaded rather easily; I would not recommend them for the Intelligence Corps. I got from them clothes, disguise materials, equipment convertible to surveillance purposes, and went about collecting data for myself.

'They do possess a rudimentary organization. Through this, via a phone call, my host learned that a large delegation of zmays was moving on the Capitol. Recalling Donna Vymezal's accounts of her background, and trusting she and you had not perished after all, I thought you might be here. To have this deduction confirmed was ... most gratifying, sir.'

Flandry chewed his lip for a while before he said, 'Those were Imperials who came to arrest you? Not Dennitzans?'

'No, sir, not Dennitzans. There could be no mistake.'

Chives spoke mutedly. His thin green fingers hauled the cowl closer around his face.

'You went unmolested for days, and then in a blink—' Flandry's speech chopped off. They were at their goal.

Well into Old Town, the party passed between two many-balconied mansions, out onto a plateau of Royal Hill. Constitution Square opened before them, broad, slate-flagged, benches, flowerbeds, trees – empty, empty. In the middle was a big fountain, granite catchbasin, Toman Obilich and Vladimir locked in bronze combat, water dancing white but its sound and spray borne off by the wind. Westward buildings stood well apart, giving a view down across roofs to Lake Stoyan, metal-bright shimmer and shiver beyond the curve of the world. Directly across the square was the Capitol, a sprawling, porticoed marble mass beneath a gilt dome whose point upheld an argent star. A pair of kilometers further on, a rock lifted nearly sheer, helmeted with the battlements and banners of the Zamok.

Flandry's gaze flickered. He identified a large hotel, office buildings, cafés, fashionable stores, everything antiquated but dignified, the gray stones wearing well; how many Constitution Squares had he known in his life? But this lay deserted under wind, chill, and hasty cloud shadows. A militia squad stood six men on the Capitol verandah, six flanking the bottom of the stairs; their capes flapped, their rifles gleamed whenever a sunbeam smote and then went dull again. Aircraft circled far overhead. Otherwise none save the newcomers were in sight. Yet surely watchers waited behind yonder shut doors, yonder blank panes: proprietors, caretakers, maybe a few police – a few, since the turmoil was elsewhere in town and no disturbance expected here. Who besides? He walked as if through a labyrinth of mirages. Nothing was wholly what he sensed, except the blaster butt under his hand and a stray russet lock of Kossara's hair.

She had no such dreads. As they trod into the plaza, he heard her whisper, 'Here we go, my brave beloved. They'll sing of you for a thousand years.'

He shoved hesitation out of his mind and readied himself to fight.

But no clash came. Despite what they told him when the move was being planned, he'd more or less awaited behavior like that when a gaggle of demonstrators wanted to invade a legislative session on any human planet he knew – prohibition, resistance, then either a riot or one of the sides yielding. If officialdom conceded in order to avoid the riot, it would be grudgingly, after prolonged haggling; and whatever protesters were admitted would enter under strict conditions, well guarded, to meet indignant stares.

Dennitza, though, had institutionalized if not quite legalized procedures like the *ispravka*. Through the officer he met on the way, Ywodh had explained his band's intent. Word had quickly reached the Chief Justice. Four hundred zmays would not lightly descend on Zorkagrad, claiming to represent the whole Obala; they could be trusted to be mannerly and not take an unreasonable time to make their points; urged by Kyrwedhin, a majority in the third house of the Skupshtina endorsed their demand. No guns greeted them, aside from those of the corporal's guard at the entrance; and they bore their own arms inside.

Up the stairs – past armored doors that recalled the Troubles – through an echoful lobby – into a central chamber where the parliament in joint session waited – Flandry raked his glance around, seeking menaces to his woman and shelters for her.

The room was a half ellipsoid. At the far-end focus, a dais bore the Gospodar's lectern, a long desk, and several occupied chairs. To right and left, tiers held the seats of members, widely spaced. Skylights cast fleetingness of weather into steadiness of fluorescents, making the polished marble floor seem to stir. On gilt mural panels were painted the saints and heroes of Dennitza. The lawmakers sat according to their groupings, Lords in rainbow robes, Folk in tunics and trousers or in gowns, Zmayi in leather and metal. After the outdoors, Flandry breathed an air which felt curdled by fear and fury.

Banners dipped to an old man in black who sat behind the

lectern. Slowly the fishers advanced, while unseen tele-scanners watched on behalf of the world. In the middle of the floor, the ychans halted. Silence encompassed them. Flandry's pulse thuttered.

'Zdravo,' said the Chief Justice, and added a courteous Eriau 'Hydhref.' His hand forgot stateliness, plucked at his white beard. 'We have . . . let you in . . . for unity's sake. My under-standing is, your delegation wishes to speak relevantly to the present crisis – a viewpoint which might else go unheard. You in turn will, will understand why we must limit your time to fifteen minutes.'

Ywodh bowed, palms downward, tail curved. Straighten-ing, he let his quarterdeck basso roll. 'We thank the assembly. I'll need less than that; but I think you'll then want to give us more.' Flandry's eyes picked out Kyrwedhin. Weird, that the sole Dennitzan up there whom he knew should bear Merseian genes. 'Worthies and world,' Ywodh was saying, 'you've heard many a tale of late: how the Emperor wants to crush us, how a new war is nearly on us because of his folly or his scheming to slough us off, how his agents rightly or wrongly charged the Gospodar's niece Kossara Vymezal with treason and – absolutely wrongly – sold her for a slave, how they've taken the Gospodar himself prisoner on the same excuse, how they must have destroyed the whole homestead of his brother-in-law the voivode of Dubina Dolyina to grind out any spark of free spirit, how our last choices left are ruin or revolution— You've heard this.

'I say each piece of it is false.' He flung an arm in signal. With a showmanship that humans would have had to re-hearse, his followers opened their ranks. 'And here to gaff the lies is Kossara Vymezal, sister's daughter to Bodin Miyato-vich our Gospodar !'

She bounded from among them, across the floor, onto the dais, to take her place between the antlers of the lectern. A moan lifted out of the benched humans, as if the fall wind had made entry; the zmayi uttered a surflike rumble. 'What, what, what is this?' quavered the Chief Justice. Nobody paid

184

him heed. Kossara raised her head and cried forth so the room rang:

'Hear me, folk! I'm not back from the dead, but I am back from hell, and I bear witness. The devils are not Terrans but Merseians and their creatures. My savior was, is, not a Dennitzan but a Terran. Those who shout, "Independence!" are traitors not to the Empire but to Dennitza. Their single wish is to set humans at each other's throats, till the Roidhun arrives and picks our bones. Hear my story and judge.'

Flandry walked toward her, Chives beside him. He wished it weren't too disturbing to run. Nike of Samothrace had not borne a higher or more defenseless pride than she did. They took stance beneath her, facing the outer door. Her tones marched triumphant:

'– I escaped the dishonor intended me by the grace of God and the decency of this man you see here, Captain Sir Dominic Flandry of his Majesty's service. Let me tell what happened from the beginning. Have I your leave, worthies?'

'Aye!'

Gunshots answered. Screams flew ragged. A blaster bolt flared outside the chamber.

Flandry's weapon jumped free. The tiers of the Skupshtina turned into a yelling scramble. Fifty-odd men pounded through the doorway. Clad like ordinary Dennitzans, all looked hard and many looked foreign. They bore firearms.

'Get down, Kossara!' Flandry shouted. Through him ripped: *Yes, the enemy did have an emergency force hidden in a building near the square, and somebody in this room used a minicom to bring them. The Revolutionary Committee – they'll take over, they'll proclaim her an impostor—*

He and Chives were on the dais. She hadn't flattened herself under the lectern. She had gone to one knee behind it, sidearm in hand, ready to snipe. The attackers were deploying around the room. Two dashed by either side of the clustered, bewildered fishers.

Their blaster beams leaped, convergent on the stand. Its wood exploded in flame, its horns toppled. Kossara dropped her pistol and fell back.

185

Chives pounced zigzag. A bolt seared and crashed within centimeters of him. He ignored it; he was taking aim. The first assassin's head became a fireball. The second crumpled, grabbed at the stump of a leg, writhed and shrieked a short while. Chives reached the next nearest, wrapped his tail around that man's neck and squeezed, got an elbow-breaking single-arm lock on another, hauled him around for a shield and commenced systematic shooting.

'I say,' he called through the din to Ywodh, 'you chaps might pitch in a bit, don't you know.'

The steadcaptain bellowed. His slugthrower hissed. A male beside him harpooned a foeman's belly. Then heedless of guns, four hundred big seafarers joined battle.

Flandry knelt by Kossara. From bosom to waist was seared bloody wreckage. He half raised her. She groped after him with hands and eyes. 'Dominic, darling,' he barely heard, 'I wish—' He heard no more.

For an instant he imagined revival, life-support machinery, cloning ... No. He'd never get her to a hospital before the brain was gone beyond any calling back of the spirit. Never.

He lowered her. *I won't think yet. No time. I'd better get into that fight. The ychans don't realize we need a few prisoners.*

Dusk fell early in fall. Above the lake smoldered a sunset remnant. Otherwise blue-black dimness drowned the land. Overhead trembled a few stars; and had he looked from his office window aloft in the Zamok, Flandry could have seen city lights, spiderwebs along streets and single glows from homes. Wind mumbled at the panes.

Finally granted a rest, he sat back from desk and control board, feeling his chair shape its embrace to his contours. Despite the drugs which suppressed grief, stimulated metabolism, and thus kept him going, weariness weighted every cell. He had turned off the fluoros. His cigarette end shone red. He couldn't taste the smoke, maybe because the dark had that effect, maybe because tongue and palate were scorched.

Well, went his clockwork thought, *that takes care of the main business*. He had just been in direct conversation with Admiral da Costa. The Terran commander appeared reasonably well convinced of the good faith of the provisional government whose master, for all practical purposes, Flandry had been throughout this afternoon. Tomorrow he would discuss the Gospodar's release. And as far as could be gauged, the Dennitzan people were accepting the fact they had been betrayed. They'd want a full account, of course, buttressed by evidence; and they wouldn't exactly become enthusiastic Imperialists; but the danger of revolution followed by civil war seemed past.

So maybe tomorrow I can let these chemicals drain out of me, let go my grip and let in my dead. Tonight the knowledge that there was no more Kossara reached him only like the wind, an endless voice beyond the windows. She had been spared that, he believed, had put mourning quite from her for the last span, being upheld by urgency rather than a need to go through motions, by youth and hope, by his presence beside her. *Whereas I – ah, well, I can carry on. She'd've wanted me to.*

The door chimed. *What the deuce?* His guards had kept him alone among electronic ghosts. Whoever got past them at last in person must be authoritative and persuasive. He waved at an admit plate and to turn the lights back on. Their brightness hurt his eyes.

A slim green form in a white kilt entered, bearing a tray where stood teapot, cup, plates and bowls of food. 'Your dinner, sir,' Chives announced.

'I'm not hungry,' said the clockwork. 'I didn't ask for—'

'No, sir. I took the liberty.' Chives set his burden down on the desk. 'Allow me to remind you, we require your physical fitness.'

Her planet did. 'Very good, Chives.' Flandry got down some soup and black bread. The Shalmuan waited unobtrusively.

'That did help,' the man agreed. 'You know, give me the proper pill and I might sleep.'

'You – you may not wish for it the nonce, sir.'

'What?' Flandry sharpened his regard. Chives had lost composure. He stood head lowered, tail a-droop, hands hard clasped : miserable.

'Go on,' Flandry said. 'You've gotten me nourished. Tell me.'

The voice scissored off words : 'It concerns those personnel, sir, whom you recall the townsmen took into custody.'

'Yes. I ordered them detained, well treated, till we can check them out individually. What of them?'

'I have discovered they include one whom I, while a fugitive, ascertained had come to Zorkagrad several days earlier. To be frank, sir, this merely confirmed my suspicion that such had been the case. I must have been denounced by a party who recognized your speedster at the port and obtained the inspectors' record of me. This knowledge must then have made him draw conclusions and recommend actions with respect to Voivode Vymezal.'

'Well?'

'Needless to say, sir, I make no specific accusations. The guilt could lie elsewhere than in the party I am thinking of.'

'Not measurably likely, among populations the size we've got.' Beneath the drumhead of imposed emotionlessness, Flandry felt his body stiffen. 'Who?'

Seldom did he see Chives' face distorted. 'Lieutenant Commander Dominic Hazeltine, sir. Your son.'

CHAPTER EIGHTEEN

Two militiamen escorted the prisoner into the office. 'You may go,' Flandry told them.

They stared unsurely from him, standing slumped against night in a window, to the strong young man they guarded. 'Go,' Flandry repeated. 'Wait outside with my servant. I'll call on the intercom when I want you.'

They saluted and obeyed. Flandry and Hazeltine regarded each other, mute, until the door had closed. The older saw an Imperial undress uniform, still neat upon an erect frame, and a countenance half Persis' where pride overmastered fear. The younger saw haggardness clad in a soiled coverall.

'Well,' Flandry said at last. Hazeltine extended a hand. Flandry looked past it. 'Have a seat,' he invited. 'Care for a drink?' He indicated bottle and glasses on his desk. 'I remember you like Scotch.'

'Thanks, Dad.' Hazeltine spoke as low, free of the croak in the opposite throat. He smiled, and smiled again after they had both sat down holding their tumblers. Raising his, he proposed, 'Here's to us. Damn few like us, and they're all dead.'

They had used the ancient toast often before. This time Flandry did not respond. Hazeltine watched him a moment, grimaced, and tossed off a swallow. Then Flandry drank.

Hazeltine leaned forward. His words shook. 'Father, you don't believe that vapor about me. Do you?'

Flandry took out his cigarette case. 'I don't know what else to believe.' He flipped back the lid. 'Somebody who knew Chives and the *Hooligan* fingered him. The date of your arrival fits in.' He chose a cigarette. 'And thinking back, I find the coincidence a trifle much that you called my attention to Kossara Vymezal precisely when she'd reached Terra. I was a pretty safe bet to skyhoot her off to Diomedes, where she as an inconvenient witness and I as an inconvenient investigator could be burked in a way that'd maximize trouble.' He puffed the tobacco into lighting, inhaled, streamed smoke till it veiled him, and sighed: 'You were over-eager. You should have waited till she'd been used at least a few days, and a reputable Dennitzan arranged for to learn about this.'

'I didn't— No, what are you saying?' Hazeltine cried.

Flandry toyed with the case. 'As was,' he continued levelly, 'the only word which could be sent, since the Gospodar would require proof and is no fool ... the word was merely she'd been sold for a slave. Well, ample provocation. Where were you, between leaving Terra and landing here? Did you maybe report straight to Aycharaych?'

Hazeltine banged his glass down on the chair arm. 'Lies!' he shouted. Red and white throbbed across his visage. 'Listen, I'm your *son*. I swear to you by—'

'Never mind. And don't waste good liquor. If I'd settled on Dennitza as I planned, the price we'd've paid for Scotch—' Flandry gave his lips a respite from the cigarette. He waved it. 'How were you recruited? By the Merseians, I mean. Couldn't be brainscrub. I know the signs too well. Blackmail? No, implausible. You're a bright lad who wouldn't get suckered into that first mistake they corral you by – a brave lad who'd sneer at threats. But sometime during the contacts you made in line of duty—'

Hazeltine's breath rasped. 'I didn't! How can I prove to you, Father, I didn't?'

'Simple,' Flandry said. 'You must have routine narco immunization. But we can hypnoprobe you.'

Hazeltine sagged back. His glass rolled across the floor.

'The Imperial detachment brought Intelligence personnel and their apparatus, you know,' Flandry continued. 'I've asked, and they can take you tomorrow morning. Naturally, any private facts which emerge will stay confidential.'

Hazeltine raised an aspen hand. 'You don't know – I – I'm deep-conditioned.'

'By Terra?'

'Yes, of course, of course. I can't be 'probed . . . without my mind being . . . destroyed—'

Flandry sighed again. 'Come, now. We don't deep-condition our agents against giving information to their own people, except occasional supersecrets. After all, a 'probe can bring forth useful items the conscious mind has forgotten. Don't fear if you're honest, son. The lightest treatment will clear you, and the team will go no further.'

'But – oh, no-o-o—'

Abruptly Hazeltine cast himself on his knees before Flandry. Words burst from his mouth like the sweat from his skin. 'Yes, then, yes, I've been working for Merseia. Not bought, nothing like that, I thought the future was theirs, should be theirs, not this walking corpse of an Empire— Merciful angels, can't you see their way's the hope of humankind too?—' Flandry blew smoke to counteract the reek of terror. 'I'll cooperate. I will, I will. I wasn't evil, Dad. I had my orders about you, yes, but I hated what I did, and Aycharaych doubted you'd really be killed, and I knew I was supposed to let that girl be bought first by somebody else before I told you but when we happened to arrive in time I couldn't make myself wait—' He caught Flandry by the knees. 'Dad, in Mother's name, let my mind live !'

Flandry shoved the clasp aside, rose, stepped a couple of meters off, and answered, 'Sorry. I could never trust you not to leave stuff buried in your confession that could rise to kill or enslave too many more young girls.' For a few seconds he watched the crouched, spastic shape. 'I'm under stim and heavy trank,' he said. 'A piece of machinery. I've a far-off sense of how this will feel later on, but mostly that's abstract. However . . . you have till morning, son. What would you like while you wait? I'll do my best to provide it.'

Hazeltine uncoiled. On his feet, he howled, 'You cold devil, at least I'll kill you first ! And then myself !'

He charged. The rage which doubled his youthful strength was not amok; he came as a karate man, ready to smash a rib-cage and pluck out a heart.

Flandry swayed aside. He passed a hand near the other.

Razor-edged, the lid of the cigarette case left a shallow red gash in the right cheek. Hazeltine whirled for a renewed assault. Flandry gave ground. Hazeltine followed, boxing him into a corner. Then the knockout potion took hold. Hazeltine stumbled, reeled, flailed his arms, mouthed, and caved in.

Flandry sought the intercom. 'Come remove the prisoner,' he directed.

Day broke windless and freezing cold. The sun stood in a rainbow ring and ice crackled along the shores of Lake Stoyan. Zorkagrad lay silent under bitter blue, as if killed. From time to time thunders drifted across its roofs, arrivals and departures of spacecraft. They gleamed meteoric. Sometimes, too, airships whistled by, armored vehicles rumbled, boots slammed on pavement. About noon, one such vessel and one such march brought Bodin Miyatovich home.

He was as glad to return unheralded. Too much work awaited him for ceremonies – him and Dominic Flandry. But the news did go out on the 'casts; and that was like proclaiming Solstice Feast. Folk ran from their houses, poured in from the land, left their patrols to shout, dance, weep, laugh, sing, embrace perfect strangers; and every church bell pealed.

From a balcony of the Zamok he watched lights burn and bob through twilit streets, bonfires in squares, tumult and clamor. His breath smoked spectral under the early stars. Frost tinged his beard. 'This can't last,' he muttered, and stepped back into the office.

When the viewdoor closed behind him, stillness fell except for chimes now muffled. The chill he had let in remained a while. Flandry, hunched in a chair, didn't seem to notice.

Miyatovich gave the Terran a close regard. 'You can't go on either,' he said. 'If you don't stop dosing yourself and let your glands and nerves function normally, they'll quit on you.'

Flandry nodded. 'I'll stop soon.' From caverns his eyes observed a phonescreen.

The big gray-blond man hung up his cloak. 'I'll admit I couldn't have done what got done today, maybe not for weeks, maybe never, without you,' he said. 'You knew the right words, the right channels; you had the ideas. But we *are* done. I can handle the rest.'

He went to stand behind his companion, laying fingers on shoulders, gently kneading. 'I'd like to hide from her death myself,' he said. 'Aye, it's easier for me. I'd thought her lost to horror, and learned she was lost in honor. While if you and she – Dominic, listen. I made a chance to call my wife. She's at our house, not our town house, a place in the country, peace, woods, cleanness, healing. We want you there.' He paused. 'You're a very private man, aren't you? Well, nobody will poke into your grief.'

'I'm not hiding,' Flandry replied in monotone. 'I'm waiting. I expect a message shortly. Then I'll take your advice.'

'What message?'

'Interrogation results from a certain Mers— Roidhunate agent we captured. I've reason to think he has some critical information.'

'Hoy?' Miyatovich's features, tired in their own right, kindled. He cast himself into an armchair confronting Flandry. It creaked beneath his weight.

'I'm in a position to evaluate it better than anyone else,' the Terran persisted. 'How long does da Costa insist on keeping his ships here "in case we need further help"? – Ah, yes, five standard days, I remember. Well, I'll doubtless need about that long at your house; I'll be numb, and afterward—

'I'll take a printout in my luggage, to study when I'm able. Your job meanwhile will be to . . . not suppress the report. You probably couldn't; besides, the Empire needs every drop of data we can wring out of what enemy operatives we catch. But don't let da Costa's command scent any special significance in the findings of this particular 'probe job.'

The Gospodar fumbled for pipe and tobacco pouch. 'Why?'

'I can't guarantee what we'll learn, but I have a logical suspicion— Are you sure you can keep the Dennitzan fleet mobilized, inactive, another couple of weeks?'

'Yes.' Miyatovich grew patient. 'Maybe you don't quite follow the psychology, Dominic. Da Costa wants to be certain we won't rebel. The fact that we aren't dispersing immediately makes him leery. He hasn't the power to prevent us from whatever we decide to do, but he thinks his presence as a tripwire will deter secessionism. All right, in five Terran days his Intelligence teams can establish it's a bogeyman, and he can accept my explanation that we're staying on alert for a spell yet in case Merseia does attack. He'll deem us a touch paranoid, but he'll return to base with a clear conscience.'

'You have to give your men the same reason, don't you?'

'Right. And they'll accept it. In fact, they'd protest if I didn't issue such an order, Dennitza's lived too many centuries by the abyss; this time we nearly went over.'

Miyatovich tamped his pipe bowl needlessly hard. 'I've gotten to know you well enough, I believe, in this short while, that I can tell you the whole truth,' he added. 'You thought you were helping me smooth things out with respec to the Empire. And you were, you were. But my main reasor for quick reconciliation is . . . to get the Imperials out of th Zorian System while we still have our own full strength.'

'And you'll strike back at Merseia,' Flandry said.

The Gospodar showed astonishment. 'How did you guess?'

'I didn't guess. I knew – Kossara. She told me a lot.'

Miyatovich gathered wind and wits. 'Don't think I'm crazy,' he urged. 'Rather, I'll have to jump around like sodium in the rain, trying to keep people and Skupshtina from demanding action too loudly before the Terrans leave. But when the Terrans do—' His eyes, the color of hers, grew leopard-intent. 'We want more than revenge. In fact, only a few of us like myself have suffered what would have brought on a blood feud in the old days. But I told you we live on the edge. We have got to show we aren't safe for unfriends to touch. Otherwise, what's next?'

'*Nemo me impune lacessit*,' Flandry murmured.

'Hm?'

'No matter. Ancient saying. Too damned ancient; does nothing ever change at the heart?' Flandry shook his head. The chemical barriers were growing thin. 'I take it, then, in the absence of da Costa or some other Imperial official –

who'd surely maintain anything as atavistic as response to aggression is against policy and must in all events be referred to the appropriate authorities, in triplicate, for debate – in the absence of that, as sector governor you'll order the Dennitzan fleet on a retaliatory strike.'

Miyatovich nodded. 'Yes.'

'Have you considered the consequences?'

'I'll have time to consider them further, before we commit. But . . . if we choose the target right, I don't expect Merseia will do more than protest. The fact seems to be, at present they are not geared for war with Terra. They were relying on a new civil war among us. If instead they get hit, the shock ought to make them more careful about the whole Empire.'

'What target have you in mind?'

Miyatovich frowned, spent a minute with a lighter getting his pipe started, finally said, 'I don't yet know. The object is not to start a war, but to punish behavior which could cause one. The Roidhunate couldn't write off a heavily populated planet. Nor would I need a genocidal mission. But, oh, something valuable, maybe an industrial center on a barren metal-rich globe – I'll have the War College study it.'

'If you succeed,' Flandry warned, 'you'll be told you went far beyond your powers.'

'That can be argued. Those powers aren't too well defined, are they? I like to imagine Hans Molitor will sympathize.' The Gospodar shrugged. 'If not, what becomes of me isn't important. I'm thinking of the children and grandchildren.'

'Uh-huh. Well, you've confirmed what— Hold on.' The phone buzzed. Flandry reached to press accept. He had to try twice before he made it.

A countenance half as stark as his looked from the screen. 'Lieutenant Mitchell reporting, sir. Hypnoprobing of the prisoner Dominic Hazeltine has been completed.'

'Results?' The question was plane-flat.

'You predicted aright, sir. The subject was deep-conditioned.' Mitchell winced at a recollection unpleasant even in his line of work. 'I'd never seen or heard of so thorough a treatment. He went into shock almost at once. In later stages, the stimuli necessary were – well, he hasn't got a forebrain left to speak of.'

'I want a transcript in full,' Flandry said. 'Otherwise, you're to seal the record, classified Ultimate Secret, and your whole team will keep silence. I'll give you a written directive on that, authorized by Governor Miyatovich.'

'Yes, sir.' Mitchell showed puzzlement. He must be wondering why the emphasis. Intelligence didn't make a habit of broadcasting what it learned. Unless – 'Sir, you realize, don't you, this is still raw material? More incoherent than usual, too, because of the brain channeling. We did sort out his basic biography, details of his most recent task, that kind of thing. Offhand, the rest of what we got seems promising. But to fit the broken, scrambled association chains together, interpret the symbols and find their significance—'

'I'll take care of that,' Flandry snapped. 'Your part is over.'

'Yes, sir.' Mitchell dropped his gaze. 'I'm ... sorry ... on account of the relationship involved. He really did admire you. Uh, what shall we do about him now?'

Flandry fell quiet. Miyatovich puffed volcanic clouds. Outside, the bells caroled.

'Sir?'

'Let me see him,' Flandry said.

Interlinks flickered. In the screen appeared the image of a young man, naked on a bed, arms spreadeagled to meet the tubes driven into his veins, chest and abdominal cavities opened for the entry of machines that kept most cells alive. He stared at the ceiling with eyes that never moved nor blinked. His mouth dribbled. *Click, chug*, it said in the background, *click, chug*.

Flandry made a noise. Miyatovich seized his hand.

After a while Flandry stated, 'Thank you. Switch it off.'

They held Kossara Vymezal in a coldvault until the Imperials had left. This was by command of the Gospodar, and folk supposed the reason was she was Dennitza's, nobody else's, and said he did right. As many as were able would attend her funeral.

The day before, she was brought to the Cathedral of St. Clement, though none save kin were let near. Only the four men of her honor guard were there when Dominic Flandry came.

They stood in uniform of the Narodna Voyska, heads lowered, rifles reversed, at the corners of her bier. He paid them no more mind than he did the candles burning in tall holders, the lilies, roses, viyenatz everywhere between, their fragrance or a breath of incense or the somehow far-off sound of a priest chanting behind the iconostasis, which filled the cool dim air. Alone he walked over the stones to her. Evening sunlight slanted through windows and among columns, filtered to a domed ceiling, brought forth out of dusk, remote up on gold and blue, the Twelve Apostles and Christ Lord of All.

At first he was afraid to look, dreading less the gaping glaring hideousness he had last seen – that was only what violent death wrought – than the kind of rouged doll they made when Terran bodies lay in state. Forcing himself, he found that nothing more had been done than to cleanse her, close the eyes, bind the chin, gown and garland her. The divided coffin lid showed her down to the bosom. The face he saw was hers, hers, though color was gone and time had eased it into an inhuman serenity.

This makes me a little happier, dear, he thought. *I didn't feel it was fitting that they mean to build you a big tomb on Founders' Hill. I wanted your ashes strewn over land and sea, into sun and wind. Then if ever I came back here I could dream every brightness was yours. But they understand what they do, your people.* A corner of his mouth bent upward. *It's I who am the sentimental old fool. Would you laugh if you could know?*

He stooped closer. *You believed you would know, Kossara. If you do, won't you help me believe too – believe that you still are?*

His sole answer was the priest's voice rising and falling through archaic words. Flandry nodded. He hadn't expected more. He couldn't keep himself from telling her, *I'm sorry, darling.*

And I won't kiss what's left, I who kissed you. He searched among his languages for the best final word. *Sayonara.* Since it must be so. Stepping back a pace, he bowed three times very deeply, turned, and departed.

Bodin Miyatovich and his wife waited outside. The weather was milder than before, as if a ghost of springtime flitted fugitive ahead of winter. Traffic boomed in the street. Walkers cast glances at the three on the stairs, spoke to whatever companions they had, but didn't stop; they taught good manners on Dennitza.

Draga Miyatovich took Flandry by the elbow. 'Are you well, Dominic?' she asked anxiously. 'You've gone pale.'

'No, nothing,' he said. 'I'm recovering fast, thanks to your kindness.'

'You should rest. I've noticed you hour after hour poring over that report—' She saw his expression and stopped her speech.

In a second he eased his lips, unclamped his fists, and raised memory of what he had come from today up against that other memory. 'I'd no choice,' he said. To her husband: 'Bodin, I'm ready to work again. With you. You see, I've found your target.'

The Gospodar peered around. 'What? Wait,' he cautioned.

'True, we can't discuss it here,' Flandry agreed. 'Especially, I suppose, on holy ground ... though she might not have minded.'

She'd never have been vindictive. But she'd have understood how much this matters to her whole world: that in those broken mutterings of my son's I found what I thought I might find, the coordinates of Chereion, Aycharaych's planet.

CHAPTER NINETEEN

The raiders from Dennitza met the guardians of the red sun, and lightning awoke.

Within the command bridge of the *Vatre Zvezda*, Bodin Miyatovich stared at a display tank. Color-coded motes moved around a stellar globe to show where each vessel of his fleet was – and, as well as scouts and instruments could learn, each of the enemy's – and what it did and when it died. But their firefly dance, of some use to a lifelong professional, bewildered an unskilled eye; and it was merely a sideshow put on by computers whose real language was numbers. He swore and looked away in search of reality.

The nearest surrounded him in metal, meters, intricate consoles, flashing signal bulbs, dark-uniformed men who stood to their duties, sat as if wired in place, walked back and forth on rubbery-shod feet. Beneath a hum of engines, ventilators, a thousand systems throughout the great hull, their curt exchanges chopped. To stimulate them, it was cool here, with a thunderstorm tang of ozone.

The Gospodar's gaze traveled on, among the viewscreens which studded bulkheads, overhead, deck – again, scarcely more than a means for keeping crew who did not have their ship's esoteric senses from feeling trapped. Glory brimmed the dark, stars in glittering flocks and Milky Way shoals, faerie-remote glimmer of nebulae and a few sister galaxies. Here in the outer reaches of its system, the target sun was barely the brightest, a coal-glow under Bellatrix. At chance moments a spark would flare and vanish, a nuclear burst close enough to see. But most were too distant; and never another vessel showed, companion or foe. Such was the scale of the battle.

And yet it was not large as space combats went. Springing from hyperdrive to normal state, the Dennitzan force – strong, but hardly an armada – encountered Merseian craft which sought to bar it from accelerating inward. As more and more of the latter drew nigh and matched courses with invaders, action spread across multimillions of kilometers. Hours passed before two or three fighters came so near, at such low relative speeds, that they could hope for a kill; and often their encounter was the briefest spasm, followed by hours more of maneuver. Those gave time to make repairs, care for the wounded, pray for the dead.

'They've certainly got protection,' Miyatovich growled. 'Who'd have expected this much?'

Scouts had not been able to warn him. The stroke depended altogether on swiftness. Merseian observers in the neighborhood of Zoria had surely detected the fleet's setting out. Some would have gone to tell their masters, others would have dogged the force, trying to learn where it was bound. (A few of those had been spotted and destroyed, but not likely all.) No matter how carefully plotted its course, and no matter that its destination was a thinly trafficked part of space, during the three-week journey its hyperwake must have been picked up by several travelers who passed within range. So many strange hulls together, driving so hard through Merseian domains, was cause to bring in the Navy.

If Miyatovich was to do anything to Chereion, he must get there, finish his work, and be gone before reinforcements could arrive. Scouts of his, prowling far in advance near a sun whose location seemed to be the Roidhunate's most tightly gripped secret, would have carried too big a risk of giving away his intent. He must simply rush in full-armed, and hope.

'We can take them, can't we?' he asked.

Rear Admiral Raich, director of operations, nodded.

'Oh, yes. They're outnumbered, outgunned. I wonder why they don't withdraw.'

'Merseians aren't cowards,' Captain Yulinatz, skipper of the dreadnaught, remarked. 'Would you abandon a trust?'

'If my orders included the sensible proviso that I not contest lost causes when it's possible to scramble clear and fight another day — yes, I would,' Raich said. 'Merseians aren't idiots either.'

'Could they be expecting help?' Miyatovich wondered. He gnawed his mustache and scowled.

'I doubt it,' Raich replied. 'We know nothing significant can reach us soon.' He did keep scouts far-flung throughout this stellar vicinity, now that he was in it. 'They must have the same information to base the same conclusions on.'

Flandry, who stood among them, his Terran red-white-and-blue gaudy against their indigo or gray, cleared his throat. 'Well, then,' he said, 'the answer's obvious. They do have orders to fight to the death. Under no circumstances may they abandon Chereion. If nothing else, they must try to reduce our capability of damaging whatever is on the planet.'

'Bonebrain doctrine,' Raich grunted.

'Not if they're guarding something vital,' Miyatovich said. 'What might it be?'

'We can try for captures,' Yulinatz suggested: reluctantly, because it multiplied the hazard to his men.

Flandry shook his head. 'No point in that,' he declared. 'Weren't you listening when we talked *en route*? Nobody lands on Chereion except by special permission which is damn hard to get — needs approval of both the regional tribune and the planet's own authorities, and movements are severely restricted. I don't imagine a single one of the personnel we're killing and being killed by has come within an astronomical unit of the globe.'

'Yes, yes, I heard,' Yulinatz snapped. 'What influence those beings must have.'

'That's why we've come to hit them,' the Gospodar said in his beard.

Yulinatz's glance went to the tank. A green point blinked: a cruiser was suffering heavily from three enemy craft which paced her. A yellow point went out, and quickly another: two corvettes lost. His tone grew raw. 'Will it be worth the price to us?'

'That we can't tell till afterward.' Miyatovich squared his shoulders. 'We could disengage and go home, knowing we've thrown a scare into the enemy. But we'd never know what opportunity we did or did not forever miss. We will proceed.'

In the end, a chieftain's main duty is to say, 'On my head be it.'

'Gentlemen.'

Flandry's word brought their eyes to him. 'I anticipated some such quandary,' he stated. 'What we need is a quick survey – a forerunner to get a rough idea of what is on Chereion and report back. Then we can decide.'

Raich snorted. 'We need veto rights over the laws of statistics too.'

'If the guard is this thick at this distance,' Yulinatz added, 'what chance has the best speedster ever built for any navy of getting anywhere near?'

Miyatovich, comprehending, swallowed hard.

'I brought along my personal boat,' Flandry said. 'She was not built for a navy.'

'No, Dominic,' Miyatovich protested.

'Yes, Bodin,' Flandry answered.

Vatre Zvezda unleashed a salvo. No foes were close. None could match a Nova-class vessel. She was huge, heavy-armored, intricately compartmented, monster-powered in engines, weapons, shielding fields, less to join battle than to keep battle away from the command posts at her heart. Under present conditions, it was not mad, but it was unreasonable that she fired at opponents more than a million kilometers distant. They would have time to track those missiles, avoid them or blow them up.

The reason was to cover *Hooligan's* takeoff.

She slipped from a boat lock, through a lane opened momentarily in the fields, outward like an outsize torpedo. Briefly in her aft-looking viewscreens the dreadnaught bulked, glimmering spheroid abristle with guns, turrets, launch tubes, projectors, sensors, generators, snatchers, hatches, watch-domes, misshapen moon adrift among the stars. Acceleration dwindled her so fast that Yovan Vymezal gasped, as if the interior were not at a steady Dennitzan gravity but the full unbalanced force had crushed the breath from him.

In the pilot's chair, Flandry took readings, ran off computations, nodded, and leaned back. 'We won't make approach for a good three-quarters of an hour,' he said, 'and nothing's between us and our nominal target. Relax.'

Vymezal – a young cadre lieutenant of marines, Kossara's cousin and in a sturdy male fashion almost unendurably like her – undid his safety web. He had been invited to the control cabin as a courtesy; come passage near the enemy destroyer they were aimed at, he would be below with his dozen men, giving them what comfort he could in their helplessness, and Chives would be here as copilot. His question came hesitant, not frightened but shy : 'Sir, do you really think we can get past? They'll know pretty soon we're not a torp, we're a manned vessel. I should think they won't be satisfied to take evasive action, they'll try for a kill.'

'You volunteered, didn't you? After being warned this is a dangerous mission.'

Vymezal flushed. 'Yes, sir. I wouldn't beg off if I could. I was just wondering. You explained it's not necessarily a suicide mission.'

The odds are long that it is, my boy.

'You said,' the earnest voice stumbled on, 'your oscillators are well tuned enough that you can go on hyperdrive deep into a gravity well – quite near the sun. You planned to make most of our transit that way. Why not start at once? Why first run straight at hostile guns? I'm just wondering, sir, just interested.'

Flandry smiled. 'Sure you are,' he replied, 'and I'm sorry if you supposed for a minute I suppose otherwise. The reason is simple. We've a high kinetic velocity right now with respect to Chereion. You don't lose energy of relativistic motion merely because for a while you quantum-hop around the light-speed limit. Somewhere along the line, we have to match our vector to the planet's. That's better done here, where we have elbow room, than close in, where space may be crammed with defenses. We gain time – time to increase surprise at the far end – by posing as a missile while we adjust our velocity. But a missile should logically have a target. Within the cone of feasible directions, that destroyer seemed like our best bet. Let me emphasize, the operative word is "bet".'

Vymezal eased and chuckled. 'Thank you, sir. I'm a dice addict. I know when to fade.'

'I'm more a poker player.' Flandry offered a cigarette, which was accepted, and took one for himself. It crossed his mind: how strange he should still be using the box which had snapped shut on his son, and give it no particular thought.

Well, why throw away a tool I'd want duplicated later? I've been taught to aviod romantic gestures except when they serve a practical demagogic purpose.

Vymezal peered ahead at the ruby sun. Yes, his profile against the star-clouds of Sagittarius was as much like Kossara's as young Dominic's had been like Persis'.

What can I write to Persis? Can I?

Maybe my gesture is to carry this cigarette case in my pocket for the rest of my days.

'What information have we?' the lieutenant almost whispered.

'Very little, and most we collected personally while we approached,' Flandry said. 'Red dwarf star, of course; early type, but still billions of years older than Sol or Zoria, and destined to outlive them. However, not unduly metal-poor,' *as Diomedes is where I put her at stake for no more possible win than the damned Empire.* 'Distribution of higher elements varies a good bit in both space and time. The system appears normal for its kind, whatever "normal" may mean: seven identified planets, Chereion presumably the only vitafer. We can't predict further; life has no such thing as a norm. I do expect Chereion will be, m-m, interesting.'

And not an inappropriate place to leave my bones.

Flandry inhaled acridity and gazed outward. With all the marvels and mysteries yonder, he wasn't seeking death. In the last few weeks, his wounds had scarred over. But scar tissue is not alive. He no longer minded the idea of death.

He wished, though, it had been possible to leave Chives behind, and Kossara's cousin.

A magnifying screen emblazoned the Merseian destroyer, spearhead on a field of stars.

'Torpedo coming, sir,' Chives stated. 'Shall I dispose of it?' His fingers flicked across the gun control board before him. A firebolt sprang hell-colored. Detector-computer systems signaled a hit. The missile ceased accelerating. Either its drive was disabled or this was a programmed trick. In the second case, if *Hooligan* maintained the same vector, a moment's thrust would bring it sufficiently close that radiation from the exploding warhead could cripple electronics, leave her helpless and incidentally pass a death sentence on her crew.

'Keep burning till we're sure,' Flandry ordered. That required a quick change of course. Engines roared, steel sang under stress, constellations whirled. He felt his blood tingle and knew he was still a huntsman.

Flame fountained. A crash went through hull and flesh. The deck heaved. Shouts came faintly from aft.

Gee-fields restabilized. 'The missile obviously had a backup detonator,' Chives said. 'It functioned at a safe remove from us, and our force screens fended off a substantial piece of débris without harm. Those gatortails are often inept mechanicians, would you not agree, sir?' His own tail switched slim and smug.

'Maybe. Don't let that make you underestimate the Chereionites.' Flandry studied the readouts before him.

His pulse lifted. They were matched to their goal world. A few minutes at faster-than-light would bring them there, and—

'Stand by,' he called.

CHAPTER TWENTY

The eeriest thing was that nothing happened.

The planet spun in loneliness around its ember sun. Air made a thin bordure to its shield, shading from blue to purple to the winter sky of space. Hues were iron-rusty and desert-tawny, overlaid by blue-green mottlings, hoar polar caps, fierce glint off the few shrunken seas which remained. A small, scarred moon swung near.

It had to be the world of Flandry's search. No other was possible. But who stood guard? War raved through outer space; here his detectors registered only a few automatic traffic-control stations in orbit, easily bypassed. Silence seeped through the hull of his vessel and filled the pilot's cabin.

Chives broke it: 'Analysis indicates habitability for us is marginal, sir. Biotypes of the kind which appear to be present – sparsely – have adapted to existing conditions but could not have been born under them. Given this feeble irradiation, an immense time was required for the loss of so much atmosphere and hydrosphere.' He paused. 'The sense of age and desolation is quite overwhelming, sir.'

Flandry, his face in the hood of a scannerscope, muttered, 'There are cities. In good repair, fusion powerplants at work ... though putting out very little energy for complexes their size ... The deserts are barren, the begrown regions don't look cultivated – too saline, I'd guess. Maybe the dwellers live on synthetic food. But why no visible traffic? Why no satellite or ground defenses?'

'As for the former, sir,' Chives ventured, 'the inhabitants may generally prefer a contemplative, physically austere existence. Did not Aycharaych intimate that to you on various occasions? And as for the latter question, Merseian ships have maintained a cordon, admitting none except an authorized few.'

'That is' – the tingle in Flandry sharpened – 'if an intruder like us ever came this close, the game would be up anyway?'

'I do not suggest they have no wiles in reserve, sir.'

'Ye-e-es. The Roidhunate wouldn't keep watch over pure philosophers.' Decision slammed into Flandry like sword into sheath. 'We can't learn more where we are, and every second we linger gives them an extra chance to notice us and load a trap. We're going straight down!'

He gave the boat a surge of power.

Nonetheless, his approach was cautious. If naught else, he needed a while to reduce interior air pressure to the value indicated for the surface ahead of them. (Sounds grew muffled; pulse quickened; breast muscles worked enough to feel. Presently he stopped noticing much, having always taken care to maintain a level of acclimation to thin air. But he was glad that gravity outside would be weak, about half a gee.) Curving around the night hemisphere, he studied light-bejeweled towers set in the middle of rock and sand wastes, wondered greatly at what he saw, and devised a plan of sorts.

'We'll find us a daylit place and settle alongside,' he announced on the intercom. 'If they won't talk to us, we'll maybe go in and talk to them.' For his communicator, searching all bands, had drawn no hint of—

No! A screen flickered into color. He looked at the first Chereionite face he could be certain was not Aycharaych's. It had the same spare beauty, the same deep calm, but as many differences of sculpture as between one human countenance and the next. And from the start, even before speech began, he felt a ... heaviness: nothing of sardonic humor or flashes of regret.

'Talk the conn, Chives,' he directed. A whistling had begun, and the badlands were no longer before but below him. *Hooligan* was an easier target now than she had been in space; she had better be ready to dodge and strike back.

'You are not cleared for entry,' said the screen in Eriau which was mellow-toned but did not sing like Aycharaych's. 'Your action is forbidden under strict penalties, by command of the Roidhun in person, renewed in each new reign. Can you offer a justification?'

Huh? jabbed through Flandry. *Does he assume this is a Merseian boat and I a Merseian man?* 'Em – emergency,' he tried, too astonished to invent a glib story. He had expected he would declare himself as more or less what he was, and hold his destination city hostage to his guns and missiles. Whether or not the attempt could succeed in any degree, he had no notion. At best he'd thought he might bear away a few hints about the beings who laired here.

'Have you control over your course?' inquired the voice.

'Yes. Let me speak to a ranking officer.'

'You will go approximately five hundred kilometers northwest of your immediate position. Prepare to record a map.' The visage vanished, a chart appeared, two triangles upon it. 'The red apex shows where you are, the blue your mandatory landing site, a spacefield. You will stay inboard and await instructions. Is this understood?'

'We'll try. We, uh, we have a lot of speed to kill. In our condition, fast braking is unsafe. Can you give us about half an hour?'

Aycharaych would not have spent several seconds reaching a decision. 'Permitted. Be warned, deviations may cause you to be shot down. Proceed.' Nor would he have broken contact with not a single further inquiry.

Outside was no longer black, but purple. The spacecraft strewed thunder across desert. 'What the *hell*, sir?' Chives exploded.

'Agreed,' said Flandry. His tongue shifted to an obscure language they both knew. 'Use this lingo while that channel's open.'

'What shall we do?'

'First, play back any pictures we got of the place we're supposed to go.' Flandry's fingers brushed a section of console. On an inset screen came a view taken from nearby space under magnification. His trained eyes studied it and a few additional. 'A spacefield, aye, standard Merseian model, terminal and the usual outbuildings. Modest-sized, no vessels parked. And way off in wilderness.' He twisted his mustache. 'You know, I'll bet that's where every visitor's required to

208

land. And then he's brought in a closed car to a narrowly limited area which is all he ever sees.'

'Shall we obey, sir?'

'Um, 'twould be a pity, wouldn't it, to pass by that lovely city we had in mind. Besides, they doubtless keep heavy weapons at the port; our pictures show signs of it. Once there, we'd be at their mercy. Whereas I suspect that threat to blast us elsewhere was a bluff. Imagine a stranger pushing into a prohibited zone on a normal planet – when the system's being invaded! Why aren't we at least swarmed by military aircraft?'

'Very good, sir. We can land in five minutes.' Chives gave his master a pleading regard. 'Sir, must I truly stay behind while you debark?'

'Somebody has to cover us, ready to scramble if need be. We're Intelligence collectors, not heroes. If I call you and say, "Escape," Chives, you will escape.'

'Yes, sir,' the Shalmuan forced out. 'However, please grant me the liberty of protesting your decision not to wear armor like your men.'

'I want the full use of my senses.' Flandry cast him a crooked smile and patted the warm green shoulder. 'I fear I've often strained your loyalty, old chap. But you haven't failed me yet.'

'Thank you, sir.' Chives stared hard at his own busy hands. 'I . . . endeavor . . . to give satisfaction.'

Time swooped past.

'Attention!' cried from the screen. 'You are off course! You are in absolutely barred territory!'

'Say on,' Flandry jeered. He half hoped to provoke a real response. The voice only denounced his behavior.

A thump resounded and shivered. The tone of wind and engines ceased. They were down.

Flandry vaulted from his chair, snatched a combat helmet, buckled it on as he ran. Beneath it he already wore a mind-screen, as did everybody aboard. Otherwise he was attired in a gray coverall and stout leather boots. On his back and across his chest were the drive cones and controls of a grav unit.

His pouchbelt held field rations, medical supplies, canteen of water, ammunition, blaster, slugthrower and Merseian war knife.

At the head of his dozen Dennitzan marines, he bounded from the main personnel lock, along the extruded gangway, onto the soil of Chereion. There he crouched in what shelter the hull afforded and glared around, fingers on weapons.

After a minute or two he stepped forth. Awe welled in him.

A breeze whispered, blade-sharp with cold and dryness. It bore an iron tang off uncounted leagues of sand and dust. In cloudless violet, the sun stood at afternoon, bigger to see than Sol over Terra, duller and redder than the sun over Diomedes; squinting, he could look straight into it for seconds without being blinded, and through his lashes find monstrous dark spots and vortices. It would not set for many an hour, the old planet turned so wearily.

Shadows were long and purple across the dunes which rolled cinnabar and ocher to the near horizon. Here and there stood the gnawed stump of a pinnacle, livid with mineral hues, or a ravine clove a bluff which might once have been a mountain. The farther desert seemed utterly dead. Around the city, wide apart, grew low bushes whose leaves glittered in rainbows as if crystalline. The city itself rose from foundations that must go far down, must have been buried until the landscape eroded from around them and surely have needed renewal as the ages swept past.

The city – it was not a giant chaos such as besat Terra or Merseia; nothing on Chereion was. An ellipse defined it, some ten kilometers at the widest, proportioned in a rightness Flandry had recognized from afar though not knowing how he did. The buildings of the perimeter were single-storied, slenderly colonnaded; behind them, others lifted ever higher, until they climaxed in a leap of slim towers. Few windows interrupted the harmonies of colors and iridescence, the interplay of geometries that called forth visions of many-vaulted infinity. The heart rode those lines and curves upward until the whole sight became a silent music.

Silent ... only the breeze moved or murmured.

A time passed beyond time.

'*Milostiv Bog*,' Lieutenant Vymezal breathed, 'is it Heaven we see?'

'Then is Heaven empty?' said another man as low.

Flandry shook himself, wrenched his attention away, sought for his purposefulness in the ponderous homely shapes of their armor, the guns and grenades they bore. 'Let's find out.' His words were harsh and loud in his ears. 'This is as large a community as any, and typical insofar as I could judge.' *Not that they are alike. Each is a separate song.* 'If it's abandoned, we can assume they all are.'

'Why would the Merseians guard ... relics?' Vymezal asked.

'Maybe they don't.' Flandry addressed his minicom. 'Chives, jump aloft at the first trace of anything untoward. Flight at discretion. I think we can maintain radio contact from inside the town. If not, I may ask you to hover. Are you still getting a transmission?'

'No, sir.' That voice came duly small. 'It ceased when we landed.'

'Cut me in if you do ... Gentlemen, follow me in combat formation. Should I come to grief, remember your duty is to return to the fleet if possible, or to cover our boat's retreat if necessary. Forward.'

Flandry started off in flat sub-gee bounds. His body felt miraculously light, as light as the shapes which soared before him, and the air diamond clear. Yet behind him purred the gravity motors which helped his weighted troopers along. He reminded himself that they hugged the ground to present a minimal target, that the space they crossed was terrifyingly open, that ultimate purity lies in death. The minutes grew while he covered the pair of kilometers. Half of him stayed cat-alert, half wished Kossara could somehow, safely, have witnessed this wonder.

The foundations took more and more of the sky, until at last he stood beneath their sheer cliff. Azure, the material resisted a kick and an experimental energy bolt with a hardness which had defied epochs. He whirred upward, over an edge, and stood in the city.

A broad street of the same blue stretched before him, flanked by dancing rows of pillars and arabesque friezes on buildings which might have been temples. The farther he scanned, the higher fountained walls, columns, tiers, cupolas, spires; and each step he took gave him a different perspective, so that the whole came alive, intricate, simple, powerful, tranquil, transcendental. But footfalls echoed hollow.

They had gone a kilometer inward when nerves twanged and weapons snapped to aim. 'Hold,' Flandry said. The man-sized ovoid that floated from a side lane sprouted tentacles which ended in tools and sensors. The lines and curves of it were beautiful. It passed from sight again on its unnamed errand. 'A robot,' Flandry guessed. 'Fully automated, a city could last, could function, for – millions of years?' His prosiness felt to him as if he had spat on consecrated earth.

No, damn it! I'm hunting my woman's murderers.

He trod into a mosaic plaza and saw their forms.

Through an arcade on the far side the tall grave shapes walked, white-robed, heads bare to let crests shine over luminous eyes and lordly brows. They numbered perhaps a score. Some carried what appeared to be books, scrolls, delicate enigmatic objects; some appeared to be in discourse, mind to mind; some went alone in their meditations. When the humans arrived, most heads turned observingly. Then, as if having exhausted what newness was there, the thoughtfulness returned to them and they went on about their business of – wisdom?

'What'll we do, sir?' Vymezal rasped at Flandry's ear.

'Talk to them, if they'll answer,' the Terran said. 'Even take them prisoner, if circumstances warrant.'

'Can we? Should we? I came here for revenge, but – God help us, what filthy monkeys we are.'

A premonition trembled in Flandry. 'Don't you mean,' he muttered, 'what animals we're intended to feel like ... we and whoever they guide this far?'

He strode quickly across the lovely pattern before him.

Under an ogive arch, one stopped, turned, beckoned, and waited. The sight of gun loose in holster and brutal forms at his back did not stir the calm upon that golden face. 'Greeting,' lulled in Eriau.

Flandry reached forth a hand. The other slipped easily aside from the uncouth gesture. 'I want somebody who can speak for your world,' the man said.

'Any of us can that,' sang the reply. 'Call me, if you wish, Liannathan. Have you a name for use?'

'Yes. Captain Sir Dominic Flandry, Imperial Navy of Terra. Your Aycharaych knows me. Is he around?'

Liannathan ignored the question. 'Why do you trouble our peace?'

The chills walked faster along Flandry's spine. 'Can't you read that in my mind?' he asked.

'*Sta pakao*,' said amazement behind him.

'Hush,' Vymezal warned the man, his own tone stiff with intensity; and there was no mention of screens against telepathy.

'We give you the charity of refraining,' Liannathan smiled.

To and fro went the philosophers behind him.

'I ... assume you're aware ... a punitive expedition is on its way,' Flandry said. 'My group came to ... parley.'

Calm was unshaken. 'Think why you are hostile.'

'Aren't you our enemies?'

'We are enemies to none. We seek, we shape.'

'Let me talk to Aycharaych. I'm certain he's somewhere on Chereion. He'd have left the Zorian System after word got beamed to him, or he learned from broadcasts, his scheme had failed. Where else would he go?'

Liannathan curved feathery brows upward. 'Best you explain yourself, Captain, to yourself if not us.'

Abruptly Flandry snapped off the switch of his mindscreen. 'Read the answers,' he challenged.

Liannathan spread graceful hands in gracious signal. 'I told you, knowing what darkness you must dwell in, for mercy's sake we will leave your thoughts alone unless you compel us. Speak.'

213

Conviction congealed in Flandry, iceberg huge. 'No, you speak. What are you on Chereion? What do you tell the Merseians? I already know, or think I know, but tell me.'

The response rang grave: 'We are not wholly the last of an ancient race; the others have gone before us. We are those who have not yet reached the Goal; the bitter need of the universe for help still binds us. Our members are few, we have no need of numbers. Very near we are to those desires that lie beyond desire, those powers that lie beyond power.' Compassion softened Liannathan's words. 'Terran, we mourn the torment of you and yours. We mourn that you can never feel the final reality, the spirit born out of pain. We have no wish to return you to nothingness. Go in love, before too late.'

Almost, Flandry believed. His sense did not rescue him; his memories did. 'Yah!' he shouted. 'You phantom, stop haunting!'

He lunged. Liannathan wasn't there. He crashed a blaster bolt among the mystics. They were gone. He leaped in among the red-tinged shadows of the arcade and peered after light and sound projectors to smash. Everywhere else, enormous, brooded the stillness of the long afternoon.

The image of a single Chereionite flashed into sight, in brief white tunic, bearing though not brandishing a sidearm, palm uplifted – care-worn, as if the bones would break out from the skin, yet with life in flesh and great garnet eyes such as had never burned in those apparitions which were passed away. Flandry halted. 'Aycharaych!'

He snatched for the switch to turn his mindscreen back on. Aycharaych smiled. 'You need not bother, Dominic,' he said in Anglic. 'This too is only a hologram.'

'Lieutenant,' Flandry snapped over his shoulder, 'dispose your squad against attack.'

'Why?' said Aycharaych. The armored men gave him scant notice. His form glimmered miragelike in the gloom under that vaulted roof, where sullen sunlight barely reached. 'You have discovered we have nothing to resist you.'

You're bound to have something, Flandry did not reply.

A few missiles or whatever. You're just unwilling to use them in these environs. Where are you yourself, and what were you doing while your specters held us quiet?

As if out of a stranger's throat, he heard: 'Those weren't straightforward audiovisuals like yours that we met, were they? No reason for them to put on a show of being present, of being real, except that none of them ever were. Right? They're computer-generated simulacrums, will-o'-the-wisps for leading allies and enemies alike from the truth. Well, life's made me an unbeliever.

'Aycharaych, you are in fact the last Chereionite alive. The very last. Aren't you?'

Abruptly such anguish contorted the face before him that he looked away. 'What did they die of?' he was asking. 'How long ago?' He got no answer.

Instead: 'Dominic, we share a soul, you and I. We have both always been alone.'

For a while I wasn't; and now she is; she is down in the aloneness which is eternal. Rage ripped Flandry. He swung back to see a measure of self-command masking the gaunt countenance. 'You must have played your game for centuries,' he grated. 'Why? And ... whatever your reason to hide that your people are extinct ... why prey on the living? You, you could let them in and show them what'd make your Chereionites the ... Greeks of the galaxy – but you sit in a tomb or travel like a vampire— Are you crazy, Aycharaych? Is that what drives you?'

'No!'

Flandry had once before heard the lyric voice in sorrow. He had not heard a scream: 'I am not! Look around you. Who could go mad among these? And arts, music, books, dreams – yes, more, the loftiest spirits of a million years – they lent themselves to the scanners, the recorders— If you could have the likenesses to meet whenever you would ... of Gautama Buddha, Kung Fu-Tse, Rabbi Hillel, Jesus the Christ, Rumi ... Socrates, Newton, Hokusai, Jefferson, Gauss, Beethoven, Einstein, Ulfgeir, Manuel the Great, Manuel the

Wise – would you let your war lords turn these instruments to their own vile ends? No!'

And Flandry understood.

Did Aycharaych, half blinded by his dead, see what he had given away? 'Dominic,' he whispered hastily, shakily, 'I've used you ill, as I've used many. It was from no will of mine. Oh, true, an art, a sport – yours too – but we had our services, you to a civilization you know is dying, I to a heritage I know can abide while this sun does. Who has the better right?' He held forth unsubstantial hands. 'Dominic, stay. We'll think how to keep your ships off and save Chereion—'

Almost as if he were again the machine that condemned his son, Flandry said, 'I'd have to lure my company into some kind of trap. Merseia would take the planet back, and the help it gives. Your shadow show would go on. Right?'

'Yes. What are a few more lives to you? What is Terra? In ten thousand years, who will remember the empires? They can remember you, though, who saved Chereion for them.'

Candle flames stood around a coffin. Flandry shook his head. 'There've been too many betrayals in too many causes.' He wheeled. 'Men, we're returning.'

'Aye, sir.' The replies shuddered with relief.

Aycharaych's eidolon brought fingers together as if he prayed. Flandry touched his main grav switch. Thrust pushed harness against breast. He rose from the radiant city, into the waning murky day. Chill flowed around him. Behind floated his robot-encased men.

'*Brigate!*' bawled Vymezal. 'Beware !'

Around the topmost tower flashed a score of javelin shapes. Firebeams leaped out of their nozzles. *Remote-controlled flyer guns*, Flandry knew. *Does Aycharaych still hope, or does he only want revenge?* 'Chives,' he called into his sender, 'come get us !'

Sparks showered off Vymezal's plate. He slipped aside in midair, more fast and nimble than it seemed he could be in armor. His energy weapon, nearly as heavy as the assailants, flared back. Thunders followed brilliances. Bitterness tinged air. A mobile blast cannon reeled in midflight, spun downward, crashed in a street, exploded. Fragments ravaged a fragile façade.

'Shield the captain,' Vymezal boomed.

Flandry's men ringed him in. Shots tore at them. The noise stamped in his skull, the stray heat whipped over his skin. Held to his protection, the marines could not dodge about. The guns converged.

A shadow fell, a lean hull blocked off the sun. Flames reaped. Echoes toned at last to silence around smoking ruin down below. Vymezal shouted triumph. He waved his warriors aside, that Flandry might lead them through the open lock, into the *Hooligan*.

Wounded, dwindled, victorious, the Dennitzan fleet took orbits around Chereion. Within the command bridge, Bodin Miyatovich and his chieftains stood for a long while gazing into the viewscreens. The planet before them glowed among the stars, secretly, like a sign of peace. But it was the pictures they had seen earlier, the tale they had heard, which made those hard men waver.

Miyatovich even asked through his flagship's rustling stillness: 'Must we bombard?'

'Yes,' Flandry said. 'I hate the idea too.'

Qow of Novi Aferoch stirred. Lately taken off his crippled light cruiser, he was less informed than the rest. 'Can't sappers do what's needful?' he protested.

'I wish they could,' Flandry sighed. 'We haven't time. I don't know how many millennia of history we're looking down on. How can we read them before the Merseian navy arrives?'

'Are you sure, then, the gain to us can justify a deed which someday will make lovers of beauty, seekers of knowledge, curse our names?' the zmay demanded. 'Can this really be the center of the opposition's Intelligence?'

'I never claimed that,' Flandry said. 'In fact, obviously not. But it must be important as hell itself. We here can give them no worse setback than striking it from their grasp.'

'Your chain of logic seems thin.'

'Of course it is! Were mortals ever certain? But listen again, Qow.

'When the Merseians discovered Chereion, they were already conquest-hungry. Aycharaych, among the ghosts those magnificent computers had been raising for him – computers and programs we today couldn't possibly invent – he saw they'd see what warlike purposes might be furthered by such an instrumentality. They'd bend it wholly to their ends, bring their engineers in by the horde, ransack, peer, gut, build over, leave nothing unwrecked except a few museum scraps. He couldn't bear the thought of that.

'He stopped them by conjuring up phantoms. He made them think a few million of his race were still alive, able to give the Roidhunate valuable help in the form of staff work, while he himself would be a unique field agent – if they were otherwise left alone. We may never know how he impressed and tricked those tough-minded fighter lords; he did, that's all. They believe they have a worldful of enormous intellects for allies, whom they'd better treat with respect. He draws on a micro part of the computers, data banks, stored knowledge beyond our imagining, to generate advice for them ... excellent advice, but they don't suspect how much more they might be able to get, or by what means.

'Maybe he's had some wish to influence them, as if they learned from Chereion. Or maybe he's simply been biding his time till they too erode from his planet.'

Flandry was quiet for a few heartbeats before he finished: 'Need we care which, when real people are in danger?'

The Gospodar straightened, walked to an intercom, spoke his orders.

There followed a span while ships chose targets. He and Flandry moved aside, to stand before a screen showing stars that lay beyond every known empire. 'I own to a desire for vengeance,' he confessed. 'My judgment might have been different otherwise.'

Flandry nodded. 'Me too. That's how we are. If only— No, never mind.'

'Do you think we can demolish everything?'

'I don't know. I'm assuming the things we want to kill are under the cities – some of the cities – and plenty of megatonnage will if nothing else crumble their caverns around them.' Flandry smote a fist hurtfully against a bulkhead. 'I told Qow, we don't ever have more to go on than guesswork!'

'Still, the best guess is, we'll smash enough of the system – whether or not we reach Aycharaych himself—'

'For his sake, let's hope we do.'

'Are you that forgiving, Dominic? Well, regardless, Intelligence is the balance wheel of military operations. Merseian Intelligence should be ... not broken, but badly knocked askew ... Will Emperor Hans feel grateful?'

'Yes, I expect he'll defend us to the limit against the nobles who'll want our scalps.' Flandry wolf-grinned. 'In fact, he should welcome such an issue. The quarrel can force influential appeasers out of his regime.

'And ... he's bound to agree you've proved your case for keeping your own armed forces.'

'So Dennitza stays in the Empire—' Miyatovich laid a hand on his companion's shoulder. 'Between us, my friend, I dare hope myself that what I care about will still be there when the Empire is gone. However, that scarcely touches our lifetimes. What do you plan to do with the rest of yours?'

'Carry on as before,' Flandry said.

'Go back to Terra?' The eyes which were like Kossara's searched him. 'In God's name, why?'

Flandry made no response. Shortly sirens whooped and voices crackled. The bombardment was beginning.

A missile sprang from a ship. Among the stars it flew arrow slim; but when it pierced air, hurricane furies trailed its mass. That drum-roar rolled from horizon to horizon beneath the moon, shook apart wind-carven crags, sent landslides grumbling to the bottoms of canyons. When it caught the first high dawnlight, the missile turned into a silver comet. Minutes later it spied the towers and treasures it was to destroy, and plunged. It had weapons ready against ground defenses; but only the spires reached gleaming for heaven.

The fireball outshone whole suns. It bloomed so tall and

wide that the top of the atmosphere, too thin to carry it further, became a roof; therefore it sat for minutes on the curve of the planet, ablaze, before it faded. Dust then made a thick and deadly night above a crater full of molten stone. Wrath tolled around the world.

And more strikes came, and more.

Flandry watched. When the hour was ended, he answered Miyatovich: 'I have my own people.'

In glory did Gospodar Bodin ride home.

Maidens danced to crown him with flowers. The songs of their joy rang from the headwaters of the Lyubisha to the waves of the Black Ocean, up the highest mountains and down the fairest glens; and all the bells of Zorkagrad pealed until Lake Stoyan gave back their music.

Springtime came, never more sweet, and blossoms well-nigh buried the tomb which Gospodar Bodin had raised for St. Kossara. There did he often pray, in after years of his lordship over us; and while he lived, no foeman troubled the peace she brought us through his valor. Sing, poets, of his fame and honor! Long may God give us folk like these!

And may they hearten each one of us. For in this is our hope.

Amen

THE DANCER FROM ATLANTIS

Poul Anderson

Duncan Reid was snatched out of the twentieth century from a cruise liner in the mid-Pacific ... Oleg Vladimirovitch came from Novgorod in mediaeval Russia ... Uldin was a Hun barbarian who lived by cunning and the axe ... Erissa had been a sacred priestess in a lost continent ... And a mistake in a time-experiment by a race from the far future had thrown these four unlikely comrades together, pulling them through a warp in the fabric of space and time to a world which was ancient history. The strange alliance that Duncan and his companions formed in that unfamiliar world was to take on a significance that none of them could have foreseen. For not only their own future, but the very future of the world they had found was at stake ...

Also by Poul Anderson in Sphere Books:

WAR OF THE WING-MEN

THREE HEARTS AND THREE LIONS

THE BROKEN SWORD

0 7221 1163 0   75p

STAR WARS

George Lucas

Luke Skywalker challenged the stormtroopers of a distant galaxy on a daring mission – where a force of life became the power of death!

Farm chores sure could be dull, and Luke Skywalker was bored beyond belief. He yearned for adventures out among the stars – adventures that would take him beyond the furthest galaxies to distant and alien worlds.

But Luke got more than he bargained for when he intercepted a cryptic message from a beautiful princess held captive by a dark and powerful warlord. Luke didn't know who she was, but he knew he had to save her – and soon, because time was running out.

Armed only with courage and with the light sabre that had been his father's, Luke was catapulted into the middle of the most savage space-war ever . . . and he was headed straight for a desperate encounter on the enemy battle station known as the Death Star!

A spectacular motion picture from Twentieth Century-Fox!

0 7221 5669 3   95p

All Sphere Books are available at your bookshop or newsagent, or can be ordered from the following address:
Sphere Books, Cash Sales Department,
P.O. Box 11, Falmouth, Cornwall.

Please send cheque or postal order (no currency), and allow 19p for postage and packing for the first book plus 9p per copy for each additional book ordered up to a maximum charge of 73p in U.K.

Customers in Eire and B.F.P.O. please allow 19p for postage and packing for the first book plus 9p per copy for the next six books, thereafter 3p per book.

Overseas customers please allow 20p for postage and packing for the first book and 10p per copy for each additional book.